Isaiah Margulies works out of New Orleans as an Able Seaman in the United States Merchant Marine. He wrote DIASPORA between time on Mississippi River tugboats, offshore supply vessels, and factory trawlers in the Bering Sea.

DIASPORA

Isaiah Margulies

DIASPORA

A Gillson Press Book
New Orleans

Copyright © 2024 by Isaiah Margulies.

All rights reserved under International Copyright Conventions.
Published in the United States by Gillson Press.
publishers@gillsonpress.com

Cover design by H.S. Nagorski.
Illustration by Stephanie Delcambre.

ISBN 9798991053310

For Yankele

With thanks to B.Y.; Stephanie, with love; Hune, the father; and Sneven, a snail.

DIASPORA

Part 1

2

***

A light! Lost beneath the blizzard, her heart leapt with joy as a distant, golden glow caught her eye. She hurried forward, breath by laborious breath.

In search of food, she had wandered farther than she knew the land could stretch. But as the snow weighed down her coat, shivering away the last of her flesh, she found no place better off than another; every crop field lay barren, the river's countless tributaries sheathed in ice, and the forest's woodpeckers silent, starved by the trees' frozen bark.

Fixated on the light, she stumbled, a branch catching her leg. She fell to the ground, cried out, withdrew within, and steadied her breath. Searching for the warmth in her heart, she felt its heat pulsing through her limbs. But her mind swirled with the wind's cold eddies, and her body's tension melted into the snow. Within sight of that warmth, so promisingly close, she felt herself fading.

Yet her spirit refused, and with feral rage, denied her the right to die. Defying the storm's will, she raised herself, fixated on the light. She pressed on.

***

DIASPORA

1

Snow Chicken Soup

DIASPORA

The village of Tolevoste rested comfortably and quietly between the banks of the clear Jeżyna River to the east and the dark tree line of the Tolezyli Forest to the west. On the right day, one may have thought it Paradise. However, in Paradise, winters did not last nine months of the year.

In the spring, as the men would sow their previous harvest's seeds; as their daughters and wives, their feet bare, would wade down the river's banks, collecting its chalky mud to patch their walls; as the boys, between the *yeshiva* and the setting sun, would repair their roofs from the forest's fragrant pine; God would hear the rabbi, quietly praying that their upcoming harvest might stave off their hunger until the next.

Their walls, their clothes, and even their buckwheat crop blended into the dark and dusty earth. They would not have known of the color blue if not for the sky. Eternally the color of dust, one may have thought that Tolevoste breathed in, slept in, and drank in dust. But make no mistake. The people of Tolevoste kept their linen sheets clean, drank the Jeżyna's clear water, and breathed in God's sweet, dry air.

With the favor of God, just before Tolevoste's harvests, a rare riverboatman could sail past it without even seeing the village. In May, their tallest house—the *shul*—fell behind the walls of their thick grain.

But if the favor of God never abated, then the people of Tolevoste would have had no need for prayers. As quickly as the snow would melt from their fields and raise the Jeżyna in the spring, piercing winds, thick snow, and blizzard clouds would return with a force three times over in the winter.

One night, centuries ago, near the end of an unusually long winter, the soon-to-be lush trees of the Tolezyli Forest languished with a sick, pallid hue; a wide, barren tundra blanketed their crop fields and buckled their thinly planked roofs; a violent blizzard danced overhead, threatening to reduce their planks to shards; and the men of Tolevoste recited the *Ma'ariv*—the prayers of the evening—no differently than on any other day.

The fathers closed their *siddurim*, concluding their dialogues with God. They said prayers for their wives, resting their hands on their dry, brushed hair; said prayers for their children, bowing down to press their lips to their foreheads; and went to sleep in their cold, straw beds, satisfied that the storm would blow not a moment longer than God ordained it must.

However, in one dimly lit house, the prayers continued feverishly into the night. Sweating, as her shivering husband wandered in an uneasy dream, the pregnant Chana Vostęvskie felt a deep, wrenching pang in her abdomen. She dug her nails into her husband's hand as an agonizing wave of pain swept through her thighs. Yitzhak rolled over, lifted his head from his thin pillow, and opened his eyes.

"Wh—what's wrong, Chanale?" Yitzhak said softly, his breath condensing in the dark air between them. "Is the baby kicking?"

"It's not a kick," she whispered.

"Hm? What was that?" he asked, rubbing his eyes.

"It's not a kick!" she screamed. "Oh God, the baby is coming."

"Now?" Yitzhak shouted into the darkness. He reached for his wife, taking her face into his open palm. Tears traced down his fingers and the valleys of her hollow cheeks.

"Yes, yes, now!"

Waisting not one more moment, Yitzhak threw off his tattered covers, leaving the scant warmth of his marriage bed.

DIASPORA

Frantically grabbing his coat, his worn out boots, and his fur hat, he ran into the dark storm, like any decent husband of Tolevoste would have done. The midwife's house stood only a few paces down the road.

Watching Yitzhak trudging through the bitter wind for Chana, God felt satisfied to see him performing his obligations. But for Yitzhak, beyond what was required of him, a unique feeling drove him forward; he loved her.

Yitzhak had known Chana for four decades, raised just two houses from his own, since their first days of life. As he cut through the snow, early memories played through his mind.

Sharing their mothers' milk as infants, he and Chana once played, chased, and ran between their fathers' legs in the crop fields. As children, wrestling one another to the ground, Chana would grab at his *payot,* and he would tug at Chana's long, dark braids. When one would be bested, the two would run to whoever's father was most near, indignant and crying, insisting that the other had started it and was not playing fair.

Inseparable through the years that followed, their fathers began to question whether the two even knew that each belonged to different parents; after all, fathers and mothers did not come in fours.

But by Yitzhak and Chana's teenage years, their parents accepted, and even believed, that their children may have just as well been siblings. On the Sabbath, their parents had no choice but to let them alternate between one house and the other; they refused to eat their meals when the other one was not present. Yitzhak remembered how, the following mornings, when he would leave his Yeshiva lessons, Chana would be waiting by the shul's door with a bright smile. He would then explain to her all the lessons that she had not been allowed to hear.

Eventually, the realities of adolescence compelled their parents to temper their unusual intimacy. After all, neither had yet a *bashert*. Yitzhak and Chana only moved their games and affection out from under their parents' eyes. He recalled a particular summer evening well. Just as the ice sheets of the Jeżyna broke apart and the men and women of Tolevoste took turns bathing in the purifying stream, he and Chana snuck away during the twilight hours. The two only wanted to play in no different of a fashion than they always had; they could not enjoy the river's cool water if they did not have their best friend's hand in theirs. While their fathers recited their prayers and their mothers mended their husbands' overalls, they left to swim together.

With changes of clothes hidden beneath a tree, they removed their garments and put on their swimwear in front of each other's gaze. As if they never considered one a boy and the other a girl, they were little aware of the sensations arising within themselves. Holding hands as they waded down, Chana broke free from Yitzhak and dove beneath the water. She stood up, raising her chin, and pulled her long, brown hair behind her ears; turned around to see Yitzhak blushing, breathless, scanning her shape under the soft, orange sunlight; imperceptibly allowed herself to drift closer as Yitzhak reached out to take her in his arms; and moments after they pressed their foreheads together, feeling a new kind of affection gripping one another's hearts, she felt Yitzhak's lips on her cheek. Chana blushed, felt the blood flowing through her neck, and turned her face to meet his.

They circled in the water in each other's arms until sunset, laid in one another's lap against the roots of the tree by the riverbank under the starlight, and whispered intimate thoughts between themselves and God. They saw mysteries uncovering themselves before their eyes; believed they finally understood the meanings in the words of prayers they had long been made to sing; probed into each other's kaleidoscopic minds, as if by stirring together the colors of their thoughts, they could understand them better as a pair; and pulled one another through the trees, out onto the dirt road, and out into the fields, each chasing the other's silhouettes and shadows through the dark.

    The following Sabbath, Yitzhak informed their parents that they were in love. His father, boisterously laughing, bragged that he knew it all along; his mother, dropping her dinner plate, tearfully smothered Chana in her strong arms, crying that she had always been her daughter; and Chana's parents, shocked and pale, insisted on restraint. But Yitzhak, holding Chana's hand tight, interjected that they had already *known* each other, and the matter was settled.

    The room fell silent. Chana's mother fainted into her husband's arms. Though not even sure what that term meant at the time, Yitzhak succeeded in his objective. That very night, after tense discussions, the wedding was scheduled to follow the very next Sabbath. Chana cried tears of joy into her pillow every night that week.

    Time passed. Within just a few seasons from their wedding day, Yitzhak's shoulders broadened. Vibrant, womanly tones wove through Chana's boyish features. The married couple, in the height of their vigor, plowed their land in the mornings, raised the planks of their new house in the evenings, and spent their remaining energy at night on their religious obligation of filling their house with as many children as Chana could hope to bear.

    The people of Tolevoste would stare at them with raised brows as they walked down the street, side by side, their hands so close as to *almost* be holding. The other wives at the shul, glancing up from their prayer books, would whisper to Chana to lower her head. Paying them no mind, she never ceased staring at her husband from across the shul with wide, glassy eyes.

    Their affection toward one another grew day by day and season by season. They consulted the rabbi, the midwife, and Chana's much older sisters. And Yitzhak reasoned with God, believing firmly that he had performed his duties correctly to Him and his wife. However, twenty-four years passed before Chana and Yitzhak, broken to His mysterious will, were blessed with just one child.

When the middle-aged couple learned of the conception, they cried tears of joy. Considering the conception happened just after the first flurry of winter, they thanked God endlessly that their baby would be born just at the beginning of spring. But though nine months passed, the following March *had* come, and the first green sprouts *should* have been rising from the dirt, God had not yet driven the cold from their land. To their horror, on that impoverished night, God would deliver their child into hunger and cold.

The shingle of a roof blew down the street, nearly struck Yitzhak in the face, and refocused his attention away from his memories. Walking to the midwife, he noticed with sorrow all of the open crates and barrels, buried in snow against fences and walls, long scraped clean by wives clawing for their family's last morsels of flour. At least as poor as his neighbors and likely poorer, Yitzhak had endured such horrible malnourishment that, for weeks, he refused to remove his shirt before Chana's gaze. Though he gave his pregnant wife the last of his scraps—meager as they were—she scarcely had more flesh on her bones than him. Lying in pain in her bed, Chana feared for her soul that she would not have milk to nurse her coming child.

Yitzhak considered seeking the village's aging rabbi, Ezra, but he knew he had nothing to give them. Rabbi Ezra never found satisfaction unless he knew he lived poorer than the poorest of his people. Even *his* shreds of food were not his, for sleeping on the floor beside him lay his own elderly wife, mother of seven children and grandmother to twenty seven more, shivering beneath a shawl in the everlasting cold. All he could offer anyone was his awareness of the Divine.

At last, Yitzhak arrived at the midwife's single room shack. He knocked forcefully on her door, shaking the young woman from her well-deserved sleep. Moments later, he saw the light of a candle glowing through her frosted window pane. Hastily throwing on a robe, the woman peered outside. The old farmer stared back, white snow frosting his long mustache and beard. She unbolted her door, bracing it from the wind against her thigh, and looked into the silent man's sullen, tired eyes.

"Do you have any idea what time it is?" she asked impatiently, fighting the wind to keep her robe closed.

"Liza! It's Chana—she…" Yitzhak began. "It wasn't a kick… it… it was supposed to be warmer!"

"Now? Tonight?" the midwife asked with horror, gathering everything from his disjointed explanation. Yitzhak nodded his head.

"*Elohim Adirim.* Oh, dear God. Okay, go—go back now!" she said, digging her nails into his forearm, jerking him in the direction of his house. "I'll be there."

Running from house to house, snow soaking her crumbling shoes, Liza woke up half the village. She demanded every dry blanket, rag, and towel that could be spared. A few neighbors, in the commotion, scrounged together candles. Others offered herbs and wine. With her bag of supplies in hand, she ran to the Vostęvskies as promised, letting herself in through their back door.

The feeble house shook. Snow swirled in. As if it were aghast at being denied entry, the wind fought the midwife as she bolted the door shut. Between the door frame and the bed, she could hardly find a floorboard to set her bag, let alone her two feet. Right by her legs, she found Yitzhak dutifully sitting by his moaning wife, enduring the numbing grip of her hand, slowly shaving off small pieces of his thin bedpost to maintain their fire. He turned to look at the midwife, letting her see the deep lines of worry across his brow.

"Don't worry, sweet Chana. Everything will be alright," the midwife said, bending down to brush her wet hair. Chana stared back with scared, distrustful eyes.

Wasting no more time, the midwife skillfully put her into a birthing position. As she dug out her tools, Chana silently questioned God: Why would He force her to deliver a child *now*, when she had no food to provide? Why insist she wait twenty-four years from her marriage day—far longer than any woman she had known of since *Sarah*—to bring a newborn into a world of deprivation? Yitzhak, while watching the midwife's deft hands, saw Chana's furrowed brow. Doing all he could, he wiped the sweat from her forehead, soaking a rag in a pot of melted snow.

"That's right, Chanale, it *will* be okay," he said, pressing his quivering lips to her burning forehead.

The time had come.

Dancing, colored lights swirled before Chana's eyes. Merciless pain overcame her.

"Give one last push!" the midwife implored, watching in horror as Chana's blood flowed down her thighs. Chana began to cry, cry for her baby, cry for herself, and cry without understanding. She came to the realization she might not live to raise her child.

"*All I've ever done is show love and kindness to anyone and everyone,*" Chana sobbed inwardly. "*What sin have I committed? Oh, dear God! Have I not shown enough love to You?*"

She cried, her thin breath floating away like the white smoke of their smoldering candles. The cold air pierced into her bones. Her arms and legs grew weak. Her head, unbearably heavy, fell back towards the cold planks of her bed. With just three hours until sunrise, her baby's cry replaced her own.

The wind stood still. The midwife held the healthy baby boy, covered in his mother's blood. Yitzhak breathlessly stroked

Chana's head, begging her to look at him. The candles' light danced across her grey, glazed, unblinking eyes.

God carried the baby's cry down the street. Their closest neighbors, awake and listening through their thin walls, heard the newborn.

"Mama, do you hear that?" a child said.

"What a miracle," everyone thought. *"The Vostęvskies' baby was born alive!"*

Grabbing their boots and coats, their rapid, excited movements alerted the next house, which alerted the next, and then the next. Within minutes, every family on their snowy street was awake, excited, and throwing on their rags. They piled towards the Vostęvskies' front door.

Yitzhak sullenly answered their knocks. The youngest children, sleepy and confused, stumbled through his legs with dolls. The men, ready to celebrate, brought glasses and schnapps. Completely forgetting the mother must have needed rest, even Menachem the *Klezmer*, who seldom played for free, came with a fiddle in his hand for all to dance the s*her*. But just as the entire street had crammed themselves into the Vostęvskies' home, they all gasped. Several women gave out shrill cries. The rest turned their children's faces away. No one could bear to see Chana, the new mother, laying in a pool of blood, barely distinguishable from the dead.

"So, you think this is a time to drink some schnapps?" Yitzhak snapped at his neighbors. Chana lay still, unaffected, staring into the face of God. All turned silent but the baby, incessantly wailing, waiting impatiently for his first meal in the young midwife's strong arms.

The silence only lasted for a moment.

"Well, are you all just going to stand there like a brood of roosting chickens?" the midwife shouted. "She is not dead yet! Go get what you can!"

Pouring out from the Vostęvskies' door, the neighbors rushed back to their homes, gathering together firewood, medicinal leaves, and any scraps of food they could find. One came back with half an onion. Another found an old turnip beneath a chair. With the women's help, the midwife managed to prepare *something* of a soup in Yitzhak's pot. The fading Chana took a sip of the watery broth, feeling it drip down her throat. But having eaten nothing but stale biscuits, roots, and watery broth for days, there was little the liquid could do.

Watching on silently, the men, with their hands on Yitzhak's shoulders, tried to console him. Yitzhak, letting silent tears fall into his palms, heard whispered assurances that *the rabbi was already on his way*. A few others gently set *hamsahs*, *tefillin*, and siddurim by her bedside. But God's will seemed clear to all, despite their prayers and good will. Chana had lost far too much blood.

One by one, with their heads turned towards the wet floor, the neighbors slowly, solemnly left the shack, kissing the *mezuzah* on the way out. Every wife pressed their forehead against Chana's hair. Others released their cries down the street. The charitable midwife—still holding the fading mother's cold hand in one and the swaddled baby in her other hand—could do nothing but sit beside Yitzhak and Chana, waiting for the rabbi's prayers.

But Yitzhak, alone with his thoughts, decided he would wait for no man's blessings—not even the rabbi's. He lifted his face from his hands, warm with tears, turned to God, and prayed for the first time that night:

"*Our God and God of our fathers; of Abraham, Isaac, and Jacob; of my wife and my son; look at me, look at my wife, and answer me—what life are you giving my boy? Without my wife, you know he will die. Shall all he know of your Earth be one night of hunger? By your own design, I cannot give milk! And yet, when you ordained in creation that a Vostęvskie must*

DIASPORA

join you in the eternal kingdom of heaven—and that that Vostęvskie must join you today, not a moment later—you decided that Vostęvskie must be my wife, mother of my son? Is this your choice? Waiting for her to see her son's bris, to decide his name, even to feed him one meal—in the eternity of time, these few days for you are just far too long?

Our God and God of our fathers; of Abraham, Isaac, and Jacob; of my wife and my son; you have never turned your eyes away from Earth; do not turn your eyes away from me. I am not asking for much. You've given us nothing but wisps of flour to ration through the winter, a few dried roots, and a sallow goat that hasn't given milk in three years! Forgive my petulance. But with your everlasting power, in all of creation, is it too much for you to find for my wife something to sustain her for the night? She needs food! Real food! I am asking for nothing more than the smallest morsel of meat!"

Yitzhak repeated his prayers several more times, laid his head in his hands, let his tears fall some more, and resigned to let God's will be done.

***

All the while, wheezing through the cold wind, she had finally clawed her way to the source of the light—the frosted window of a derelict cabin at the edge of a frozen street. Though much dimmer than when it first caught her eyes, that enchanting glow, directly overhead, flooded her heart with excitement.

Deep within her, however, a foreboding instinct urged her to stop in her tracks; primal fear flashed down her spine. But what good could apprehension do for her? Before her lay light, and therefore, warmth; behind her, only the cold void she would soon succumb to. Just moments from collapse, she raised her arm, and with the remainder of her strength, clawed desperately at the lighted shack's door.

***

DIASPORA

Hearing a gentle noise at the door, Yitzhak's eyes shot open. He lifted himself up, went over, and cautiously opened it with a small crease. Mindful not to let out their little warmth, he peered through the dark blizzard with one eye—nothing there. He glanced at the midwife watching in suspicion, shook his head, and looked downward.

"Oy Gevalt!" he shouted, jumping back in fright. A small, shivering animal, barely taller than the snow piled around it, was taking shelter under the eaves of his entrance. He stared, bewitched, at the miserable sight. Covered in dirty snow, a black cat looked up into Yitzhak's eyes. Yitzhak stood paralyzed as she stepped forward, brushing up against his warm legs. Snow from her coat melted down his threadbare pants. She braved one tap at the father's boot, and realizing the leather could offer her no love, looked right back at Yitzhak. Letting out one pitiful mew, she seemed to ask if his humble house had room for one more.

Yitzhak, trembling where he stood, considered the meaning of the sight. He spat three times at the snow, shook the cat off his boot, closed the door gently, and stepped a few paces back towards his wife's bedside. Plunging his head back into his hands, he was too distraught by what he had seen to even pray.

The midwife, her mouth agape, scoffed in frustration.

"Oh my God, you *schmendrick!*" she cried, thrusting the baby into Yitzhak's lap. "What was *that* out there?" She ran to open the door, and to her great relief, saw *it* was still there—a sad cat standing exactly where Yitzhak had left it.

"Here, here, *kleine ketsl*," the midwife whispered, inching closer to it. But the cat did not move. They locked eyes. Its pupils widened.

It knew.

Yitzhak gasped in sudden realization.

The midwife pounced in the snow, her arms wide, as the cat jumped away.

"For the love of God, grab a lamp—catch that, catch *that!*" she shouted down the street.

The Vostęvskies' neighbors, still trudging back to their houses, turned around.

"Catch what? What is it?" A neighbor asked, watching the midwife give chase.

"Wait, I see it too!"

"There it goes!"

One by one, squinting at the dark creature scurrying away from the Vostęvskies' glowing window pane, neighbor after neighbor followed suit. A cry erupted down the street. The men took hold of their hats, the women lifted their hemlines, and through the darkness, slipping one after another, they pursued the apparition throughout all of Tolevoste. Over their fences, behind their houses, and into their neighbors' bushes, they slowly homed in on the poor animal, miserably struggling to get away. Unable to see where she was going, the cat ran up against a wooden fence. The neighbors closed in behind the midwife. With a few trailing behind, lamps in hand, they surrounded it on all sides.

The cat arched its back, raised its tail to the sky, and hissed at the midwife, baring its fangs with its last strength. Just before everyone else could make out clearly *what*, exactly, they had been chasing through the darkness, the midwife pounced. She snatched its scruff. Raising it in the air for all to see, the neighbors gasped in unison.

Its yellow eyes reflected their lights.

"We got it!" the midwife said. "Quickly, someone go find a butchering knife! The rest, bring any more firewood you can to the Vostęvskies! *Gib a loif!* Let's go!"

No one moved as nervous, distrustful glances spread around the circle. Children cautiously snuck between their parents' legs to take a look. The eldest people of Tolevoste, hearing the commotion from inside their houses, peered through their shutters and doors.

"Well, what's the problem?" the midwife asked, feeling their heavy glares. The silence endured.

"You can't be suggesting we…" one man cautiously spoke up.

"Where is the rebbi…" said another through rising whispers.

"It's a *dark omen!*" shouted a white haired woman with disgust. "Drop it! Let it go!"

"Don't be ridiculous!" The midwife forcefully retorted. "This is no omen! What has gotten into you all? You're talking like *Goyim*! It's meat—nothing more. Sure, it's not *kashrut*, but under the circumstances… frankly, I don't care what any of you —or the *rabbi*—thinks."

A communal shriek erupted around the circle.

"What I meant is… well, fine! *Get* the rabbi! He will tell you himself!" she said, flustered and indignant. "Where *is* he?"

Everyone glanced around.

At the far end of the road, yanked out his door in his slippers, the rabbi slowly trundled forward. A child by each arm helped guide the old, frail man, fighting his robe from carrying him aloft. As far as he could gather from the children's excited explanations, there had been a birth, and the parents *insisted* he bless the child and mother that very night. Privately, under the circumstances—with his toes freezing, feeling like his nose was a strong gust from breaking off—he held that the Vostęvskies were quite too far, and his blessings for the new mother and child could have *at least* waited until the morning light. Low on breath, he inquired from the children once more what the urgency seemed to be. But before they could speak, he got his answer from the shouting just up ahead.

"Rabbi!" he heard called out through the darkness.

"There he is!" others said. "Go get him!"

He squinted his eyes. Half of his village, with the midwife in front, was charging at him with furious speed.

"Oh God!" he thought to himself. *"Is this about Rivka's baking tray? I told Pitale to return it yesterday!"*

With a fearful cry, he raised his shaking hands in the air, turned around, and hurriedly tried to shuffle back home. But before he could retreat two paces, the midwife, along with the rest of the neighbors, surrounded him. Candle lamps brought his bearded face into deep relief.

"It's back at home! It's just an honest—" the rabbi shouted in astonishment.

"—Rabbi, listen to this!"

"What's back at home?"

"Wait—is he talking about my tray?"

"Alright, alright! Can I speak? Is that okay?" Liza frantically asked the crowd. They quieted, she caught a deep breath, and she began to calmly explain everything that had happened in the rabbi's absence.

Liza gestured right down the road, began her story, and explained the situation of the new mother. The rabbi covered his mouth in shock. She lifted the wriggling cat for all to see once more, boldly making clear her intentions. With his approval, she was ready to prepare Chana a meal.

The rabbi looked at the animal hanging pitifully from her fist; glanced around to the crowd, zealously hounding him in the dark snow; gazed into the midwife's sad eyes, anxiously hoping for his approval; and thought, in eighty-one years on Earth, he had never seen such a sorry sight. The poverty of the night, the sadness of the birth, the desperation of his people, and the poor creature in the center of it all—a profound weight settled on his heart.

The rabbi, knowing God very well, and ready to get back into his little warmth, did not truly have anything difficult to consider. Frankly, he was surprised the issue had persisted thus far. Gathering his strength to address the crowd, he opened his mouth to speak.

"Do you *understand* what she's asking, rabbi? Are we really going to butcher a *cat*? It's unspeakable!" the old woman shouted with disgust from her window. Several more raised their voices in concurrence.

"She's right! It's an affront to the Torah," added a gray old man, scarcely younger than the rabbi, from his own doorstep.

"There are still roots left she can eat!"

"Yes, we must *banish* the dark omen—not *eat* it!"

"*I* would sooner eat sticks than a black cat!" added another, spitting three times at the thought.

The rabbi lifted his shaking finger, tilting his head in disapproval. His people's talk of supposed dark omens—from animals or otherwise—always bewildered him. But gathering his breath to speak, he was interrupted again.

"As if *you* understand the *halacha*," said one young woman in the crowd to the gray haired old man, courageously coming to the defense of the midwife. "And besides, it's not *you* who must eat it, but Chana!"

"She's right, we're wasting time!" cautiously added another.

"Rabbi, why do you want Chana to be hungry?" asked a little girl in a floral dress, soaked to her neck with snow, tugging on the rabbi's sleeve. The rabbi slapped his forehead. Yet again, he tried to get in a word—and again, he was interrupted.

"*Sheket* rabbi, look, Yitzhak is coming now!"

Yitzhak, having engaged a neighbor girl to temporarily hold his son back in his house, marched through the crowd, up to the rabbi's face, and accosted him without hesitation.

"Rabbi, what is this insanity?" he said.

The rabbi stepped back in fright.

"Are these people saying that the life of *some miserable cat* is worth more than my wife's? My child's? Surely *you* know better! My wife is dying and my baby starves while these people speak for God from their windows. How could it be *treif* to save a life? Impossible! And how can you remain silent on all of this? For God's sake, these people came to you for an answer; it's your duty to speak out, so speak already!"

Yitzhak's irreverent outburst caused an even greater uproar. A few felt as if they could faint. The rabbi, practically ready to collapse as well, bent down, took one last breath, and whispered to the little girl.

"Sweet child? Will you *please* go find for me the butcher? Tell him to bring his sharpest cleaver," he implored, peering at the crowd from the side of his eye.

"What—what did the rabbi just say?" someone said.

"Did you all hear that?" Yitzhak shouted.

"Heard what? What did he say?"

"*Ribono Shel Oylem*! Let's get this over with already!" the rabbi shouted, shaking his hands in the air. "Someone bring me a knife!"

The crowd turned deathly silent.

"You all heard the rabbi! There is nothing more to debate!" Yitzhak said, hastily grabbing the cat from the midwife's hands. "I'm taking *this* to my house. Liza—help the rabbi over. So, where is the butcher?"

"He's right here!" the little girl called out, pushing the butcher into the center. The old man stared back at them like a startled deer. His mustache quivered. Anxiously trading glances, the crowd leaned in to hear what the old man would say.

"Well? Will you bring a knife or not?" Yitzhak asked.

"Rabbi," the old, devoutly religious man began nervously. "Yes, I have something I can bring. But... this little girl said you asked for my *best* cleaver... perhaps, not my *best*? Considering I must use it for..."

Yitzhak listened to the sound of his beating heart. Rage boiled over in his soul.

"So, that's how you feel!" he said, unwilling to hear any more of the butcher's appeal. He marched past the butcher, pushing his neighbors aside, and with fire glowing from his eyes, ran to the closest houses' stone well. With a deep breath, he raised the cat high above him.

"Wait, dear Yitzhak!" the rabbi cried. "We will settle this. We will slaughter it! But it *must not* be done like that!"

Yitzhak, ignoring his words, and with all of his power, thrashed the cat against the stones. She let out a pitiful shriek. With a snap, her limp body fell into the snow. Blood drained from a deep gash in her head. Within seconds, she breathed her long life's last, shallow, laborious breath.

"There! We don't need to ruin your precious cleaver!" Yitzhak shouted with wrath.

Everything stood in silence; every man and woman in the crowd looked on in abject terror; the butcher hurriedly fled to his house, dragging the little girl away too; the rabbi's eyes bulged from his face; and the howling blizzard, still blanketing the ground with snow, seemed to pause with bated breath. Even God, seeing what he already knew would come to pass, let fall one celestial tear.

Yitzhak, panting, stared at the dead carcass lying by his feet. Though frightened by his own actions, he made peace within himself. Liza, the midwife, shocked as anyone, was the first to break the enduring silence.

"Rabbi, what do we do *now*?" she murmured softly.

The rabbi, staring vacantly into the air, shook his head as if he had been awoken from a dream.

"What did you say, sweet child?"

"I asked what we do now," she repeated, struggling to hold back tears.

The rabbi, delving deep into his understanding of the *Talmud*, searched for a precedent to guide him.

"I—Well, I must bless a new mother and child," he answered in awe, as if divining the answer as he spoke. Rabbi Ezra then looked at Liza, sighed, wiped his face off with his wet sleeve, and knocked the snow off his hat.

"You, my dear," he added, "must now help me save her life. So help me there. I imagine there is a hearth to light."

The midwife softly gasped, covered her mouth, closed her moist eyes, and obediently nodded her head.

He extended his arm to her, and obeying his words, she took his arm in her hands. They walked in silence to the Vostęvskies' house. One by one, the rest of the neighbors returned to their homes, closed their windows, and tightly bolted their doors. Yitzhak was the last one in the street. With a furrow over his brow, he collected the carcass from the snow and followed the rabbi and Liza at a short distance.

Back behind his house, with his rusted scythe, Yitzhak began his preparations. With an expressionless, sunken face, he coarsely shaved her coat, cleaned her, and crudely chopped her meat into sections. Meanwhile, on the other side of the wall, with the crying baby once more in her arms, the midwife raised their fire. In Yitzhak's pot, she prepared a broth with more snow, wild flowers, dried herbs, and the rest of their wine. She waited in silence, gently petting Chana's hand, for the concoction's final ingredient. Yitzhak, silently approaching through the back door, swiftly dropped the dreadful meat into the pot.

As the soup cooked beside them, the rabbi, still catching his breath, gave the silent mother and child a simple blessing. He gently kissed the newborn boy on his head. Sitting down in contemplation, Rabbi Ezra considered that all of God's gifts on Earth had a blessing spoken for them since the creation of time. However, just as he sensed the soup had finished cooking and the air in the house smelled of herbs, flowers, warm alcohol, and sinewy meat, the rabbi hastily stood up. He kindly bowed to the midwife, to Chana, and to the baby. He picked up his coat, opened the door, and after briefly exchanging a severe glance with Yitzhak from the corner of his eye, left into the storm alone.

Despite all he had seen, the rabbi could not bear to watch a new mother fed a meal which he *could not* bless. As he meditated over the night, he acknowledged that the cat must have been the answer to someone's prayer. However, could an unblessable meal have been sent by God at all? He could not find an answer to this problem. In troubled thought, following the tracks he had carved earlier in the night, he returned to his rest on a thin pallet beside his old, sleeping wife.

The midwife, understanding the rabbi's profound dilemma, could no longer abate her tears. How could she serve Chana such an abhorrent meal? How could she be a part of it?

Yitzhak saw this and nudged her aside. He picked up his ladle, his spoon, and prepared the bowl himself. He was no less aware of the halacha, understood his own actions, and understood the significance of the rabbi's severe glare. But fully aware that God had answered his *own* prayer, he tasted the soup, decided it was good, and muttered a blessing for it of his own design.

When the first spoonful touched her lips, Chana tasted it on her tongue and let the warm, oily broth slowly melt down her throat. She opened her mouth by a crease, lifted her eyelids by a hair, and by her second sip, Death had already dejectedly shown itself out their door.

Yitzhak lifted his baby from the midwife's arms, still bloody, awake, and silent. Chana coughed, moaned, and turned her head. Seeing her baby clearly for the first time, she cried in joy. She hungrily drank the soup, nearly choking, swallowing whole spoonfuls as Yitzhak fed her.

"Slow down, Chanale," Yitzhak said, smiling. "It's not going anywhere."

Sighing in deep relief, she felt life soak through her muscles, her skin, her bones, and her breasts. Not thirty minutes later, she sat up in her bed, took her baby on her lap, named him Abraham, and fed him his first meal.

In other times, God's miracles parted the Red Sea or brought forth water from a stone in Refidim. For the Vostęvskies, a sick cat from the snowy tundra proved God's grace all the same. For their neighbors, however, lying awake in their beds that night, doubts and questions—even dark fears—lingered in their minds.

But if anyone in Tolevoste had doubted that God was with them at all, by sunrise, the wind abated, the sky cleared, and spring's warm air suddenly enveloped their land. The entire village awoke to the sound of songbirds late in the morning. Walking through their dirt streets, they felt the warm sun on their skin, the gentle breeze on their foreheads, and the soft, melting snow crunching beneath their feet. Many cried. Others smiled. All said a deep prayer of gratitude. And honoring their humility, God answered them as one, deciding that the people of Tolevoste would never endure a winter as long as that one again.

With the new season having come, new weddings to be celebrated, old dances to warm the *mashke*, and ancient prayers to brighten the shul, the horror of that impoverished night faded from their collective memory. Nonetheless, for most in the village, a vague fear of Yitzhak persisted.

For Chana Vostęvskie, the version of events Yitzhak recounted to her, days later—of the heroic midwife, her dutiful husband, and her beloved rabbi, wading through the wind and snow for her—stayed close to her heart until the day of her death. And the people of Tolevoste, in sympathy for both Chana and the baby Abraham, with great discretion, never contradicted Yitzhak's version of events with the truth. Therefore, up until the cruel destruction of the Jews of Tolevoste two centuries into the future, every Vostęvskie would eat *snow chicken* soup for the

DIASPORA

Sabbath in remembrance of the "chicken," sent by God from the snowy tundra, that saved the life of a new mother generations ago. Prepared in a similar way—braising the meat in wine, seasoning it with wild herbs and dried flowers—Chana and Yitzhak's descendants would know just as much as Chana Vostęvskie did of the true ingredient for the original *snow chicken* soup; that is to say, they would know nothing of it at all.

But despite the many blessings that would flow through Tolevoste and even the Vostęvskie household for several generations more, Yitzhak's severe trespass lingered in God's eternal mind. God did permit Chana's strength to increase many times over. Yitzhak, seeing this, tried countless times more for children with his bright and virile wife. But Chana, inexplicably, could never conceive another child. Her nieces and nephews joined the aging Chana, Yitzhak, and their cousin Abraham, for dinners on the Sabbath. Her cousins crowded the shul with little girls in white frocks and boys in oversized Kapotas. But in the Vostęvskies' house, to their great dismay, their daily meals remained quiet, cold, and short. Chana and Yitzhak called upon the ever-tormented rabbi for guidance in the matter of her inexplicable infertility many times. With his wisdom and discretion, he would lower his head, close his eyes, and with a tinge of guilt, bid Chana and Yitzhak to accept God's mysterious will.

God did permit Yitzhak's line to continue for generations more. However, proceeding the night Yitzhak disobeyed the rabbi's simple order for patience, thrashed a cat to death with *wrath* against a stone well, and fed his nursing wife from its unblessable flesh, God forbade Chana, and any other women who married a Vostęvskie, to ever bear her husband more than one child.

To ensure His will be done, God scanned across Heaven, found a minor angel, confirmed it had been occupied with nothing of great importance, and assigned it to watch this particular family. So in service to God, one angel would proceed to keep the Vostęvskies under its gaze.

DIASPORA

2

The Schlemiel

Decades passed. Like a rock under the rain, Tolevoste sat where it was placed. Small enough to be out of sight, no one had yet kicked it aside. Every year, this inconsequential rock fell beneath a soft dusting of snow; reemerged for the sun; overgrew with weeds, tall grass, and moss; and shivered beneath the frost once more. For every person born in Tolevoste, another person died. For those gone and arrived, they could ask for no more than that.

However, in the decades that followed the birth of Abraham, the weather did moderate, as God promised; the harvests proved bountiful; and with God's particular favor, Tolevoste happened to rise into a moderately greater condition than it had at most other points in the past. The planks of the ramshackle cabins of the previous generation, largely eaten away by termites, were steadily replaced with good, stained hardwood. Though there were no Rothschilds in that part of Poland, many families of Tolevoste had, through rigorous discipline, amassed modest fortunes.

Although the people toiled over their fields in the same way they had always done and in the same way people did in other villages nearby, their frugality and diligence slowly began to be noticed around the region. The Christians from the nearby village of Revnokita, for example, knew of the Jews of Tolevoste by their clean and rugged wool jackets, their well-fed horses and mules, and the aromatic carts of carp and herring they pulled every Sunday back from the market.

Yet despite all of this, no money had yet entered the village except what they earned from their fields. From buckwheat and buckwheat alone, most of the elders of Tolevoste could expect to leave their children with not only their love and

DIASPORA

wisdom, but with enough money to bury them, and plenty extra for a good many meals to follow.

Abraham, too, lived, married, and died. In this way, he fulfilled all his duties to his child, his wife, and his God as he understood them. What's more, he lived, married, and died in much the same fashion as his father, Yitzhak; guiding his plow and swinging his rusted scythe until his beard had grown silver to the tip; spending a short retirement in his straw bed beside his dutiful wife, Sarah; and sustaining his breath just long enough to see his only child, Chaim, marry Miriam, a young girl of startling grace. For Abraham, this was enough. Having finally fathered just one child at the late, unexpected age of sixty-one, he could not have asked from God for anything more.

His son, Chaim, was similar to many of the Vostęvskies before him. However, in one particular way, and against great odds, he would stand out from them all. The only way to hear that unlikely story in its truest form—as Chaim would keep its enigmatic details close to him throughout his life—was to sit down with Chaim's son, Moishe, with a bottle of Slivovitz in hand. If one cleared their evening of all responsibilities and accepted that they would find Moishe's retelling of the history almost impossible to believe, they would hear the truth about how the Vostęvskies came to be among Poland's finest creators of kosher wine.

Moishe's story of his father began with the portrait of a typical *schlemiel*; from one "ingenious" escapade to another, his father had flung money out of his hands as hastily as if it were a parcel of pork, and he had mistakenly picked it up at the *Goyish* market in Revnokita—the further away it landed from him, his family, or his friends, the better. His patient wife, Miriam, grew to lament the evenings he would come home from his buckwheat crop with a newspaper in one hand and the key to their coin box in the other.

"Miriam!" Chaim burst into his house one evening, slamming his door, sending his two chickens in his front yard into a frenzy.

"My God. You almost gave me a heart attack! What is the matter with you?"

"Miriam, oh, the blessing! Our problems are over! Tell me, we have no time to waste, do you still have your grandmother's pearls?"

"Dear," she began, horrified, and raising the collar of her shirt ever so slightly. "We still have several months before the harvest—"

"No matter, my darling wife, no matter! I'll be back in the morning, and believe me, we shall be king and queen of Tolevoste by sundown!"

Stuffing his satchel with the silver kopecks from his coin box that Miriam could never figure out how to hide well enough, he grabbed his fur hat, flew out his door, and caught an overnight train to Ribnyvosk. There, he got a bed in their only inn. By the first morning light, he let himself in at the door of a machinery shop advertised in the corner of his regional newspaper. He held all the money to his name in one hand. Minutes later, he left through their back door with a crate the size of a calf, towed by the machinery shop owner's donkey, back to the train station.

How, exactly, a steam-powered *ice cream maker* could have turned Chaim's capricious goat's odd quart of milk into riches—with no sugar or ice to speak of—no one could have said at the time. But to Chaim, nothing could have made greater sense.

"Ice cream... *ice cream* he says! And with what cow? Dear God, this man will be my death!"

A pattern like this continued from the day of their marriage and beyond the birth of Moishe. Miriam would plead with her husband; *when* she would fail, she would fall on the

DIASPORA

rabbi's feet; the rabbi, hearing the trying task before him, would gather strength from the words of wisdom in his siddur; and soon after Chaim would return home with the spoils of his caprices, the two of them, as the most influential figures in his life, would accost him sufficiently into undoing the financial harms he caused—to whatever extent was even possible.

But following the day he dejectedly rolled his steam-powered confectionary contraption back onto the train to Ribnyvosk, Miriam desperately sought a more lasting solution to this problem. The rabbi, mentioning in passing frustration that Chaim took greater inspiration from the newspaper than the siddur, inspired Miriam with what she had to do.

With the help of the rabbi and for the sake of their darling baby Moishe, she persuaded all of the village to agree to an outlandish proposition: no newspapers could be seen on the streets of Tolevoste anymore, lest Chaim get a hold of one again. Even the monger at the far end of Tolevoste's main road, who happily sold cigarettes to children by the stick and Slivovitz to the drunks by the shot, eventually agreed. He hid his newspapers whenever a man, fitting the description of a wild-eyed buckwheat farmer in an oversized fur hat, approached him in the distance.

For a time, the solution appeared to work miraculously. With nothing left to occupy his fancy but the clear sky and his iron scythe, the next harvest passed for the Vostęvskies in peace. Fair weather and high grain prices had refilled much of the silver lost to his whims; baby Moishe stood up on his own wobbly feet; and the creases Chaim had carved into the edges of his young wife's eyes imperceptibly faded away.

From the day of that decision, two happy years passed. On one spring morning, before the Sabbath, the contented wife awoke late. The three year old Moishe slept quietly by her side while her husband—she assumed—ever the dutiful father, toiled over his buckwheat crop in the field.

Miriam had much to do. In addition to preparing for the Sabbath, the village anticipated a newborn baby's bris. Several travelers, mostly distant family members of the child's parents, had taken up lodging in the village's few open beds. Miriam knew, if she were to find any candles for the Sabbath still left for sale, she had to leave for the shops right away.

Miriam made her way to Tolevoste's general store with the heavy Moishe in her arms. All around the village, men prepared for the upcoming celebration with freshly slaughtered cuts of beef and lamb. The sisters and friends of the newborn boy's mother collected baby clothes and toys as gifts. The rest of the women salted herring and prepared white fish salad for the reception at the shul.

Miriam found the store's very last candles sitting on its shelf. She wanted to make sure her husband would enjoy his hard-earned Sabbath, so she spent a few of her own groszy to buy a pack of sugar, intending to bake some cakes. But before Miriam could place her candlesticks and sugar on the counter, she saw something wholly unexpected in the corner of her eye. Her heart dropped. Slowly, she turned her entire body to see. In one of the visitor's hands, under his squinting, monocled gaze, she saw *it*.

"Where did you get that?" Miriam asked with disgust.

"What, my dear? The Warsaw Gazette? Why, I brought several copies. Would you like one?"

Miriam's eyes shot around the store. Newspaper after newspaper floated by in people's hands.

"Ribono Shel Oylam!" she shouted, flying out to the street.

It was only 9:30 a.m. Having had no idea when that man had even come in, she prayed she still had time. Miriam ran desperately to the Kalinasevka station, an hour's walk to the north of Tolevoste's crop fields. But the Warsaw bound train had left a half hour earlier, and with it, her husband, with the

DIASPORA

advertisement section of the Warsaw Gazette in hand, and their entire savings of recently replenished silver kopeks.

As if he were a drunk and the water in his canteen had mistakenly been replaced with schnapps, Chaim's suppressed habit erupted from dormancy with a vengeance. Not only did he spend every last kopek he could scrape from his coin box, his wife's purse, and the hidden flap in his Sabbath shoe, but Miriam's heirloom pearls, innocently left defenseless on her nightstand, traveled to Warsaw as well.

But for this brazen caper of Chaim's, his family's meager life savings could not bring him very far. So in exchange for the extent of his family's wealth, Chaim secured a high-interest loan from a loan shark stationed right across the street from the First Bank of Warsaw—the bank, he learned, refused to give loans to Jews.

What were the fruits of this labor? Miriam was the first to learn. She sat disconsolate at the train stop all the next day, with Moishe playing in the dust beside her, waiting for her husband to return. The last train of the evening came to a stop. At the end of the line, on its very own flatcar, a giant, shining, mechanized crop thresher, recently shipped from America, contrasted obliquely against the wooden passenger cars it had been tacked onto at the final minute.

Miriam, utterly horrified, understood everything immediately.

How, exactly, that farcical monstrosity was supposed to increase the profitability of Chaim's four acres of buckwheat, no one but Chaim, and perhaps God, could have explained. The following events played out not only as Miriam guessed, but to her dismay, with far greater irony—perhaps humor—in God's eyes.

Just in time for the summer harvest, Chaim had to ride the twelve-hour train ride back to Warsaw for the second time to consult the manufacturer; his thresher lay hopelessly dormant on its pallet, broken from the moment the village people first managed to unload it off of the train. His loving wife, with her husband missing, and desperate to save their crop, took up his scythe for herself.

"*If my husband can do this, surely I can,*" Miriam thought to herself.

In the fields, with a choir of oxen, surrounded by the men, and with Moishe tugging at her skirt, she tried to harvest her husband's buckwheat. Every third step through the mud, she slipped out of Chaim's old boots, muddying her knees and face on the ground. Meanwhile, in Warsaw, despite Chaim's meek insistence that the machinery importer should honor his crumbled warranty, he could only secure a twenty-five percent discount on a replacement threshing cylinder to fix the problem.

"Will you ship it to Tolevoste for me?" Chaim asked.

"Shipping is separate," the salesman said curtly, not looking up from his paperwork at his desk.

Back in Tolevoste, just after fully disassembling, reassembling, re-lubricating, and extensively adjusting his machine, a fungal infection rapidly swept across not a single other field but Chaim's. Everything Miriam had not yet harvested had been destroyed. Considering Miriam had no previous experience with a scythe, this happened to be nearly all.

Beseeching his young wife for help once more while he searched for a solution, Chaim prostrated before her, laboriously convincing Miriam to keep their household together through nightly shifts as a seamstress. Meanwhile, the rabbi, to both of their dismay, could not find a prayer to rid Chaim's dying crops of their infection. Chaim tried everything—growth tonics, poisonous powders, and even the purchase of a horticulturist's tome in Revnokita, soon to languish in dust on Chaim's small shelf above his bedroom study. As it often happens when it is

God who is trying to teach someone a lesson, Chaim could not catch a break.

He had run out of good options. He burned what remained of his crops, decided the thresher bore the mark of the evil eye, and though ostensibly having remedied its original mechanical issue, declared it had to be scrapped. In regards to his debt, since his days in the yeshiva, Chaim had been inculcated with the threat that unpaid debts would be judged very harshly by God on *Yom-Kippur,* the day of atonement. But fearing his loan shark would judge his debt at least as harshly as God, or more, he decided his debt had to be repaid immediately. Chaim planned his third, and hopefully last, trip to Warsaw.

For the following month, Chaim made the somber preparations for his trip back to the big city. By the time the wind had cooled, he had skimmed just enough money from his wife, bought a third ticket, and waited by the Kalinasevka train stop on one *Yom-Sheni,* a Monday. Early that same afternoon, with the sun shining brightly over the finely polished city, Chaim stepped foot onto the platform of the Warsaw Central Train Station.

A light flurry began to dust the city. With his head down, he tore through the crowds of Polish, Armenian, and Czechian travelers anxious to board, all dressed in fine suits, tall stockings, and dark, leather shoes. Chaim, under his oversized fur hat, with hanging payot; in a long, black, cotton kapota; felt uneasy about his conspicuousness.

He nearly smiled at the smell of the city's stoves and fireplaces burning with sappy wood. In the air, shipments of tea, Asiatic spices, dried meats, fine leather, pets, old books, and mothy luggage swirled around him. The brisk breeze quickly awakened him to the attitude of the city. But at the thought of what he prepared to do, the entire city and all its people, at other times delightful in his eyes, seemed loathsome.

His first stop, as he had unhappily decided the previous evening, would be to pawn his prized, silver-cased *Breguet* pocket watch. He looked down at its shimmering *grand-feu* enamel dial and single, blue-fired hour hand. Shamefully, he did not even need to look up to see where he needed to go; he knew well his way from the station, to the pawn shop, to his creditor.

"*Where did it go wrong?*" he thought in a rare moment of somber reflection.

As images came to his mind of his Bar Mitzvah, the day his father bestowed upon him the family heirloom, the gravity of his compounding mistakes hounded him. The loss of his wife's pearls, however, equally irreplaceable; her silverware, gifted by her father on their wedding day; and the long days she spent rebuilding what *he* had squandered away, still hardly crossed his mind.

Before pawning his timepiece, he had to make a brief stop at Kalina Timepieces, the French Horologist's authorized Warsaw dealership, to re-certify the heirloom's authenticity. He knew his grandfather Abraham had paid eighty-six zloty for it when new, and he would need it to pawn for fifty, along with his satchel filled with sixty-five, to fully pay off his loan shark that day.

The recertification, to his relief, took little time—the watch was a well-kept classic—and with the document in hand, he left the store. Only two streets down, clutching his Breguet and holding back tears, Chaim pushed his way through the pawn shop's deceptively light, double swinging doors. They slammed against the wall. The pawnbroker glanced up at the small, anxious man with annoyance.

Of all the places to make an entrance... Chaim thought ruefully.

He glanced around—the shop seemed much the same as he remembered it. Darkened oil paintings, muskets, dresses, and bizarre stringed instruments cluttered the dimly lit and tightly organized store. Behind a display case of etched pistols and tarnished pocket watches doubling as a trading desk, the pawnbroker sat with his arms folded. Chaim delicately placed the timepiece and paperwork atop the counter.

"What'll you give me for it?" He asked dejectedly.

Ignoring the document, the young pawnbroker picked up the timepiece in his hand and inspected the rare, shimmering timepiece with familiarity. His eyes instantly betrayed delight.

"This isn't stolen, is it?"

"Of course not!" Chaim said, aghast.

"Fine, fine. I need to ask these things you know."

The pawnbroker cleared his throat.

"I'll do three hundred right now. Nothing to scoff at, no? We have a deal?" he said, extending his hand.

"Three hundred!" Chaim shouted in disbelief. "You must be out of your mind!"

"Now, now—I was merely talking aloud," the shopkeeper countered, already expecting to haggle. "We can find an arrangement suitable to us both."

Still in disbelief over the sum, Chaim looked at him so strangely that the pawnbroker could only surmise he was discontented.

"Come now, don't look at me that way. There are limits to what a humble pawnbroker can pay! See, there are things you must consider, from my perspective—"

"—You mean to say you're offering me *three hundred* zloty for my grandfather's timepiece, purchased sixty-five years ago? Impossible! There is simply no way such an amount is fair!"

"You must temper your expectations! Obviously, you've no doubt seen an early Breguet *Souscription* on a mantle in a fine department store with a price of six hundred, yes? Okay, but ahh, doesn't the simple pawnbroker have to earn his share? The authenticity has been assured, but there is still the cost of adjustment, of the oiling—in fact, I believe there is a small scratch just here," the pawnbroker said evasively, pointing to a barely noticeable mark on the crown.

Chaim stared at him, slack-jawed. A bead of sweat formed on the pawnbroker's temple.

"Now, I see you are not a fool, and I may have offended you, for which I apologize. As a final offer, I can do three hundred and twenty."

"Three hundred and twenty!" Chaim blurted out in astonishment, before finally forcing his own mouth shut. At last, he managed to restrain himself. Looking into the pawnbroker's anxious eyes, for once, the gear train in his brain began to turn. He preened his hand, reached over the desk, and dignifiedly removed the watch from the pawnbroker's hand.

"Now hold on," the pawnbroker began, holding his finger up.

"Yes, very well—" Chaim's voice subtlety cracked. "I've thought about your offer, but I think the timepiece speaks for itself. After all, it is a Breguet *Sous-crip-tion*," Chaim said, deftly mimicking the pawnbroker's French. Turning around, he feigned to leave. "Perhaps the *Tomasz* Pawnshop–"

"Just a moment!" the pawnbroker interjected. "Three hundred and fifty, final offer. *Tomasz* is always avoiding his debtors, and… and I have the money right here!"

Chaim stopped.

Well, I'm taking a loss here, but…" he said with his back to the pawnbroker, averting his gaze so as to not reveal his excitement. I can accept three hundred and sixty. Then it's yours."

"Fine, fine. Excellent, then hand it over—three hundred an sixty, we have a deal!"

The pawnbroker grabbed Chaim's hand, shook it, snatched the timepiece, briefly left through a backdoor to get his coin-box, and came straight out with Chaim's payment. One after another, he carefully counted out 360 zloty into Chaim's simple-mindedly outstretched hands. After every fifty pieces, Chaim unceremoniously dumped the coins into his bag, weighing down his shoulder with bright silver.

Throughout the entire exchange, Chaim had unconsciously begun holding his breath. He felt too afraid to betray his guise of calm with a large gasp of air. When the pawnbroker finally turned away to draft a receipt, lightheaded, blue, and unable to contain his excitement any longer, Chaim hastily fled out the door.

Clutching his heart, he gasped. The cool breeze dried the sweat on his forehead. He threw his hands in the air, feeling ready to sing, reveling in his first victory since last Pesach when he won back his only chicken from David the *Shikker* over a game of Mizerka at the *mashke*. He had been in the store for longer than he thought; he took in the freshly lit lamplights and the headlights of the quietly rolling carriages and carts all around the street. All of the people around him suddenly seemed cheerful and smiling, as if joining in Chaim's revelry just by virtue of being in that softly lit, breezy city, passing the golden hour of the evening.

Chaim sauntered forward. His breath finally steadied. The air that entered his lungs displaced months of failure and frustration. His newfound financial freedom outweighed the sorrow of losing his heirloom; even just thirty zloty would be enough to sustain his family through the winter!

Dusk settled in. The cool breeze, pleasant under the sun, started to pierce through Chaim's thick wool overcoat.

In more troubled times, a sweat would have broken out over his brow by then; his creditor lay just ahead. But in that moment, every step Chaim took forward held more determination than the last.

Chaim's time in the loan shark's dimly lit office was brief. With the courage of Moses, he took a great breath, and confidently threw apart the double doors. The plump, bald, unshaven usurer before him jumped in fright.

Chaim fixated on the man's frightened eyes. He smelled a strong odor of vodka on his breath. A cheap, pot-metal crucifix hung from his neck.

"This is the man I feared?" Chaim thought, internally mocking the precarious stacks of paper and folders, not two promissory notes away from toppling over, surrounding him. To the lender's horror, he cavalierly spread the mountains of papers apart, clearing a large area, and poured forth a heaping pile of silver coins all across his desk from his ragged, goatskin satchel. The sound of the flowing silver stopped passersby on the street. The lender stared silently at the bewildering apparition.

"That's thirteen, fourteen—one hundred and fifteen," Chaim said, counting aloud to the loan shark's astonished sneer. "Mark my account cleared, please."

"Now just a moment—" the lender tried to interject.

"I'll take my receipt now. The name is Vostęvskie. Vos-tęv-skie!" he said, signing out the spelling in the air.

A moment passed in silence. Never breaking eye contact, the loan shark briefly scrawled a receipt on a thin piece of receipt paper, tore it away, and handed it to the strange Jew. He held onto it for a moment longer, searching the face of his former client for a hint of an explanation. But Chaim's grip overcame him. Ripping it away from his arms, God had freed Chaim from his debt, his fear for his family's finances, further reproaches of the rabbi and his darling wife, and most importantly to Chaim, any need for him to face the causes of his continued desperation.

Satisfied with Chaim's good fortune, but somewhat frustrated by his lack of awareness, God turned to His angel for insight. Together, they decided that Chaim would benefit from a test; all the money in the world could do no good for a fool.

DIASPORA

3

Strange Wine

44

With several hours to spare before his train would depart back east, Chaim rested his legs on a stone bench in Gdansk Square. He pulled up his collar to protect his neck from the wind, retrieved an apple from his satchel, and basked in the lightness of his mind. At long last, with nothing at all left to worry about—he could buy back his goat from the butcher, fix his leaking roof, and even replace the candlesticks he had "borrowed" from the rabbi for the past three Sabbaths—he considered what obligations he had to his wife.

"*Maybe I should get her something*," he said to himself. "*A gift—a new set of pearls—yes, that'd be nice. I'm quite a rich man, after all.*"

After nonchalantly standing up, stretching, and tossing his half-eaten apple into a bush, he made his way back to the street.

Taking a wide look around, seeing an array of upscale shops encircling the square, he turned towards a dazzling jewelry shop, the *Karenina*, glowing through the darkness. He looked through their floor-to-ceiling windows displaying everything from hats and dresses, candelabras and chandeliers, to jewelry, perfumes, and dolls. At the edge of the window, he saw it: the perfect pearl necklace, hanging from a velvet-lined bust, vaguely reminiscent of the one he had pawned away.

He was just about to enter, his hand on the door handle, when he stopped in his tracks. His nose flared. Like the serpent's whisper, a gentle aroma tempted him away.

Is that mulled wine? he asked himself, craning his neck.

Just next door to the Karenina, he found the source—the *Yordania*, a lively pub, crowded by young, well-dressed, festive Warsovians, warmed by their hot mugs, sharing one another's laughter under the pub's awning. Forgetting altogether the gift for his wife waiting in anguish for him back in Tolevoste, Chaim made his way toward the pub.

"*I'll just be a minute… No one will have to know*," Chaim thought, dismissing his awareness that the Yordania's wine was certainly not kosher. Clearing his way through the crowd by the entrance, he brushed the light dusting of snow off of his boots, shoulders, fur hat, and opened the door. The instant he crossed the door frame, the noise from the street vanished.

His world shifted sideways by a hair.

He felt faint; his vision blurred, as if standing too fast from his bed; he heard a powerful ringing in his ears; but a moment later, his world came back into focus. Feeling the luxurious warmth of the pub's air, he sighed with relief. Warsaw's cold winter did not penetrate the Yordania.

Chaim's eyes adjusted to the dim, gently flickering lamplight. Contrasting the Yordania's polished, well maintained facade, its derelict interior atmosphere took him by surprise. The wall panels, floor boards, tables, and chairs all appeared to be cut from the same rough, gray, knotted lumber. Two or three people, hunched over their drinks, sat alone in the pub's distant booths, their faces hidden beneath tall collars and broad shadows. A layer of fine dust, like fresh snow, coated the floor. Contrasting all its dilapidation, the pub's myriad polished oil lamps, encircling the walls, gave Chaim the impression of being inside a dusty chandelier.

The barkeeper, with white shoulder-length hair, wearing the ragged tunic of an ascetic, stared straight ahead. Polishing a mug, he betrayed no awareness of Chaim's entrance. Chaim felt uneasy, struck by the sight of that biblically old and ragged man overseeing a backbar with every drink he could imagine. He cleared his throat and approached.

"Quiet tonight, isn't it?" Chaim began, taking a seat, laying his satchel on the ground beside him.

"Quiet? I'm not so sure. The world is spinning fast; the wind is howling; the snow is dancing in the clouds," the barkeeper countered, still looking distantly past him.

Paying no mind to the old man's strange comment, Chaim glanced suspiciously around him once more. The ethereally quiet pub had completely emptied of its few patrons. He felt thoroughly unsettled, but with wine still preoccupying his mind, decided his stop would be brief.

"Yes, sure, well if you're still serving—" Chaim began.

The barkeeper interrupted him by placing the mug on the bar and ladling it with fresh mulled wine—exactly what he was about to request.

"Ah, yes. Perfect!"

Grabbing the mug, Chaim breathed in its intoxicating fumes, closing his eyes as he smelled its warm cinnamon, allspice, orange peel, and sliced green apple, hypnotically twirling in the concoction's center. He took his first sip and felt the warm wine, thick like oil, spread throughout his chest. As quickly as they had arisen, he felt all his apprehensions wash away.

"The quiet is good! I needed this," he said, stretching his muscles, getting comfortable in his chair. Still breathing in his drink's aroma, he took a second gulp. A heavy warmth settled behind his eyes. His body began to feel light.

"*Oy va-voy, that's some mulled wine,*" Chaim thought.

The combination of the drink's otherworldly scent, the softness of his wool-lined coat, and the dance of the oil lamps seemingly swaying around him led Chaim to rest his head on the bar. He closed his eyes. The last of his thoughts floated away. He faded off into deep sleep.

An unknown amount of time passed.

Chaim coughed, sat up, rubbed his eyes, and looked around. Though unconcerned, he felt intrigued that he could not fully remember where he was, nor how long he had been sitting there—or how he even got there.

"*Wasn't I—I was about to do something. But what was it?*" he asked himself. "*Was it something to do with my wife?*"

Looking away in thought, he noticed a drink right in front of him. He smelled its sweet steam, still rising in thick clouds, as if still boiling in its pot.

"Ah, mulled wine! You read my mind!" he said, recalling the enchanting smell that had brought him inside there in the first place. "May I?"

The barkeeper nodded, watching Chaim take his third, hearty draft.

Chaim's vision faded to gray. Eclectic shapes, indistinct voices, vibrating colors, and confused thoughts swirled around in his head as if his brain were a stew God was stirring over a fire. When Chaim had at last lost the last of his bearings, God removed his ladle, the motion of Chaim's mind slowed down, and a vision of Miriam came into deep relief.

He saw Miriam sitting at their small kitchen table, in an old shawl wrapped tightly around her, mending the sleeve of another's *bekishe*. Meanwhile, Moishe sampled her charcuterie board of buttons, laying delectably, defenselessly on the floor. The smoldering ashes of a spent fire glowed in their small, cold hearth. He gazed into his wife's sad, dark, brown eyes as if noticing them for the first time. Dread filled his heart; he felt as if she were an insurmountable distance away. He tried to hold back his tears, but God added fuel to the inextinguishable flame beneath his mind. Shame overflowed from the bottom of his soul.

He realized everything and remembered it all.

"Oh, what I've put that poor woman through!" Chaim lamented. "How sad she looks now. How miserable of a husband I've been, going behind her back, cleaving away every kopek she earned, stealing her late grandmother's pearls! Then what do

I do? I see a necklace in a window to replace what I stole, and that's that! Ha! Even at that, I failed, my nose carrying me away before I could take one step in that jewelry store... and all the while, my wife sits at home with Moishe, repairing paupers' dresses for groszy and kopeks! How can I show my face to her again? *Gottenyu*, I'm ashamed!" He said, dropping his head in his hands.

The barkeeper stared at him, betraying no emotion, though listening deeply to every word Chaim uttered.

A tear trickled down Chaim's face. He clenched his mug for comfort—bizarrely, the only thing in that moment that felt *real*. He felt its warmth, seemingly growing in magnitude; he noticed the fine crystal glowing in the light; and with the delicate steam floating away, saw feelings he had long tamped down swirling before his eyes. For a moment he sat in silence, mesmerized, as waves of the potion hit him with greater and greater force. Unable to hold his tears back any longer, he cried. He took one more sip of his wine, now glowing, swirling, and iridescent, as if it were milk of emeralds and sapphires.

Like a snuffed out candle, he fell into a calm, silent stupor. The old man behind the bar, satisfied with all he had heard, answered back.

"Chaim, child," he said kindly, "Enough of all that. You torture yourself over a pearl necklace long pawned away. Yes—you were wrong to do so. But is a pearl necklace what Miriam needs right now? Are pearls what she lacks? She has suffered at your hand, but you suffer from it beside her. Your field lies in ruins. Your ambitions leave your house poor. Baby Moishe is growing up fast without guidance. And now, you see what you have done. You admit your sins, you supplicate before me, and yet, you are clueless as to what you must do.

Chaim Vostęvskie, son of Abraham, father of Moishe! *He* has decided that you and your family have suffered enough. You shall pay back your wife one thousand times over. Hear me now.

Soon, you will forget your paltry buckwheat and the fungus which ravages it. In its place you shall grow sweet, violet grapes, and *He* shall see that your vines grow."

Placated and hypnotized by the words of the old man, he listened in silence, overlooking altogether that the barkeeper's knowledge was inconceivable. He pondered the old man's words for a moment, and leaving aside everything that had just brought him to tears, erupted in child-like laughter.

"Did you say *grapes*? In Tolevoste! Is that what you suggest I do? Grow grapes! Our fields are hardly sufficient to sustain buckwheat, let alone vineyards. You're a funny man!" he said, shaking his head. The barkeeper stared at him patiently.

"*Moykhl*, that's a very sweet blessing. Thank you. And look, if there existed such a grape that could grow from my cold field, then let God give me its seeds—*I'd gladly give up every zloty to my name*—and mark my words, I would make such a grape grow," he added, with a good natured laugh.

"*As you wish*," the barkeeper intoned.

Something nearly out of sight caught Chaim's attention for a brief moment, like a passing shadow. His gaze shifted away. But not a second later, when he looked back ahead, he saw the barkeeper had vanished. Half lit by the pub's dim lamps and half veiled in darkness, Chaim found himself in the Yordania alone.

"*Oh well, it must be closing time*," he thought, questioning nothing, much like one does in a dream.

He took out a zloty for payment, lifted his mug into the air, and quickly poured back the very last drop of his drink. Just as he slammed his mug onto the bar, the warm air turned deathly chill.

He rubbed his eyes, seeing faint colors and swirling shapes gently re-encroaching on his vision. When he opened his eyes again he saw something in the place of his mug, directly in front of him—a glossy wooden jewelry box, dimly glowing, producing its own light. Cautiously intrigued, staring at it, he had the inexplicable feeling that the pub had been reverently erected precisely around where the box had already been.

Adorned with intricate carvings of flowers and vines, its mysterious gold-like heaviness mesmerized him. Overcome by his curiosity, he opened its delicate, silver latch. Fingering through the contents—little paper sacks—he noticed the names of exotic plants, with prints of what appeared to be Goyish deities printed on each one. He lifted one, shook it by his ear, and heard the sounds of its contents. *Seeds?*

He recognized none of the crosshatched divinities and could not have known what they signified. Glancing through them, he glossed over Apollo, Athena, and the last, Hercules' poor mother, Hera, weeping over her burned children from beside a cliff. Moved by this image, Chaim took out *that* packet and read the inscription:

VITIS FERINA—ZILGA GRAPE

He experienced an ineffable, dark chill, shoved the seeds back in the box, pushed it away, hurriedly stood up, and picked up his satchel.

"It is no longer yours to leave behind," the barkeeper said softly in his ear, materializing behind his shoulder.

"Dear God!" Chaim shouted, placing a hand on his chest. "How did you do that? Never mind, I—I have a train to catch, allow me to pay," he said, extending out his zloty.

But quietly murmuring, under Chaim's dumbfounded gaze, the barkeeper walked away. Moving silently, his feet glided across the floor. The dim candle flames grew into a fury as he passed them by and dimmed once more as he left them behind. He disappeared behind a creaking back door, closing it agonizingly slowly. The heavy, brass latch audibly closed.

"I'll just leave this?" Chaim called out timidly.

DIASPORA

With a bang, the door swung back open not one moment later. Chaim, jumping out of his skin, launched the zloty across the pub. The barkeeper, still murmuring strange intonations, burst forth in a cloud of purple, iridescent dust.

"Oh God, what was in that drink..." Chaim thought, beginning to realize the bizarreness of the reality around him. He watched the barkeeper gently waft back to the bar, clenching something heavy in his two hands, and felt that he wanted no part of it.

"Okay, I'll just be heading out—" Chaim said, backing away.

"From *Him*! This will fertilize your soil," the barkeeper interrupted, extending out his small burlap sack.

"Leave me alone!" Chaim shouted. "Enough of your absurdity! I've had a long day, my head is killing me, and I can't even think straight... this is *not* what I came in here for. Your money is on the ground. Now I'm leaving! Good day!"

He turned his back and took a step towards the door.

"What did you say to me?" the barkeeper cried, his voice rising like distant thunder. "The foolishness! The arrogance! The chutzpah! What did you come here for, then? Do you even remember? Can you even say?"

Chaim turned back around, visibly shaking.

"I only came for a..." Chaim began in an indignant tone. But it struck him that, in that precise moment, he no longer knew at all. He looked to the barkeeper, terrified, as his dizziness and confusion overcame him.

Quieting his wrath, the old man moved closer. Reaching out, he felt his way down Chaim's shoulders, his arms, and eventually, his icy hands. Chaim's breath slowed to a halt. For one moment, the bewitched buckwheat farmer was permitted to see the true, cavernous face of the man before him. He realized the man's eyes were blind, utterly white, glowing, and belying a cloudy darkness. As the angel peered a thousand miles into Chaim's soul, Chaim's fear melted away.

"Take your fertilizer. You will need it," he said.

Fully entranced, Chaim reached around his shoulder for his satchel. But he lost his balance and fell on his knees.

"Worry not—it will be in there," Chaim heard him say faintly as if from the other end of a distant tunnel. The ringing which passed when he first entered the Yordania came back to his ears, growing louder by the second; his vision, already fading, went in and out of focus; his limbs grew weak; and just before he fully collapsed, he felt someone bump into his back.

He shouted in alarm as he sprang to his feet, feeling completely and suddenly sober.

"Forgive me!" said a petite young lady, two handfuls of colorful shopping bags hanging at her sides.

Chaim stared first at her and then, as if just awoken from a fever dream, frantically surveyed the surrounding world. He listened to the chatter of the crowded shop seeing children, young women, and various store attendants bustling through the festive aisles of—of the *Karenina?!* Little girls tried on flowery hats, little boys chased their brothers with model guns, and the attendants, mindful to not damage their products, carefully toted large handfuls of fine shirts, dresses, and suits over their heads. His memory clouded over. He could not pinpoint exactly where he had just been; all he could remember was the silhouette of a bizarre old man who had been there.

"Do you have any other earrings like these under five?" the woman said to someone behind Chaim, raising her delicate voice above the din of the shop.

"I believe we have something similar, ma'am," answered a shopkeeper in a youthful voice.

When Chaim turned around to see him, a boyish, cleverly dressed store clerk briskly walked around the counter to help the lady. Chaim searched everywhere around him once more. There was no old man anywhere in sight.

"What did *you* come in for, *sir*?" the young clerk said curtly, briefly stopping in front of Chaim, scanning him from *fur hat* to toe.

"What?" Chaim asked hysterically. The store clerk stepped back.

"Are you drunk? Is there something *you* want?" the clerk asked impatiently. Chaim searched his face, seeing nothing but the clear eyes of a young man.

He instinctively checked inside his satchel—the money, where was his money?! Digging further down, he felt a burlap sack, a receipt of payment, a train ticket, and some mysterious, loose seeds at the bottom.

"My money! Where has my money gone?!" Chaim shouted. The shopkeeper only stared at him, horrified.

"Listen to me," he pleaded. "I came in here with over two hundred zloty! It's around here somewhere, it must be here! Someone has stolen from me!"

"*Sir*, you just came in here seconds ago!" retorted the shopkeeper. "Don't be causing any trouble now, *Jew.*"

Chaim saw people staring. The shop grew quiet. Behind him, the store's guards walked closer. He hastily tied his satchel closed, hurried toward the door, and nearly running out from under his fur hat, managed to slip through their fingers.

Outside the shop, he frantically looked to his left. He had an inclination; *that* was the place! He had just gotten something to drink next door! But running to the entrance, rather than a pub, he found the building next door to the Karenina languishing destitute, boarded up, its facade blackened from streaks of smoke. An old man dressed in rags, scratching his arms, took cover under the building's awning. Chaim approached him with a sense of trepidation.

"Alms for the poor?" the old man said beseechingly, facing Chaim. Strong hints of spiced wine came from his breath. Chaim desperately took his hand, held it for a moment, searched the poor man's face, and found that he was blind.

"Alms for the poor—Chaim?"

"Chaim!? How do you know my name?" he asked, hysterically.

"Alms for the poor?" the man continued softly, looking distantly through Chaim. Utterly horrified, Chaim turned to run, the man's rising voice following him down the street.

"Alms for the poor! Alms for the poor!"

DIASPORA

4

The Debate

Chaim sat alone on an open bench by the window in his dimly lit passenger car. His satchel lay beside him. He laid his head in his hands. On any other train ride, he would have been reading a page of the *Gemara*, intermixed with short breaks gazing out the window, watching the silhouette of the trees speeding by. But he could do none of it. With a pulsating headache, he closed his eyes and rested his head against the window. From out of the darkness, a pair of blindingly white eyes jolted him upright.

He rubbed his face, glanced at the few sleeping passengers around him, and looked at his satchel.

"Oh God, how am I going to explain this to Miriam!" Chaim thought.

He slowly clawed back pieces of his hazy memory. He speculated that he had had a drink of some dubious wine from a bizarre old man, subsequently fainted, and ran out of a jewelry shop he had no memory of entering. It occurred to him that he may have had one too many drinks. That, or he walked into the Karenina at the moment of a nervous fit—yes, no other explanation made sense.

However, if I lost my money at the Karenina, where did these... things come from? he asked himself, inspecting the contents of his satchel, lifting a seed between his fingertips.

He tried again to recall that person. He searched his memory for the features of his face, but the harder he looked, the hazier it became. A great hand veiled a corner of Chaim's mind from him, just as a fisherman might mollify his catch by shielding its eyes from the light. He feared, as he often did, that he may have been a victim of the evil eye.

DIASPORA

Chaim tied his bag shut, looked around once more, opened his window, and prepared to throw the entire accursed thing out into the countryside. But just as he lifted the bag, the wind, rushing through the window, seemed to force his hand back.

Chaim's eyes opened wide. In an instant, his head cooled, his heartbeat slowed, his grimace relaxed, and he took a deep breath. Gazing out his window, he noticed the rolling hills of the dark countryside. The moon burned bright and clean, like a lamp of whale oil, as the scent of larch sap and burning firewood from the houses nearby wafted through his train car like perfume.

Within his mind, an image of himself standing motionless on the planks of that very railway, by a solitary switch lever, came into relief. He watched his own train steaming towards him, with a fork in the track, just paces ahead of where he stood, making possible his salvation. If he pulled the lever, he understood the train would turn and skirt him by. But uncertainty arrested his movements. He turned to God, pleading with Him to tell him what to do. God, satisfied to let pass what may, said nothing. He gestured to His angel to release his benevolent grip of Chaim's arm. The angel obliged.

The two watched as Chaim, staring into the train's blinding head lamp, looked at the lever and back to the train. He closed his eyes, took a deep breath, dropped his arms to his side, and made no effort to prevent himself from colliding into the weight of his own rushing soul.

"No—not everything in my life can be the fault of the evil eye!" he said to himself. His clear thoughts began to flow. "Yes, it is true; I am a poor man. But how long has my trust in God been a function of my wealth? The Talmud teaches us riches are the greatest deception of the evil eye, but when God removes them from my hand, to whom do I turn? Do I trust in His design? Do I thank God for His mercy? No—I overlook my beautiful *wife, my darling child, and my health. My faith becomes callous, my thoughts become bitter, and my soul corrupted with desire!"*

Chaim saw years of happiness squandered by his vain ambition, stupidity, and greed. He asked God to judge the ambitions of a poor and foolish man with mercy. A tear rolled down his cheek. He wiped his eyes, took a deep breath, and nodded his head resolutely. He could lament for the rest of his life how two hundred silver zloty escaped his grasp, or he could thank God for the endless blessings bestowed upon him which he had failed to notice at every turn of his life. After all, he remembered that he was, for once, no longer in debt.

"Never will I doubt a *gesheft* from the almighty Himself," he concluded. "Who else's work could this be but His?"

God, hearing this, felt satisfied. He knew that Chaim would never recall his deal with His angel as a clear, unambiguous memory. However, He was pleased to see, all the more, Chaim had remembered the pledge he had made within his heart.

Chaim closed the window. His eyes softly rested on the horizon. In silence, the moonlit fields passed him by. Eventually, fatigue overcame him. He fell into a deep slumber, awaking when the conductor at the Kalinasevka train station jostled him, early the next morning.

Arriving home by noon, he greeted his wife, hurriedly kissed her forehead, kissed his baby Moishe, disappeared into his bedroom study, and shut the door before she could fit in another word.

"Ah, the great *Macher* arrives home from his business!" she cried. "What jewelry of my grandmother's must we sell now?"

"Yes, yes my *libe*! We shall talk soon!" Chaim answered kindly, latching his door closed to concentrate.

He lit his lamp, performed his morning prayers, and hurriedly studied a page of the Gemara. Immediately upon flipping the holy book shut, he turned to his horticulture book that he had barely opened twice and now, miraculously, could not have been of greater use.

He had two mysteries to resolve. For the first, he reached back into his satchel and referenced the inscription on that torn packet of seeds:

VITIS FERINA—ZILGA GRAPE

He perused the table of contents, found the section on fruits and the subsection for grapes, and diligently read through the chapter. He noticed the textbook paid great attention to the vanguard species of the greatest wineries in the world—the likes of Merlot, Syrah, Zinfandel, and Malbec. After cursory summaries, it began delving into the various specific regional and climatic differences between one family of grapes and another.

"*...the majority of which flourish in temperate climates with brief, rainy winters,*" Chaim read, scratching his beard. He turned back to the previous page to read it again. The words 'France' and 'Italy' appeared frequently; the exotic lands of 'Argentina' and 'California' received passing mentions. But nowhere did it mention grapes being grown in any place within 500 kilometers of his Tolevoste.

He sighed, somewhat baffled by this realization. A tinge of anxiety flashed across his face; doubt over this 'gift,' which he had so quickly attributed to God, entered his mind. Nonetheless, he turned the page and read on. As the chapter shifted into more and more esoteric and scientific topics which he did not understand, his attention alighted onto a small entry near the very end of the chapter, tacked on almost as an addendum. The publication deemed it appropriate to mention how, by highlighting one uncommon and rather unpopular variety of grape as an example, certain cultivars had been known to endure climates susceptible to uncommonly cold winters better than others. There, in tiny italics beneath a single, crosshatched diagram, Chaim found the words:

Figure 4.1: VITIS FERINA—ZILGA GRAPE

In shock, he shut the book quickly. With his jaw agape, he peeked inside his bag to confirm once more what he thought that seed packet stated. There it was in print: *Zilga Grape*.

He felt a shiver. There could be no question. It *was* from Him.

He rapidly collected himself, flipped the book open once more, and poured through the pages. His wife cooked him stew but he did not smell it. The sun began to set but he did not notice the passing time. Chaim lost himself in the pages, ingesting every morsel of information he could. With God's good graces, he *would* grow the grapes.

Learning Zilga grapes were precisely what he needed for his climate, he had solved his first mystery. Later that evening, near the end of the book, he arrived at the chapter that would prove most insightful for the second mystery—the purpose of the heavy, burlap sack.

III - NUTRIENT FERTILIZATION

Chaim read the chapter quickly the first time, slower the second, and word by word on the third. With his finger, he marked certain words which were unfamiliar to him, and grabbing handfuls of pages at once, compared the words and passages in one section to definitions and explanations in another.

Sentence by sentence, in the Talmudic tradition, he carefully studied what the textbook explained to be the elemental compositions of fertile soil. Distinguishing between the different plant requirements, the textbook clearly stated the importance of nitrogen, phosphorus—and in the particular case of grapes, ammonium sulfates—to aid in their growth. Up until that point, Chaim had only known the simple fact that crops grew healthier when the ground was first mixed with manure—he never knew that *scientists* had much to say about the inner workings of God's own mind.

Turning to his strange gift—his burlap sack—his excitement grew. C*ould it be*? He cut it open, touched the contents with his finger, and raised it before his face. It tickled his nose, had a faint yellow hue, and felt like flour as he rubbed it between his forefinger and thumb. He turned his gaze back to his book, reading the last passage he had read once again. It matched the description perfectly.

"It's *ammonium sulfate*!" Chaim shouted, hardly containing his excitement, jumping to his feet. He rushed out of his room to his wife. She was sitting on her sewing chair beside Moishe, just having finished cleaning her boiling pot. Chaim picked her up and lifted her into the air.

"Dear, it's ammonium sulfate!"

"Oh God, he's speaking in tongues! Chaim, please—"

"I need to talk to the rabbi!" he said, rushing to put on his shoes and socks.

"Chaim, you're making *me* want to see the rabbi!"

"No, my sweet, I really need—"

"What you *need* is an exorcism! Oh God, he's a *Dybbuk*, a shapeshifter, a *Golem—and* it's after dark!"

Chaim looked out the window.

"Ah! So it is," he said, still in his socks, holding his shoes, and with a foot out the door. Miriam stared at him, horrified.

"Miriam, don't look at me like that," he said, grabbing her wrist, shaking the satchel inches before her face. "Look! I have been given a treasure!"

"A treasure! The world's smallest ice cream machine?"

"No, My wife," he said, slapping his forehead, exasperated. "I know I've told you this many times, but now, *bli neder, ani mavtiach,* with my hand on my heart, we won't be poor buckwheat farmers for long. This gift is from God!"

"Last I checked, God doesn't live in America!"

"Listen! We will grow grapes! We will grow a lush vineyard, straight from our own fields, and God will see that it thrives!"

"…A vineyard… Fine, Chaim…" Miriam said, deeply sighing. "You can grow anything you like. You can grow weeds for all I care. If they fail to grow too, *Baruch Hashem,* I'll till the land once more beside you. I'll till it for you. But *not* tonight. I haven't slept well in a week. *Come to bed.*"

Still excited, Chaim took a breath, ready to interject. But Miriam placed her hand on his shoulder, looked him squarely in the eye, and gestured with her head to their bedroom. He noticed how well she quieted her own deep exasperation within her and within him. He quietly nodded, and as the Talmud instructs a good husband to do, obeyed his endlessly patient wife. He made sure to quietly prepare for the following morning, placing everything he would need back in his satchel. He lifted Moishe into his crib, laid down beside his wife, and slept soundly through the night.

Waking up at dawn, Chaim carefully lifted his covers, put on his socks *and* shoes, picked up his satchel, brushed off his coat, grabbed his hat, and hurriedly left towards the Synagogue down the cool and softly lit dirt street. He threw open its door, interrupting a yeshiva lesson that had begun just moments before, and dropped his satchel amidst the students' siddurim on the reception table.

"Rabbi, I've got something you must see, and it can't wait," he announced, as the students whispered in confusion to one another.

"*Oy vey*, is it from America?" said the rabbi with his voice shaking.

Chaim was about to respond, but thinking better of it, turned right back to his bag. Sifting through his belongings, he pulled out the horticulturist's book, the seed packet, various articles in the way, and finally, the burlap sack of fertilizer sitting at the bottom.

"Rabbi, listen to me. I've had the most unbelievable trip to Warsaw. I paid off my thresher, as promised; I had quite a bizarre wine—kosher wine... well, what I mean is," he took a breath, suddenly finding himself stumbling over his words, "I have here before you *ammonium sulfate,* which my horticulturist book says..."

His head already spinning, the rabbi put his hand on Chaim's shoulder, beckoning him to slow down. After a moment, he collected his thoughts.

"Chaim, what are you asking—what is this... *Babylonian*—?"

"*Ammonium,*" he politely corrected, opening the burlap sack carefully. A swirling plume daintily rose into the air. He gestured for the rabbi to take a sniff, but the rabbi backed away.

"Rabbi," Chaim assured him. "It's only a new kind of fertilizer—nothing more. I'm here with one, simple question that only you can answer."

"Well, yes?" the rabbi asked, as the students all leaned in to hear.

"Rabbi—is ammonium sulfate kosher?"

Taken aback, the rabbi looked left, then right, then back at Chaim.

"You want to eat it?" the rabbi asked.

"No! Well, yes, it's... like I said, it's fertilizer! It will be for the *grapes*," he said resolutely. The yeshiva students burst into laughter.

"His grapes!" one student said.

"At least France is closer than America," another joked.

The rabbi squinted his eyes severely at his pupils, instantly turning them deathly silent. Turning back to Chaim, he grabbed the burlap sack, scrutinized it, cautiously touched the powder between his fingers, and sniffed it. A brief moment passed.

"I see, I see..." he murmured, satisfied that it did not burn or bewitch him. He quickly came to a decision, but held his tongue. He passed the powder around to his students, concealing a small grin.

They gasped in unison at the scent—reminiscent of rotten eggs.

"The evil eye!"

"Brimstone, straight from Gomorra!"

"Quiet, kinder, restrain yourselves," the rabbi said didactically. "Now, one at a time. Yes, Levin, you can speak. What do you think of this powder?"

"*Hilul HaShem,* it's a desecration of the name of God!" Levin, the oldest child, answered confidently.

"How do you know?" asked the rabbi.

"Rabbi, I have watched my father sow seeds for years, and he has never needed *ammonium sulfates* to grow his crop. He will say the same—we have never needed anything but what came from God on the seven days of creation. This! This is the evil eye challenging our faith. You can smell brimstone wafting in the air."

The other children, having felt more or less the same, nodded in agreement. But the rabbi, disinclined to such a hasty dismissal, challenged his star pupil.

"That is a very interesting thought, Levin. But I propose to you this: what does your father use to fertilize his fields?"

"Well, manure, rabbi."

"Ah, and can you show me where in the Torah it says God created manure?"

"Ha, rabbi, you know that manure comes from the cow, and the cow was created on the sixth day!"

"And what if the cow did not create manure until day number eight?" the rabbi said.

"What do you mean?"

"I think you know well what I mean!"

All the children but Levin, red in the face, chuckled.

"So?" the rabbi pressed on. "If the cow did not create manure until day number eight, would that mean something on Earth was *not* created during the seven days of creation?"

"Rabbi, you're embarrassing me," Levin said. "Of course, some things took more time than others..."

"So then, some things may take more time! But *livonia* sulfates—"

"*Ammonium* sulfates..." Chaim interjected.

"...*Ammonium* sulfates," the rabbi continued, "took just a little too long for you, dear Levin? Let us begin the *Amidah*, so we may ask God to hasten His plan already, lest Levin get impatient!"

"Alright, alright, *I get it,*" Levin said, sitting down, looking cross. The rabbi, laughing at his own humor, patted Levin on his shoulder.

"Tonight, you must study more of the oral tradition, my star pupil," he said with a warm smile. He turned back to the matter at hand.

"Chaim, you seem to have a word waiting on your tongue. You came to me to ask a question, I understand. Now, what do *you* think is the answer? Are... what was it, *begonia* sulfates kosher?"

"*Ammonium* sulfates, rabbi," Chaim said, as he tried desperately to prepare his thoughts. He feared, for a moment, that he would not be able to express himself. The feelings in his heart outpaced the words in his mind. Could he have been wrong about it all? But before his lips could move, calmness fell over him. Chaim took a deep breath, felt wisdom enter his lungs, and spoke freely, sensing His hand resting on his shoulder.

"Young Levin is correct," he began magnanimously, "that his father Yaacov—my good friend—has never needed anything but what God created during the first seven—or *eight*—days of creation. However, we cannot say, with honesty, that we have never wanted anything more than Tolevoste and what its buckwheat fields have offered us. God sent Moses to show us a better land, after all, and like you said rabbi, He did not see any urgency in revealing it to us right away. After all, we did not lay our eyes on the Holy Land for over two thousand years!

Now, does ammonium sulfate, in particular, come from the days of creation? I cannot say because I was not there. But I know that it came from God, as nothing on the Earth could come from outside of His domain. It is a gift like any other, and when God sends his gifts, in whatever form, I believe we must accept them as they come."

The students stared at each other, the rabbi, and then at him, finding no fault in anything he said.

Chaim murmured a brief prayer under his breath, thanking God for gracing him with such wisdom. In that moment, however, God had not been standing beside Chaim to any greater or lesser degree than any other creature of creation; His angel, too, had been observing it all in silence. Every last of Chaim's words were his own.

The rabbi nodded his head, in awe of what he just saw unfolding before him. He briefly contemplated the meaning of Chaim's miraculous new clarity.

"Why would God select such a simple man for a duty like this? He is no scholar of the Torah, and if I recall, has a strong propensity for the schnapps. But... who am I to question the almighty," he decided in his modesty.

He stroked his beard, touched the powder again, stared at it on his fingertips, and decided on a teaching. With Chaim and the yeshiva students politely waiting for him to speak, he opened his mouth.

"The truth is, my dears," the old man said solemnly, as the students leaned in closer to hear, "we could spend an eternity in debate over this one speck of yellow powder—this one here among an infinite more—and we will be no nearer to understanding it than we are to the fathomless depths of God's mind.

If I had eternity, my children, I would gladly discuss it forever," he added, lowering his head, concealing the wetness in his eyes. "Alas, I do not. A prayer must suffice."

He placed his hand on the burlap sack and settled on a blessing for the *ammonium* sulfates. He then placed his hand on Chaim's head to bless him. He noticed uncanny warmth radiating from his skin.

Chaim kissed the rabbi's hand that blessed the fertilizer and himself, politely concealed a grimace from the scent off his fingers, and left the rabbi and the yeshiva students to resume their study.

Chaim—with Miriam beside him, as she had promised—made quick work of building their small vineyard the following spring, fertilizing the earth, and sowing the seeds. Months went by as vines emerged from the once sallow, cold ground behind his house, just as the horticulturist book divined.

For the next three years, every night, coming home from tending his buckwheat crops, Chaim studied one page of his horticulturist's book for every one page of the Gemara. Next, with the last light of the days, he would inspect the vines, the leaves, and the budding Zilga grapes growing from his cold earth, from the vast sky, from the science of the horticulturists, from the wise blessings of the rabbi, and from the favor of God. Lastly, before bed, he would kiss his baby Moishe and hopeful wife. After many years more, his vines crept onto the land where his buckwheat had once been ravaged by fungus—to the point where he grew no more buckwheat at all. Little Moishe watched his father wander within the eternity of every grape, enjoying simply the sweet scent of the vines; the dark, rich soil; and the way the grape leaves rustled in the spring breeze. Through daily devotion, his vineyard expanded for no less than one hundred acres behind his home. Chaim discovered the exact and perfect scent, bounce, and color of flesh—as well as the time of day, down to the minute, down to the second—when his grapes were ripe to be picked, mashed, and fermented. With this discovery, his wealth expanded beyond his own belief. He did make one more trip to Warsaw in his later years, but not to pay off any debts. Returning to Tolevoste one evening, greeting his wife waiting at the train station no differently than when she was young, he placed the most beautiful pearl necklace around her neck. He then brought back to his house a set of new silverware for the Sabbath—more magnificent than the one they received on their wedding day—and gifted to Moishe, his star apprentice, a new *gold* cased Breguet, with a silvered Guilloche dial, to replace his grandfather's heirloom watch pawned away so many years ago.

    The Vostęvskie winery, now revered by countless people from Warsaw and beyond, contended with travelers seeking Chaim for his enigmatic winemaking advice. When his closest neighbors would inquire about the origins of his mysterious fertilizer, rather than remain coy, he replied with the simple truth: he had a unique source. What he would not tell them, however, is that since the day he had first been gifted it, he had never needed one ounce more. Only Miriam and Moishe would learn, seeing it before their own eyes, that Chaim's small burlap sack of ammonium sulfates, given to him by an angel, could pour forth ceaselessly without ever running out. Even they, oftentimes, prodded him to explain how such a thing was possible. The old man would die only offering the same small piece of wisdom to them time and again. There were no secrets. One just had to listen.

"If you do, just maybe," he told Moishe over a glass of their wine, "everything will turn out just right."

And so everything did—for a time. Immediately after Chaim's death, however, Moishe had to contend with his first great challenge as a master winemaker. When his father closed his eyes for the last time, his endless bag of ammonium sulfates ran dry.

5

The Pogrom

DIASPORA

Moishe tended to trail off into this fantastical story if someone asked even the most tangential question related to his winery. Whoever heard it politely listened—especially when over a glass of Moishe's wine—but there were few who believed it.

Moishe had reached the age Chaim was when he returned from Warsaw with a bag of seeds and endless fertilizer. Though the realities and stresses of overseeing a sprawling vineyard weighed greatly on him—so much so that he had not even contemplated marriage—he stoically and in good spirits carried on the winery of the Vostęvskie name.

One summer morning, with his field's harvested, his fermenters full, his casks aging, and his assistants paid, Moishe made preparations to make a small journey. In Lubelsk, a day and a half north of Tolevoste, Moishe would display his bottles in the largest market in the Ternopil Oblast.

Many of Tolevoste's timeless fables, such as the origins of *Snow Chicken* soup or Chaim's endless fertilizer, may have well been myths; but as the end of almost all Tolevoste's inhabitants inched closer, their stories, for better or worse, became more real.

Kissing his elderly mother, Miriam, goodbye—who was, by then, permanently assigned to a large, padded rocking chair in their two-story family home—Moishe put on his late father's thick wool coat, field cap, and fine, wool-lined glove. Leaving his mother behind, Miriam thought she saw an apparition.

"The devil himself returns," Miriam said in bewilderment. Chaim laughed. Harnessing his donkey and wagon, he left with his wine.

He expected to sell out at the market. His creations, much like his father's, earned wide praise amongst the Jews and Goyim alike; no one doubted his bottles deserved to carry the same name—*Winnice Vostęvskie*—as when the late master, Reb Chaim, had created them. After all, the vineyard had never fundamentally changed. But status aside, sales had declined marginally since Chaim had died three years earlier. The declining profits did not bother him directly. But in his heart, Moishe feared a certain quality of his father's wine could not be found in his.

Moishe prayed to God, humbly asking only that the people of Lubelsk would disagree with his apprehension—*and that not a single one of his bottles would return with him to Tolevoste after market day.*

Leaving Tolevoste under the brilliant winter sun, he smelled the air, filled with the scent of endless buckwheat fields and pollinating weeds. The wagon rolled easily under the pull of his tireless Mordecai, eating from a pouch hanging in front of him.

Keeping a steady pace, he crossed a stone bridge built over the Jeżyna River by the evening. By sundown, he rested within the tree line of the Tolezyli forest. Moishe slept peacefully, wandering within a recurring childhood dream, resting on his donkey's heaving abdomen. He spread his blanket over them both. Mordecai dreamt of his favorite snack of ground barley and rye, periodically sighing with satisfaction.

Many hours into the night, Mordecai tossed, shook his head, huffed, and awoke. He tugged at the blanket covering them both. He began to bray. Only when his cries were louder than the chirping crickets did Moishe roll over, pull the blanket back, and awaken.

"Easy, Mordecai," he grumbled, sitting up, trying to understand what had just happened. He scratched his donkey behind the ears, doing his best to mollify him in the way that usually worked. But Mordecai shook his head, pulling away from Moishe's hand.

"Don't be like that. Is it the blanket? You tore your other blanket in half, remember? Now we must share."

Mordecai huffed.

"Fine, it got caught in the wheel. Now, look—this one is just fine for us both. It's new. It has roses on it—pretty flowers. Mother made it. So go to sleep, okay? You can take my share."

But just then, Moishe heard it too—the clopping of hooves on the road up ahead, followed by creaking wheels and the heavy, truncated march of a crowd. Grabbing Mordecai's mouth shut, he peered through the leaves. Torch-bearing men, dressed in black, passed him by. Once they were out of earshot, seeking something to say to his donkey, he tamped down the fear in his heart.

"Drunks from Kalinasevka, Mordecai. Perhaps they lost a goat. They're nothing to worry about, sweet boy," he said, stroking his neck.

Kalinasevka, however, was not south, but northwest of Tolevoste. If they did not intend to sleep in the dirt, they should have been going in the opposite direction. Moishe realized this, and as if needing to explain the logical conundrum to Mordecai, added that they were just too drunk to know which way was up.

"Okay, my dear? Now, go back to sleep. Get under the cover."

His donkey may have submitted to Moishe's half-hearted explanation, but Moishe still needed to explain the bizarre scene to himself. Who would need to go to Tolevoste in the middle of the night? After hours of laying on the warm abdomen of his sleeping donkey, he found no solution. But lulled by the sweet rustle of the forest leaves, sleep at last overcame him.

The canopy of the Tolezyli forest shielded them from the early light of the sun. Moishe awoke late in the morning, refitted Mordecai to his harness, and lazily continued north. The road felt cool and breezy—the ground beneath their feet, hard and dry.

As he traveled further from the Jeżyna River, a scant few travelers and merchants began to appear along the dusty road. If Moishe had paid them greater attention, he may have seen their disquieted glares at the sight of an apparition such as himself, wearing all black from his cap to his jacket.

Passing the people without a thought, Moishe and his donkey kicked up a light cloud of dust behind them. He meditated on the creak of his wheels, the sound of the wind, and the rustle of the forest's leaves. He had learned from his father at a young age to tamp down any disquiet within him. Nonetheless, the band of men who passed him the night before lingered in his mind.

Out of the distance, a pair of Cossack cavalrymen at a gentle trot rose plumes of dust greater than his own. As they approached, Moishe pulled his donkey to the edge of the road. He had no specific reason to fear the Cossack and had done nothing wrong. However, raised with the doctrine that the less interactions with the Cossack, the greater the fortune of the Jew, he kept his head down. As the Cossacks passed, he chanced a glance and gathered just a few brief words of their conversation:

"…and you're sure it's only a few hours down the road?"

"Oh, yes, they're likely already done. We'll meet them soon enough this way."

Just as they peered down over their mustaches, he averted his gaze. The horsemen, eyeing the passing Jew from top to bottom, looked at one another with amusement.

"Three hours down the road by horseback—could they have business in Tolevoste?" Moishe wondered. He found no good answer to this question. He decided to put it out of his mind. He had wine to sell, and whatever reason they had for heading south was their own—Moishe had learned from his father to accept God's plan. He quickened his pace.

DIASPORA

Hours passed, the sun rose higher, and the last trees of the forest withdrew into shrubbery and golden fields. By noon, Moishe and Mordecai approached the gates of Lubelsk, smelling the sweet fermenting wine from a brandy distillery just on the outskirts.

He neared the village center. Cobblestones and freshly planted yellow flowers encircled a wide fountain. He filled his water canteen, gave Mordecai a drink, set his cart on its stilts, and sat down alone.

Several moments passed before Moishe noticed something out of the ordinary. There were no other carts present. Every door and shutter around the square was closed.

"That's odd," he thought. "Today *is* market day, no?"

Noticing a flier languishing in a dirty puddle, he walked over to pick it up, squinted his eyes, and read the few words written across the top:

Lubelsk CENTRAL MARKET
CLOSED March 16, 1888

PORUCHIK III CLASS Vladamir Petrosky

Moishe read the few terse words again carefully. Perhaps he did not understand the connection between this flier and the men he saw marching towards Tolevoste the night before. But more likely, he chose not to. He scratched his beard, laid the flier back down, and continued looking around.

He wandered the paved streets to the east a few blocks from the square, leaving Mordecai and his cart in their place. More than once he heard a shutter snap close. With a deep sigh, and his hands in his pockets, he turned back around to head west. He hoped old man Noam Blau, owner of the *Pokład*, his favorite Tavern in Lubelsk, would enlighten him on the news.

The Tavern had never been closed on market day. Merchants were known to crowd to Noam's bar for his famous *Latkes*. Moishe found it all the more surprising that the doors and windows to the Pokład were boarded up. Large panels of timber forbade the sun's entry. Moishe approached the store to peer through the cracks in the wood.

"Go away!" a shaky voice shouted from inside the shop.

"Noam? It's Moishe, the winemaker. Boy, am I hungry! Hey, I was wondering—" Moishe began, before hearing the click of a rifle's hammer.

"I warned you, whoever you are. Go away!" the frightened man shouted again. Moishe hurriedly turned around.

As it appeared to him at that moment, the people of Lubelsk had either gone crazy or vanished into the air. With a great sigh, and one last good look around the village, he raised a finger towards the sky.

"Alright, very funny!" he said to God, and shaking his head some, he re-harnessed Mordecai, and prepared for the long walk back to Tolevoste.

He wondered for a good part of the afternoon how he would explain to his mother why he returned without selling a single bottle of wine. Maybe there was a holiday? Could the entire village be hopelessly drunk? The *Goyim's* traditions, he argued to himself, were as mercurial as the wind.

Despite his failed objective, he reminded himself he was still blessed, as always. Yes, God had not exactly answered his prayers that day; however, he would return to home in good health, no poorer than he left, and despite his prayer to the contrary, with a cart still full of the best Kosher wine to be found in Poland.

He walked all day, and without stopping to sleep, continued after sunset. The moon shone brightly overhead. As quickly as they had disappeared as he left, the farms, the familiar forest trees, and the flowering buckwheat fields bordering his village enveloped him. Tolevoste lay just ahead. Mordecai had made this journey countless times as a foal with Moishe's father; his knowledge of every dip in the dirt road guided Moishe and his wagon through the dark.

Far down the road in front of him, the two of them caught wind of an unexpected smell.

"Could that be meat roasting on a fire?" Moishe thought. He managed to make out the faint glow of a campfire cutting the darkness. He felt immensely hungry, but his skepticism slowed him down. *"Who would be out in these fields, at this time of the night, roasting meat?"*

He did consider that, many years ago, he and his father, on their way home from Lubelsk, sometimes made camp just outside of the village. They would fall asleep by a small fire, finishing together whatever bottle of wine his father had opened for the journey. Moishe would ask his father about the names of the shapes in the stars. His father would make up different names and stories every time. But they never roasted meat on the roadside. Moishe's attention turned back to the present.

He advanced a few steps further. The fire's smoke, rising straight into the air, veiled the moonlight. He heard raucous laughter.

"Shh, Mordecai," Moishe whispered. "Stay a few paces back."

He approached the group of at least twenty men, only a stone's throw away, around what turned out to be not one fire, but three. Reposing in the dirt by the firelight, the group of men were slowly cutting pieces off a freshly slaughtered lamb.

"Could these be the drunks from the night before?"

They were, Moishe was sure. Various carts surrounding them were stacked high with fine furniture, barrels of fruit, and silver glinting in the firelight. Several strong work horses, donkeys, and other livestock were tied to several trees. He was sure most of those animals had not accompanied them on their way south the night before. In the flickering light, he noticed the mustached faces of the cavalrymen who raced past him.

Creeping closer, a stick snapped under his boot.

"Who's there?" one of the men shouted in the dark.

Moishe panicked and ran back to his donkey.

"Stop!" the man shouted, as two men hoisted themselves up to make chase. Catching up to Moishe just as he unlatched Mordecai's harness, they pummeled him against his wagon. With a wild bray, Mordecai broke into a gallop towards the village, kicking dust into all of their eyes. But at the same time, before they could strike the stranger, Moishe's glass bottles, all covered with a tight tarpaulin, sweetly clinked. The two men looked at one another, tossed Moishe to the ground, then tore open the tarpaulin.

"Christ almighty! It's a cartload of wine!" one of them shouted back to the other men. Wasting no time, the rest ran to see.

"God's grace—it's all here!"

"So that's why the stock was low at the village," he said, squinting at the Hebrew letters on the label.

"See, I told you they weren't hiding it with *Jew magic*," another one sneered, uncorking the first bottle. Within seconds, each man had opened his own. Through it all, Moishe, too frightened to move, watched ruefully as they stole his prized wine.

"What do we do with him?" one of the men asked, gesturing to the ground. Backing away, Moishe began to run, but they quickly grabbed him by his coat and pinned him against his wagon. He felt their alcoholic breath on his face.

"Don't you worry about a thing, Jew. Just empty your pockets," one of the men said.

Moishe kicked him in his shin. The man punched him in his gut and held him as one of the accomplices wrestled a fine, gold timepiece from his pocket.

"Give that back! That was my father's."

"It was *his father's!*" the man mocked. He ripped the timepiece off the chain, dropped it in the dirt, and crushed it beneath his boot.

"The gold will be worth a few kopeks at the pawnshop. Now give your Jew father my regards," he said, bringing a knife close to Moishe's throat.

Moishe, aware they were only holding on to the sleeves of his jacket, managed to slip himself out. The murderous bandits, who never truly cared to keep him, broke into amicable laughter. They sauntered back towards their camp. As Moishe ran, tears streamed down his face. He had finally accepted that those bandits had, indeed, known where they were going the day before, and were now on their way back from their *Pogrom*—their ransacking of Tolevoste.

Moishe ran, failing to catch his breath. His village lay in ruins only a few parcels of land ahead. Down the main street, he ran past husbands and wives nursing broken ankles and bleeding foreheads in the street.

He could not hear the glass beneath his boots, drowned out by his miserable panting and the blood pounding in his ears. Blood, laying in puddles beside dead chickens and goats, splattered across his pant legs and white cotton shirt with every step. Seeing his house up ahead, with the door flung wide open, he quickened his pace. He flew in, briefly catching himself on the jagged door frame.

"Mama!" he shouted, clearing a path towards her through the broken chairs, dressers, and table.

His old mother, laying on the bare floor, covered in a blanket, quietly wept. He ran up to her and held her as she laid withdrawn, repeating a short prayer. He looked her over, and despite his horror, felt a moment of relief. She survived untouched. Hoisting her upright, stroking her thin hair, and holding back his tears, he slowly raised his eyes. He saw past his shattered kitchen window to his vineyard.

"No—" Moishe said. His breath stopped. He felt his legs grow weak. Tears welled in his eyes. Carefully letting go of his mother, Moishe ran through his back door onto the field.

His three fermenters lay pierced and dented, his tool shed reduced to ashes, and flies circled above crunched vines and rotting grape husks. For as far as he could see into the distance, a hundred acres of the greatest grapevines Moishe had ever known, and his father's lifetime's work, were burnt down, hacked into pieces, and strewn across the land. He saw everything that God had once given them, and that man had taken away.

He walked past his fermenters through pools of dark wine. He fell on knees. He thought he might pray. He turned his face toward God. But for the first time in his life—perhaps among the very first times in the thousand year history of Tolevoste—when he thought of something to say to God, not a single thought even came to his mind. With utter disgust, he turned his head away from God, stood back up, and walked away. In that moment, with hatred in his heart, Moishe decided he would never speak to God again in his life.

***

For seven nights and days, the village sat in shiva for the dead, numbering four. They butchered their remaining carcasses, fixed what windows they could, and their broken ankles, in time, began to heal. With no vineyard remaining, by the following summer, Moishe and the elderly Miriam plowed the dead vine's roots, laid dried manure across his land, and sowed the buckwheat kernels his neighbors generously saved for him from their own.

DIASPORA

The buckwheat grew back on the Vostęvskies' land like it had always grown for a thousand years—battling fungal infections, pests, and the bitter winds all the same.

6

Meir

DIASPORA

The residents of Tolevoste never expected to see the promised land in their lifetimes. However, a promise is a promise; they did not shy away from beseeching God to answer when his promise may be fulfilled. After all, God did not promise the impossible—everlasting life, endless wealth, or unconditional peace, as examples. He promised a land—a *place* where, despite enemies all around them, they would be free. They knew, as the Torah had taught them, that Tolevoste—that the Ternopil Oblast—was not the land which God had promised. Nonetheless, could they still expect a modicum of peace? Despite the freezing sea within which they floated, could they, if huddled together, gain enough of a degree of warmth to survive? This is the question which raised itself seemingly from the dust, year after year, generation after generation. The pogrom which Tolevoste suffered on March 16, 1888 was not the only one in the Ternopil Oblast that year, let alone that day. The Cossacks penciled in that date like so many others with bureaucratic precision. The Jewish people suffered through violence and destruction. They counted their blessings in chickens and the sun's warmth. But practically speaking, despite their prayers, they had precious few blessings to count on. For the previous millennium, it seemed nothing changed. But as the decades marched on, their few blessings seemed to dwindle.

The world expanded beyond belief. Even a pebble like Tolevoste could not avoid the landslide of industry. In this regard, Tolevoste saw one of the few ways in which change came to it. Railroads had for decades begun sprawling across the vast, barren land, but by the start of the 20th century, Tolevoste had its own name on a train stop. Factory smokestacks rose across the horizon. The specter of change encircled them, ensnared them, and engulfed them as the coal dust of the factories to the west engulfed their fields. Through it all, they continued their toil, farming their land, and praying to God in much the same fashion they had since time immemorial.

Unlike the adjacent Christian villages, the village of Tolevoste strictly never grew larger than its initially allotted borders. In fact, Tolevsote seemed to grow smaller. The vibrant, whitewashed houses lost their lustrous coats; the stones in the streets fell into disrepair; and the wind, briefly banished from their homes, chilled their bedrooms and dining rooms once more. But in spite of all this, they were able to keep the bulk of their land. The same could not be said for every Jewish village in the region. They had managed to survive the fall of the Tsar's empire; the guns and artillery of the Great War only singed their edges of their fields, finding scant few fighters to drag along; and the son of the son of Moishe still wandered around the same sallow field in which his grandfather's vineyard once stood. No differently than the descendants of the great Rabbi Ezra, of Rabbi Micha, of Rabbi Saltzman, and every other family that long ago carved a plot in that field, they lived like grains of rye in a pot of water; as their enemies stirred them, the closer they drifted together.

Tolevoste benefited from its relative isolation. Not far enough east to be bothered by the Soviets' Red Army, and not far enough west for the West to care, they had enjoyed being somewhat forgotten. However, they did hear rumors of the changing times from the newspapers coming in from neighboring villages and cities. Politicians in Germany, as the papers said, blamed their economic problems of their own making on the Jews. Jewish merchants, such as Lisa Blau, the great granddaughter of Noam Blau, began to close their shops before darkness fell. Even in proud Vienna, the number of Jewish names on the rosters of university faculty, art galleries, and research laboratories dwindled for one reason or another.

DIASPORA

Closing their papers and feeding them to their kitchen fires, the people of Tolevoste believed they could dismiss their own worries. After all, how could one worry about lands so far away? There was far too much to worry about right in front of oneself. Life in Tolevoste carried on for each and every family, including the Vostęvskies, and for the young Meir.

Meir knew as much about his respected grandfather, Moishe—who died of liver disease shortly after fathering Aaron, Meir's father—as he did of the world outside Tolevoste. That is to say, he knew very little. Neither did he know very much about the vineyard which once stood on the now rocky, dry patch of dirt behind his home. Nonetheless, his home—the same one that had been rebuilt at least a dozen times in a thousand years—sat on the same plot of dirt where his great grandfather brought the wonder of ammonium sulfate to Tolevoste and where his great-great grandfather Abraham had first been fed through the soup of a desperate cat. Into his mind, the adults and teachers of Tolevoste poured the rich, ancient history of King David, Joseph's coat of many colors, and the Menorah which burned on scant oil for eight nights. But most of the stories ended right around there, as if the residents of Tolevoste, and the Jewish people more generally, were oblivious of the hundreds or thousands of years that stood between them and the stories they loved and revered.

Nonetheless, the songs Aaron sang to Meir as a baby had not strayed far from the ones Moishe sang to Aaron, Chaim sang to Moishe, Abraham sang to Chaim, and Yitzhak sang to Abraham. In this particular way, the memories of Meir's forefathers continued. Those melodies soaked into Meir's blood just as the rain once soaked into the long-gone vineyard behind his house.

By the age of five, Meir had shown his parents his own beautiful singing voice when one night, at the Sabbath dinner, his voice shone brightly above his father's.

His parents, taking strong notice of his talent, fostered it well. For his son's sixth birthday, after tireless months of scraping by on worn-out shoes, tasteless meals, and candleless nights, Aaron had saved enough money to buy Meir a violin to accompany his voice. While Meir continued to sing, the moment he first held his violin, his heart flooded with joy. Meir quickly grew to love his violin no less than he loved his mother or father.

Within months, after studying and practicing for long days and nights, he played well enough for the entire shul to enjoy his music. He began to play it every evening for his mother and friends, cleaned the finger-plate and its case after every Sabbath, and taught smaller children to play during the week, forming a small school in his kitchen. His mother adored inviting anyone who passed by to come to Sabbath dinner, ending with, "Do come, and you'll get to hear Meir play!"

For every occasion in the village, from weddings to the sale of a donkey, someone invariably would say to Aaron, "bring Meir over with his fiddle, why don't you, and we'll celebrate!"

His popularity had grown to such a degree that, by the time Meir turned fourteen, through all the kopeks that had been tossed in his violin case since he was a child, he had amassed for himself seventy-five silver zloty—an impressive fortune, and not just for a young man. This did not even include the money his uncle Abel from Warsaw gave him on his Bar Mitzvah—a three-ruble coin of imperial gold.

Meir resisted showing off his wealth to the adults, let alone his friends in the yeshiva. Even on his way home from teaching a violin lesson, earning two copper Kopeks—for which he had to lend his very own violin, bow, and rosin—he made sure to hide his change in his shoe. He would turn out his pockets and say, "they could not pay me today!" when his eager friends would catch him down the road, hoping to go buy sweets. He lived this way for years, only giving money to his mother to buy new candles from the general store and meat from the butcher, so they could enjoy more than matzah ball soup on the Sabbath. As the years passed, and Meir grew to be taller than his father, and possibly even wealthier, his violin's patina only grew in depth and richness.

But if only money, music, and decent cuts of meat alone could make a person happy! Meir gave joy to his parents, his friends, his teachers at school, and even the rabbi in his astute interpretations of the halacha. But Meir, though he had flowing love to give, had not yet found happiness within himself.

The prayers on the Sabbath had grown stale. The boys in the yeshiva could not understand the questions he asked, and the pretty girls his mother introduced him to lost his interest when they spoke. The Vostęvskie family had lived and died for countless generations in Tolevoste, but at the age of fifteen, Meir faced a simple problem—he had grown tired of it all. His parents saw this, ruminated over it, and could not think of what to do. His mother only prayed to God, asking for an answer as to what her son needed to be happy.

One foggy summer evening, Meir could not be found. The boys coming home from the buckwheat fields said they had not seen him all day, and the rabbi, in the yeshiva, told his mother Meir said *she* had kept him at home for some chores. Not even missing for half a day, his mother nearly melted away, crying all evening, wondering what she had done to drive her beloved son away. Aaron comforted her, insisting it had only been a few hours; Meir would come back.

Out on the street, as people whispered that Meir had been missing since the morning, they passed the Vostęvskies' house in solemn silence. His mother's crying drowned out the street's sporadic cowbells and squeaking cart wheels. The wind chilled the air. The last of the villagers still outside wrapped up their evening chores. Just as his mother had wept her last tear, the sun settled below the horizon.

Moments later, a new light rose across the dusty fields. Bands of yellow rays cast themselves through Tolevoste's windows and onto its walls. A distant, rumbling noise crescendoed down the street.

"Ms. Hoffman! Hi!" Meir waved, speeding by through the wind.

Braap braap!

"Good evening, Reb Levi!" Meir said.

Braap pap pap!

"*Oy Gevalt!*" several people along the road were heard to say.

"Run for your lives!"

"What in Creation?"

"Slow down, Meir!"

Hearing the commotion, children and teenagers ran out of their houses, slipping between their parents' legs.

"Oh quiet, Ma," many were heard to say. "Meir has a *motorcycle!*"

As bright as a polished brass bell and as fast as a horse, but needing no food, few things as beautiful had come to Tolevoste in a thousand years—except for the Torah—as Meir's brand-new motorcycle. Each of his classmates ran up to him as he slowed down, groping to touch some shiny part of it. Meir had to stop abruptly and take care not to fall to the ground. He had just learned to ride it several hours earlier outside the dealership in Kalinasevka. He had been scared to death that he might fall on his way home and mar the motorcycle's dazzling blue paint.

A crowd larger than if the Messiah had materialized in Tolevoste flocked around Meir. With no other way around it, each and every child in the village insisted they needed to have a seat on the back; several parents had to form a line to make sure their children did not scratch it or hurt themselves getting on and off.

DIASPORA

"*This* is what you missed class for today," said the rabbi, scurrying down the street. "Liar!" he scolded him, grabbing his ear.

"Oh, but Baruch Hashem!" he added with delight, admiring the impossibly thin spoked wheels that reflected the moonlight through the clouds. "*Mazel Tov! Mazel Tov!*" he shouted, still holding Meir's ear, only letting go to swing a leg over it himself.

"Careful, rabbi. This is very hot," Meir said laughing, delicately tapping the soft, silver exhaust pipe, sculpted in the resemblance of a dove in flight.

Meir's mother and father, just moments before having opened their door to see what all the commotion was about, frantically made their way through the crowd. His mother gasped at the sight of the motorcycle.

"Mama, papa!" Meir said, beckoning them closer. "I'm sorry for not telling anyone where I went. I wanted it to be a surprise!"

"Oh, my darling, don't ever give me such a fright again!" his mother admonished, shaking him by his arms, wiping her tears on his face.

Aaron, paying no attention to her, ran his fingers over the glossy paint on the gas tank, blue and subtly wavy, reminding him of a giant raindrop from the moment of creation. He felt the weight of the fine steel when he went ahead and raised it off its kickstand. Tears welled in his eyes.

"I've been eyeing this one at the dealer's store in Kalinasevka for months," Meir explained to his father, still trapped in his mother's arms. His eyes glowed as he explained to everyone around him how it worked and what it could do. He restarted it with the kickstand, revved the engine, and a cry of almost frightful wonder spread down the street.

He did not explain its greatest quality of all—that it could, if he wanted, take him far away from there. His mother, who had only glanced at the motorcycle for the briefest second, finally let him go, briefly putting her hands on her child's head. Aaron said a small prayer, kissed his son's forehead, and returned inside to prepare for dinner.

By the time the entire village had come and gone, the night turned late. Although everyone went to bed past their normal bedtime, the next morning, each resident of Tolevoste would say that they had not had such good rest in weeks.

It surprised no one that, the very next morning, just before the ultimate destruction of the residents of Tolevoste, Meir was out riding his motorcycle down the main road, far from his village.

One morning like any other, when the distant steam whistles of the flour mill just north of Tolevoste blew and the factories to the south lit their furnaces, Meir awoke. The sun had not yet risen. He rubbed his eyes and got dressed. He had some errands to run outside of the village—including getting his bow restrung—so before helping his father in the buckwheat fields, he planned to ride like the wind to Kalinasevka where his violin maker worked, drop off his bow, and return home just before the men reached the fields.

Meir grabbed a few kopecks from his hollowed out copy of *Yitzhak Leybush Peretz' Collected Works*—a clandestine coin box that not even his parents knew of. He hung his bow over his back, put on his tattered cotton cap beneath which he wore his *yarmulke*, and imperceptibly left his house. A thin dirt path beside the rails, though narrower than the road beside the Tolezyli forest, allowed him to carve a straighter path to Kalinasevka. When riding west, he felt himself flying from the sun.

His motorcycle could carry him far, but the tracks always went further. He often thought about where they went—perhaps deep into Germany, or grander yet, all the way to the *sea*. If he had no family, he had the passing thought of continuing on and never returning to old, tired Tolevoste. He secretly prayed to God, asking Him to show him more of the world than the Ternopil Oblast.

"Don't let me die in the same spot that every Vostęvskie has died before," he said beneath his breath. He made prayers like these frequently, and each time, he felt ashamed.

Turning his attention back to the road ahead, he considered, if he kept up speed—nearly sixty kilometers per hour—he would be in Kalinasevka before six in the morning. If he had time, he thought, he might ask the shopkeeper if he could try out some of the new violins in stock.

He felt a sudden shiver. That morning felt unusually cold, even for the beginning of fall. His new coat, in the modern style popular in Warsaw, was not made to keep a man warm at those speeds.

After thirty minutes of riding and intermittently shivering, he passed the Kalinasevka train stop. The village lay only minutes ahead.

Meir noticed that something about that morning was not quite right; the usual fading of soft blue emanating over the horizon at that hour had not appeared. Something seemed to have scared the sun away from shining its light. Perhaps, above the horizon, the factories' black smoke covered the first morning rays, he considered. Of course, that day had to be like every other in the truest sense. Every day the sun rose, gave all the plants and animals its warmth, and went back to bed as did they. Meir appealed to his reason whenever his heart felt unsteady. However, *something* felt undeniably different, no matter what reason he came up with. A profound heaviness settled over his heart.

Just then, on the rails far ahead, the faint sound of an east-bound steam locomotive rose above his engine's thrum. Moments later, the ground beneath his tires shook. Trains did not usually come that way on those tracks at that time, he knew. As

Meir continued to ride, the distant train barreled closer. He squinted as its lights blinded him. The engine passed him with a shrill, desperate cry. Plowing the wind, it nearly knocked Meir off his leather seat.

Many trains had passed him by while riding before, but none had ever raced with such fury. The engine steamed across the plain, with its boxcars of Polish passengers in tow, as if escaping something's grasp.

The train eventually grew distant. His engine, as if no longer frightened by the cry of the locomotive, sung through the night once more. Meir adjusted himself to get comfortable. The first rays of the sun finally rose over the horizon. He smiled and briefly closed his eyes, feeling the sun's warmth caress his eyelids; noticed how the fields to his left reflected the sunrise's deep orange; and heard the songbirds waking in the field's furrows in between his engine's rhythmic pulse.

And yet, riding through the gentle wind, unbeknownst to him, a last moment of peace—a last moment of everything—had come and gone.

Far into the west, a second thunderous noise rose, but this time, emanating from the sky. Crossing over his head, he could make out scores of planes cutting through the sunburnt clouds. He had seen airplanes before—small, canvased biplanes, such as those which battled in the Great War—but those dark, monstrous, steel machines cruised above him with a deeper, sinister, bellowing drone. To his horror, their engines' awful symphony turned into an unbearable, piercing shriek. In the direction of the train, one after another, a wave of *dive bombers* plummeted from the sky.

Several kilometers behind him, just as that attacking squadron crossed paths with the east-bound train, they released their heavy payloads. With hit after direct hit, the entire expanse of the passenger train erupted into volcanic ash and flame, striking Meir's eardrums like a dagger.

The ground jumped beneath his tires as the sound wave hit. From kilometers away, he felt the heat from the flaming steel on his neck.

He pulled in his clutch, turned straight away from the rails, and rode through a rocky division between one crop field and another. Nearly being bumped off his seat, he kept up his speed through the field until he came upon the old dirt road by the forest. He set his motorcycle on its kickstand and turned off its engine, but left in the key.

He cautiously peered over the fields to the horizon ablaze with flame. As he stood there watching, the planes flew back towards the clouds, turned north towards the old flour mill, and diving again, released scores of bombs on their target.

Consumed by the horrific sight, Meir barely noticed that, coming down the same dirt road on which he stood, several tracked cars were fast approaching. When he heard them, he froze in fear, connecting those approaching vehicles with the planes that just dropped bombs before him. They saw him just as he saw them, with his motorcycle's headlight still casting light across the tree line.

"*Wer ist das? Stoppen!*" one of the drivers shouted.

Scared by the harsh command, Meir quickly ran back into the buckwheat field he had just ridden through. As that tracked car stormed by, one of the soldier's in the back raised his rifle, shooting several rounds vaguely in the direction in which Meir had disappeared. Luckily for Meir, he had tripped and fell over one of the field's furrows, blooding his nose against the cold, jagged ground, just as the soldier's bullets whizzed past him. Meir laid still, shivering with fear, but as soon as the sound of the vehicle disappeared, he picked up his cap, stood back up, and ran.

Panting from exhaustion, he made his way back through to the other side of the field beside the railway tracks. He would have continued running the twenty-six kilometers home, but he stopped, gasped, and turned back around.

"*My bike! I forgot my bike!*"

The burning flames to the west lit the morning more brightly than the sun in the east. Gunshots rang from above the clouds as humble Polish planes battled the Luftwaffe for control of the sky. Just then, piercing through him like a cold wind, the terrible siren of the dive bombers crescendoed directly overhead.

Following the same path he had trampled earlier through the buckwheat, he reached the other side of the field on the edge of the Tolezyli forest once more. About to collapse from exhaustion, he nearly fell on his knees. Thankfully, he heard no cars, and except for the moon, saw no lights. Peering through the crops, he knew he stood in the same place he was before, with his motorcycle tracks clearly carved into the dirt. Along with the cars and soldiers, his motorcycle had vanished.

Meir felt a knot in his throat. His heart sank. He was too far and too tired to make his way home, but he could not rest where he stood. Fearing the road would soon see more soldiers like before, he realized what he had to do. Feeling for the small canteen of water by his hip, he crossed the road and ran into the thick trees.

***

Meir found refuge like many others in the Tolezyli forest, as the Germans advanced from the west and the Soviets marched in from the east. That immeasurable, old-growth forest, boasting precipitous hills through which ancient, mountainous roots weaved, made a Panzer less capable than a cow at crossing. Like everything else in Poland in 1939, it could be bombed from above, but its dense canopy prevented any bombsight from picking out a target on the forest floor. To attack the Tolezyli

DIASPORA

Forest would be to throw a match from a bomber aircraft over the sea with the intention of burning a herring. The hunted naturally ran for cover, and the Tolezyli forest provided cover like no other.

Only the most foolhardy of the German or Russian brigades tried to cross the forest rather than circumnavigate through the countryside around it. The forest imposed a sure death sentence for anyone who did not properly prepare. In this way, Meir survived the hunt of the German infantry. But how he crossed the forest, boarded a loaded hopper car, rode across German occupied Poland, and found himself loaded onto a civilian cargo ship at the port of Gdańsk, remained shrouded in mystery to everyone but God beyond his death.

PART 2

DIASPORA

1

Pachamama, or the SS La Pampa

Several hours deep into the Atlantic Ocean, a solitary cook, having just finished preparing his ship's first hot meal of the day, went to the forepeak hold of the bulk carrier, the SS La Pampa, to begin organizing his provisions. Common with ships departing in both times of peace and war, the port of Gdansk billed wharf space by the hour. Like a businessman late for his train throwing together his briefcase, the holds of the SS La Pampa were haphazardly piled with everything the captain and cook divined their crew of sixteen would need for twenty-five days at sea. The tireless cook had already cleaned his galley; his last duty that day was to thoroughly inventory and organize his hold.

Clouds darkened the sky. A drizzle washed the deck. The SS La Pampa lightly rolled from the sea's budding swells. The cook sighed upon seeing the disorganized mess epitomizing his days of late. He felt the pain in his back that had built over a life of service at sea. Much as he suspected, the ladder and escape hatch had been covered, open potato sacks leaned against the rocking bulkheads, and the smell of spilled flour filled the stuffy air. From port to starboard side, tight against the bulkhead, he slowly arranged his dry provisions in his own way, taking comfort in the order as he created it. He cleared a walkway to the hatches, organizing the potatoes, carrots, onions, and thick-skinned apples into their respective crates.

In the corner of his hold, the cook noticed a barrel of molasses had been opened, its lid slightly ajar, with a sticky puddle beside it.

"*Tarado,*" the cook said, aggrieved by the carelessness of the longshoremen who must have abandoned it like that. "Just wait till the captain hears about this."

DIASPORA

He picked up a rag, lifted the lid, and just before he could wipe off the rim, shouted as though he had seen the devil. Silently shivering, crouched up to his shoulders in the dark goo, a young man—Meir—looked at him with terrified eyes. The cook dropped his lid.

"A stowaway! You're in trouble!" the old man shouted.

Meir stared at him in trembling fear. The cook wanted to run for help. But before the cook could turn his eyes away, he thought he saw a second apparition. He vividly saw a different child who had also once been a stowaway on the SS La Pampa. Realizing that over fifty years had passed since that child first boarded her, he siphoned, from the lowest bilges of his mind, the memory of that boy so distant, foreign, and forgotten, that he nearly forgot that boy was actually himself.

At sixty-two years old, the cook had spent more than half of his life in the rusted steel bowels of one merchant ship. For his first ten years, he had not once seen the sea. Raised in the village of Huapampa, in the Argentinian province of Salta, mere feet from the wide Rio Rosario and just on the foothills of the Andes Mountains, he would have died in the same place nearly every other Huarpe did, never straying further from his Adobe house than the river could carry him when he tried to swim across.

The mountain's wild coca leaves would power the young Huarpe boy on his daily trips over the bluff towards the mountain's higher ridges. He would lay his Viscacha traps overnight and collect them in the morning—his modest attempt to earn his family some meat. His father's two-hectare parcel of a corn field near the Chilean border had fed them meagerly. His mother's colorful quilts and shirts staved off the death grip of the winter ice. Though seasonal flooding had encroached on their doorstep and famine rested menacingly just above the foothills, the young boy's family took solace knowing they lived in God's sacred land, the valley protected by the Cosompa mountain.

His parents were some of the last Huarpe people living in the Salta Province on the banks of the celestial Rio Rosario—as it was then called after the Catholics had renamed it from the original Quechua. Their land would have sold for a high price, even then, if only the immigrants arriving on steamers from across the Atlantic Ocean could more easily reach it. Nestled tightly in the interior of the wide continent, between a river to nowhere and a mountain range blessed by God, the only way to reach Huapampa in the last days of the 19th century would have been to wade through ninety kilometers of bristly grass to reach the closest train tracks. But missionaries and prospectors did indeed cross that shallow valley to scout those virgin hillsides, and in this way, began to erode the land once occupied by countless nations of indigenous people.

The missionaries, white like the snow caps, eventually hung their crosses from the village's *Pukara* walls; informed the Huarpe people through signs of their choice to be baptized or shot; and collected and burned the village's wooden and textile depictions of their deities. They established a church on the same mound where, on the day of the solstice, the Huarpe used to watch the Sun God, Inti, rise straight above the peak of the Cosompa mountain.

Shortly after the young boys in the village erected the timber walls of the new church under the barrel of the missionaries' guns, the boy's mother died of a virulent strain of typhus. By the time the first winter with their Christian neighbors had passed, none of the Huarpe people had faith in their new crucified god, and the fifty five residents had buried the boy's mother and five more.

In the spring, the boy prayed nightly to Pachamama to free him from the curses of the crucified devil and his idolaters. Pachamama, in Her infinite mercy, answered the boy as a female boa constrictor, streaked with interwoven bands of green and dark blue, mirroring the banks of the Rio Rosario. The very next

DIASPORA

night, just as the boy returned from an evening of trapping to his single-roomed adobe house, he saw the serpentine incarnation of Pachamama coiled comfortably on his late mother's multi-colored woven mat.

"Dear Mother Earth," whispered the boy. "I can see you."

The snake remained silent. While it sat there, the boy spotted his pet Opossum, Cayancura, crawling out from under his blanketed pallet, just as he always did when his owner returned. The boa hissed, sprang from its coil, wrung the life from his dear friend, and in carrying the carcass out the door, cleaved from the boy his last loving attachment to the land on which Huapampa stood.

When his father stumbled home from drinking Chicha in the corn fields with the other men, late into the night, he found his son sitting on his mat, his back to the door.

"What's wrong, boy," the father said.

"I've been given a sign from the Gods," answered his son. For a moment, the two stayed in silence. The boy spoke once more.

"You can die here too, if you like, but I will not."

That morning, while his father lay asleep, the boy left with a carpet bag over his shoulder, fashioned from his late-mother's multi-colored mat. With the boy gone, the father did as he said, and died as well.

The boy wandered west through the fields of the San Juan province, far across the Rio Rosario. He put his faith in the belief that the distant land to the west, where Inti rested at night, could spare the space for a small Huarpe boy's colorful mat. He forded the muddy Rio Calchaqui, and for nights and days endured the thrashing of the sharp grass, the biting insects, and a diet of uncooked corn rising from the mineral rich plains of Cachi Adentro.

A week passed. By then, though the boy's aching legs *surely* had brought him near the end of the Earth, Inti kept His same distance from him; the land where the Sun rested ruefully remained just out of reach. When night came again, lost in the great expanse of creation, the boy still rested alone.

The next morning, feeling hungry and tired, he looked behind him to the Cosompa mountain—his protector from birth—seeking strength to continue on his journey. But rather than gather strength from it, the boy was stunned to see something he could not have imagined before. The eternal Cosompa mountain had descended part way beneath the horizon; her ridges danced and swayed in the hot air, as if blending into the sky; and having crossed enough land for the air to be visible, her once lush peaks had a cold tint of blue. To him, with no knowledge the world was spherical or that air could be visible in great enough expanses, there could be no other explanation; his protector was being swallowed into the Earth, immaterialized by the wind, and drained of its warm, eternal life.

Seeing the spirit of God's own mountain fading into the ether, the boy realized that the humble Huapampa village, planted on Cosompa's foothills, must have long fallen to its grave. If Pachamama could swallow his protector, what would She make of him? With his home gone and on the verge of death, the boy laid down in the grass content to die. But as the Sun baked his dark skin, before he could fall asleep, an idea came to him.

With his cunning sense of logic, he considered the depth to which the mountain had sunk. He calculated the days elapsed since it sat entirely above the ground. He reasoned that, while Pachamama could open up the ground and swallow a mountain hole, She could only digest it slowly, like a snake does a rat. Therefore, if he went higher, across the adjacent mountain range's ridge, he may have weeks to find the Sun's resting place before the last of the sacred valley mountains were swallowed. The boy, trusting in his logic, would try.

DIASPORA

Reinvigorated by his new plan, the boy roused himself and continued west, methodically scaling the mountains he no longer knew the name of, but trusted were kindred spirits to his deceased protector, Cosompa. Drinking from the crystal water flowing from the ice caps in the sky and chewing on the abundant wild coca, the boy climbed higher. The thinning air taxed his lungs. As his breath became strained, spirits began to appear to him in the clouds.

Seeing the ghosts around him, believing that Pachamama had decided to fade him into the ether, the boy could not hold back his tears. And yet, when he looked down from just beneath the clouds, the grass in the valley stood above the Earth just as it always did. Though spirits filled the air, the mountain beneath him had not been swallowed.

The boy dried his tears. Realizing that wherever his feet stepped, Pachamama had kept the ground firm, he finally understood what his mother meant when she said he was a chosen child of God. The boy felt deep love and thanks to Pachamama. He abandoned his dangerous pursuit of the mountain range's highest ridge. Slowly descending the weaving hills for the rest of the day, oxygen re-entered his lungs, and the spirits disappeared from before his eyes.

Still, he had come no closer to his goal. Several more weeks passed as the boy's hunger outpaced his diet of coca, wild amaranth, and the rare eggs stolen from a condor's nest. He felt utterly alone. The boy had never seen another village, but he knew that Pachamama had not kept the sacred valley lush just for his people numbering fifty-five. He searched for others. At times, he thought he smelled roasting Guanaco from the hills in front of him. But he never did see a camp, or even the smoke of a fire. Time passed as the mountains descended into the valley, the valley withered into the desert, and the desert piled up into verdant hills once more beneath his feet.

One morning, when the Sun awoke him at the same distance, he felt as if Inti was taunting him. Preparing to rise, he found that his legs refused to move.

"Fine, don't move, you haven't brought me anywhere!" cried the boy to his tired legs.

In tears, but with the sagacity of an ancient man, he undid the lace tying together his mother's multi-colored mat, chose two sticks from around his body, and fashioned a viscacha sized snare. His snares had failed him twice so far on his journey. But satisfied that he had done all he could in the eyes of God, he laid his head down, covered his eyes with his hat, and said, "Now, Pachamama, I have tried, and I may die."

The boy fell asleep. If it weren't for a group of land surveyors encountering him while conducting routine work for the state, Pachamama may have done as he said and took him where he slept. If so, he would have died before he learned he had wandered as far as the Antofagasta province, in the country of Chile. He collapsed just behind the hills of the city of Antofagasta, adjacent to the Pacific Ocean.

DIASPORA

2

Antofagasta

As the boy slept, in his dream, he felt his mother's hands holding him against her chest. On a warm night, while his father stumbled drunk through the fields, his mother lay on her back, staring into the loving eyes of Qoyllur, the goddess of the stars. Sweat flowed from her body, soaked her multi-colored mat, watered the ground beneath her, and drained into the Rio Rosario, running high from the Cosompa mountain's melting ice peaks. She glowed an iridescent purple as her fever drew her blood closer to her skin. At dawn, her body evaporated under the burning Sun. The boy tried to hold on to his mother's dress, but he could not keep hold to something that was not there. He crashed back down onto her multi-colored mat. As he cried, laying on the mat, he felt the earth beneath had gotten softer. Lifting it up, he saw purple and yellow flowers had grown into a bed beneath where she laid, fortified by the vital spirit that his mother had sweated out the night before. He laid back down in the flower bed. Feeling warmth from the ground, he slowly stopped crying. The boy heard someone shouting from the sky. He rolled over in his flower bed but felt the flowers getting drier, harder, and turning to dirt.

"Boy, boy! What's your name?" A man shouted, holding smelling salts to his nose. The boy opened his eyes. A bearded man in a long, white coat stared at him, leaning towards his face. The boy immediately tried to get up but felt too weak to move. His head lay comfortably on a pillow. The boy looked around at the dim, stuffy, hospital room. He picked up an enticing scent. White women in white frocks were passing out small tin bowls of soup to the patients. The boy felt incredibly hungry.

"He can't speak a word," the bearded man said, shaking his head. The boy stared at the nurses with their bowls.

"*Want... eat?*" the doctor said in his best attempt of the Quechua language. He gestured his hand to his mouth. The boy nodded yes. When the nurse brought the food, the boy hungrily grabbed it from her hands, nearly spilling it on them both. He drank the lukewarm porridge and licked the bowl clean.

The party chief of the land surveyors stood watching beside the doctor, spoke with him for a moment, and relinquished his custody. He and his instrument-men had just minutes ago walked through the doors of the Antofagasta Mission where they laid the boy, then unconscious, on a roller bed. The thirteen kilometer walk down the hill taxed their lungs —even just carrying their stakes, books, and theodolite. They had taken turns carrying the sleeping boy on their backs.

"Family?" the doctor tried to say in Quechua to the boy. The boy stared at him.

"Papa, mama?" the doctor emphasized.

Understanding, but suddenly realizing he did not have his mother's mat, the boy lifted his head and frantically searched around him. Seeing it laying on the floor by his metal bed, he sighed with relief.

Fed, and no longer interested in the man standing over him, he felt his legs with his hands. They seemed to be working. The air felt thick as it flowed through his nose. He turned to put his feet on the ground, stretched his legs, and felt the pleasure of moving his calves. He grabbed his mat off the ground and quickly stood up—he saw the Sun still had several hours left of daylight through the window of the mission, so his journey could continue—but his legs collapsed from under him when he tried to take his first step.

"Sister Marie," the doctor called back to the nurse who just helped him. "Can you make sure this boy stays in bed?"

Sister Marie helped the doctor lift him back on the bed, put the blankets back over him, and folded his mat by his side. The doctor, wiping the sweat off his forehead, left to attend another patient.

"We'll introduce you to the rest of the boys in the morning," she said, unconcerned if he could understand her. As soon as she turned her back, the boy lifted his sheets and tried to stand once more.

"No. You stay," she said, gesturing commandingly at his bed. Breakfast is at the first bell."

The boy was not sure why the strange people seemed to not want him to leave. But gazing out the window again, he accepted that his legs were not cooperating, the bed felt comfortable, and perhaps, they might give him another meal in the morning. Resigning to wait until sunrise to continue his journey, he got comfortable in the dimming room; in the mysterious, large brick house; in the bizarre village of men and women dressed in white; and fell back asleep on clean sheets, dreaming in vivid colors, as he did when he slept by the banks of the Rio Rosario.

The boy opened his eyes when the first light warmed his face. He gazed around. The hospital room was quiet. Just as he did the evening prior, he looked for his mat, finding it neatly folded by his bedside. Relieved, he stretched his legs and stood on his two feet. Although he felt sore, they managed to carry him forward. Surreptitiously leaving the hospital room, he walked down the stairs, through a cloister hallway, and opened the heavy, wooden doors of the mission. When his eyes adjusted to the brightness, he nearly lost his breath.

On a gentle hill, the mission overlooked the port of Antofagasta. The wind sat still and heavy over the wide bay, its blue water glittering in his eyes like the wings of millions of blue butterflies. Tallships, steamers, tugboats, and sailing yachts peacefully rested on the blue sea as countless little figures wandered through the tightly packed rows of colorful houses, along the port, and up the ships' gangways. He smelled burning conifer logs, hot sawdust, sweet molasses, and the brine of dried fish as merchants, teachers, sailors, and students rolled their carts and carried their packs down the shiny, cobblestone road laid before the mission and its church.

The boy nearly cried. He did not know Pachamama had created such beauty. But before he could take another step, he heard the light scurry of soft shoes behind him.

"There he is!" cried Sister Marie. Two other nuns walked up to him and put their hands on his shoulder.

"You like to go wandering off," she remarked, feigning anger. "It's breakfast time, come back inside, and don't be causing us to worry."

He began to feel frustrated, but remembered that they were likely to give him another meal if he went with them. So with no great reason to resist, he resigned to let the overly attentive people take him back inside the strange house one more time. They brought him where a score of other orphaned boys stood in a line. Unbeknownst to him, prayer in the orphanage's steeple was requisite every morning before their breakfast of tostadas and black tea. He followed the procession past the cloisters, running his hand against the arched wall's cool, thick stone. He entered the church as the rest of the boys were taking their seats.

As the boy stepped inside, smelling the sweet frankincense and woody aroma of the steeple's old leatherback books, he looked around him. He saw *it*. Behind the pulpit, a giant statue of the crucified devil hung between the stained glass windows letting in the Sun's soft, morning light. His face was writhing in pain, blood poured from his hands, and figurine idolaters in colorful robes supplicated by his feet beside him. The boy shrieked.

"Devils!" he shouted, backing toward the door. Sister Marie and the assistants tried to stop him, but when they put their arms on him, he kicked one in the shin. "Murderers!"

"You rotten child," Sister Marie growled, grabbing his ear. But the boy had been grabbed by his father like this before and knew how to twist her wrist. Screaming in pain, she let go. The boy ran from the church, through the cloisters, and out the door of the mission. With no direction in mind but *away*, the boy ran straight through the village. No one bothered to give chase. He dropped his multi-colored mat by the mission's door, but he could not turn around. Nearly toppling over carts of fish and fruits, people shouted at him in a language he did not understand. Flushed with fear, he paid them no mind. His feet carried him all the way to the edge of Antofagasta, by the seaside, far down the hill from the mission.

Tall wooden pilings jutted out from the raised, gravelly pier. All around him, continuous processions of longshoremen and sailors disappeared behind the bulwarks of their massive ships with barrels and grain bags slung over their shoulders, preparing to disembark at high tide. Believing the devil's idolaters were still tailing him and with no other way forward, the boy picked up a grain bag from a pallet; followed a group of longshoremen up a gangway to an ironside steamer; snuck into the starboard side hold instead of turning back around to follow them; and laid down in a corner out of the light. There, in the hold of the strange dark boat, he finally felt safe.

Not soon after the last of the longshoremen stowed their cargo, the deck was secured and the steam whistle sounded. The tugboats took hold of her stern and her bow, the entire hull shuttered as the stokers raised hell fire in her furnaces, and the tired sailors hauled their wet manilla lines over the bulwarks, salt water dripping down their torn sleeves.

As the SS La Pampa pressed her hull into the rolling sea, the boy, still laying in the dark hold, acutely aware that the large boat was moving, began to feel worried.

DIASPORA

He wondered how wide that blue lake was, if the devil's idolaters would be waiting for him on the other side, and above all, how he would get back his mother's multi-colored mat.

3

The Cook

DIASPORA

And so the boy went sailing. Nine hours deep into the Atlantic Ocean, the crew found him, bound his hands, and sent him to the wheelhouse. The boy did not resist. The captain severely reproached him, questioned him, and threatened him with the brig, never concerned with the fact that he clearly did not speak Spanish. With quiet sympathy, satisfied he had been sufficiently chastised, and impressed by his stoic silence, he sent him below to get a warm bowl of stew, a piece of bread, and a glass of milk. He then had the mate ration him a bar of soap, towel, toothbrush, and assign him a berth with a fresh, clean set of linens. For the captain of the SS La Pampa, whether he be stowaway or crew, no man would be treated without dignity. That did not mean, however, the boy would find free passage on the captain's ship.

For the month-long steam across the sea, on his knees, they made the young boy scrub oily soot from the lowest bilge. Standing on his tiptoes, he cleaned the tallest wheelhouse spire. He shoveled coal beside the stoker, and eventually, reeved manila lines with the bosun and his deck crew. He listened with his eyes, answered with his hands, and worked with his heart. To much of the crew's amazement, he seemed to fall into his shipboard duties with natural ease. There was no duty he could not grasp, from lookouts on the bridge, to oiling journal bearings in the engine room.

When the crew next went ashore, he followed, and when they stayed the night at a brothel in the port of Hedland, he laid beside them on the floor. With the month having passed, and despite having paid back his passage in labor, no one could compel him to leave. After an entire season had gone by, no one tried. Eventually, he was given a sailor's wage. Port after port, season after season, and year after year, he clung to the SS La

Pampa as he grew taller, his shoulders broadened, and dark hair came to his face.

By the time he was no longer a boy, the young Huarpe man had not left the SS La Pampa for more than three straight days during his first five years of sailing. Without a passport or any documents in his name, he could not have gone far even if he wanted to. Nonetheless, like many of the others, the Huarpe man found comfort in domestic life, and there existed few lives more domestic than those of sailors. Yes, the SS La Pampa crossed vast swaths of the Earth, but so too would a hermit's cabin wander great celestial expanses while atop the remotest mountain. He had a claim to a cabin kept warm by the ship's coal, stores of dried beef and flour, and a thick, surplus blanket from the Chilean Navy atop his bed. While not the resting place of the Sun, the Huarpe man had not known a more peaceful home since the earliest days of his life when, as a baby, he laid atop his kind mother's chest.

Beyond his worldly comfort, the Huarpe man had found more aboard the SS La Pampa to satisfy him as well. He loved his captain. An aging man when he had first found the Huarpe boy as a stowaway, the captain saw how the young man regarded him with a childlike love. The captain's long, gaunt, bearded face, and eternally searching green eyes, cut through the young man. He saw a place that the Huarpe man had not yet found within himself. The Huarpe man poured the captain's coffee each morning and protected his cigars, as he lit them, from the sea breeze blowing through the wheelhouse's portholes. Despite his devotion, he could never quite understand fully what had led the captain to treat him with such kindness and grace.

Seasons upon seasons passed. Fresh seamen came and went. By the time he turned thirty three years old, his beloved captain could delay his retirement no longer. The captain patted the sailor on the shoulder, walking off the SS La Pampa one last time. With him gone, the last soul to know where the Huarpe seaman had come from, and why, had gone as well. The ship sailed on.

Older, unsettled, and deeply alone, the Huarpe man decided, as all seamen at some point do, that he had sailed enough. But why recount in detail a story that every sailor knows so well? He walked off the gangway one foggy, spring morning at the port of La Boca, Buenos Aires; payed for a top bunk at a brightly painted, bed-bug infested tenement house; laid beside the *bandoneón* musicians, criminal vagrants, and poets-for-hire; and fell into a dark stupor fueled by Quilmes and cocaine for the remainder of his short stay. The SS La Pampa crossed the wide Atlantic without him, exchanged cargo in four ports, and returned to the port of La Boca. There, the ship's crew found the enigmatic Huarpe sailor, sleeping on the ground, beside the same bollards they had moored to two months earlier. Sweating under the Chilean army blanket he pulled tightly against his body, he woke up to the sight of a young deckhand starring down at him. He left his tall beer bottle on the dock, walked back onto the ship, and took back the bunk he had left behind. His clothes, jacket, and rain gear still hung on the bulkhead where he had left them.

Years pressed on as the SS La Pampa pressed on through the rolling sea. He never tried again to leave the ship that had once cast a lifeline to a young boy, adrift. As the Huarpe man would dream in his bunk, on rare nights, the memories of Huapampa would still come to him in a mysterious fog. He wandered unfamiliar cold mountain passes and chalky fields. The ceaseless rocking of the ship transported him back through the deepest primordial memories of his early mind. Long years and countless thousands of miles continued to flow beneath his feet.

By the time his beard had gone gray, his back grew sore, and his duties relegated to the galley; by the time he nearly forgot Quechua, talking with a broken Castellano like the other sailors on the La Pampa; and by the time his heart had hardened like the ship's steel, he no longer dreamed of anything at all.

On the night before he would find Meir in a barrel of molasses, similar to most nights, the old man stood on the fantail, smoking a cigar, wide awake. The night was misty, still, quiet, and short. He watched the moon rise and fall. The Sun finally brightened the sky and the air, spackling gray, murky streaks of light over the black water and through the endless mist. The peaks of the waves awakened into a soft hue of blue. The Sun's orange crown rose over the horizon and melted across the bay. The water grew brighter, brighter, *brighter*, until jumping sparks of glitter danced atop each of the tiniest ripples of water. Pellets of the Sun, just as far as He ever was, bounded across the sea and accosted his old, tired eyes.

"Leave me alone. I can see you… I can always see you!" the old man shouted, with a quivering lip. He looked away, his heart overflowing with sadness.

"Torment an old man no longer."

He closed his eyes and cried so deeply, and for so long, he could have melted through the scuppers, carried away by his tears. Moments later, the seamen of the SS La Pampa hauled her lines, stowed them, and secured the ship for sea.

DIASPORA

4

The Barrel

The weather had rapidly deteriorated. As the ship's hull rose and fell atop the Atlantic's high swells, a portly, young deckhand rushed into the forward hold. He stumbled over the ledge as he walked through the door.

"Is everything alright, sir?" he said, catching his breath. "I heard shouting!"

The cook forced the barrel lid down just before the young man had a chance to see the stowaway.

"Well, everything *would* be alright... if you deckhands could secure your cargo correctly!" he answered, pointing to the molasses stains on the deck.

"Sir, I'm so sorry. Let me help—"

"—*Help*? I'm not so sure you didn't already *help* yourself to this molasses!" he said, eyeing the oil stains on the boy's overalls.

The deckhand stared at him, his face burning red.

"Where do these kids keep coming from?" the cook added, staring directly at him. "This isn't a daycare. Get out."

As fast as he entered, the deckhand rushed back out the door.

When the cook was sure he was gone, he hurriedly lifted the barrel's lid once more.

"Sit tight," he whispered, firmly gesturing to Meir with his hand. "I'll be back with a plan very soon. Just don't move."

Not understanding his language, Meir only stared at him, his heart pounding.

The cook mopped up the mess. He repositioned the barrel where it belonged against the bulkhead, put aside his mop bucket, and left in a hurry back through the ship.

DIASPORA

All became silent in the forward hold. Meir, frozen in fear, listened to the thrashing of the waves against the hull. He tried to adjust himself, alternating between putting weight on his feet and his back. He felt the molasses squishing between his toes, between his fingers, and on his eyelids. A sliver of light shone on him, but he could see nothing. The sugar ran down his forehead and into his eyes. He tried not to cry.

The steel hull creaked. Cargo knocked to and fro as the waves pounded the ship's bow. Had it really only been three days since Meir was in Tolevoste, sitting by the buckwheat crop with his father, playing their favorite tune on the violin, *Ve-David Yafeh Einayim*. He closed his eyes, began to hum it, and lead his mind through that day.

His mother had come around the back of the house, waiting respectfully for Meir to finish playing his melody. He opened his eyes, saw his mother waiting, but turned his focus back to his violin.

"Bubbeleh," she softly said, placing her hand on his shoulder. "Yemima is here for dinner with us, remember? From three houses down? She is such a lovely girl—"

"—I'm sure, Ma," Meir answered coldly, playing just quiet enough to hear his mother speak. After a moment passed, he felt she had not moved, stopped playing, and stared at her severely.

"And? Tell her I hope her dolls are doing well."

"That's not fair. You've hardly talked to her, dear," his mother said, seeing another *shidduch* off to a poor start.

"You know, when Aaron and I first met, we were just around your age—"

"—Fine, Ma! Since *Yemima* can't get the message, should I tell her myself?"

He raised his voice, with fire in his eyes, and instantly regretted it. His father looked away. A bizarre anger in Meir boiled over; he had no choice but to let it flow. His mother had looked at him ready to cry. He wanted to tell her not to. But when he said it in his mind, he heard a mocking abuse in his tone. In that moment, and for the rest of his enduring memory, he could do nothing but stare at her sad eyes.

Sitting in his barrel, Meir lamented having spoken so cruelly to his loving mother. And Yemima—he never did speak a word to that sweet girl. In his darkness, he wondered—perhaps, if he took her offering of love... He could find no answer that satisfied him.

Nor could he find an answer for the soldiers, the planes, the fiery bombs, the rapid guns—out of all the people to start a war with, the people of Tolevoste seemed the least deserving. The thought of those soldiers driving through his quiet village; how his family had certainly been woken up by the bombers; how his mother and father would have gone to look for him—his lip quivered. The tears he had kept bottled up overflowed from him.

Had it been only three days prior that Meir dreamed of seeing the sea? He could not believe, through his miserable seasickness, that the beauty he had envisioned was endlessly rolling beneath him.

At every turn, he had tried to stop—he had tried to turn around. But at every chance, he had no choice but to continue on the path inexorably rushing forward beneath him. Leaving the forest, he could have chosen only the soldiers' guns or the train tracks; in the hopper car, the rails ahead or the dark, bitter wilderness of Poland's vast interior; at the port, the cover of the cargo or the police inspecting papers at the dock; and in his barrel, his continual suffering or the untold retaliation of the ship's crew.

But now, at last, he had no choices left to make. What that old man had in store for him, only God knew. Meir decided he would not face his fate cowering any longer.

He slowly lifted himself up as his eyes adjusted to the bright, yellow light. He sighed with physical relief, stretching his calves, and tried to scrape off as much molasses from his body as he could. He saw the cook's bucket, still filled with soapy water; stepped from out of the barrel and into the water; took off his shirt, his pants, and his shoes; and began to clean his body.

After a moment, the ship's bow rose abruptly over a high swell. Meir lost his balance, the bucket flew from under him, and with nothing to grab onto, his head slammed onto the steel deck. Blood from a deep gash poured into the soapy, sweet smelling mop water.

Meir felt his spine tingle. His limbs grew light. With his ear pressed to the cold deck, he heard the sea beneath the hull. No longer thrashing, the water flowed like a gentle wind. Cutting through the SS La Pampa's bubbling rust, he heard Poland's autumnal breeze meandering through Tolevoste's fields. As the SS La Pampa heeled side to side, delicately draining the Blood from Meir's brain, he felt his mother rocking him to sleep in a small, single room house by a buckwheat farm, not yet drenched with blood.

The yellow light dimmed. Blackness swirled in his eyes. As his thoughts faded away, he saw a calm, shadowy, pockmarked face. Although the man's eyes stayed closed, he felt a deep, loving warmth radiating off of his gently glowing skin. The face smiled as if every face Meir had ever loved smiled at him at once. Slowly drifting closer, the face lifted its eyelids. Meir's breathing slowed. As alert as a cat under the moonlight, he felt the ancient angel's glowing, white eyes pierce a thousand years through his tired soul.

The cook, meanwhile, had just finished feverishly compiling everything he knew Meir would need; a bar of soap, towel, toothbrush, and in this day and age, sea-service paperwork, hastily forged and signed. Should his captain ask why he had not seen the new galley-hand before, the commotion of the war-time port could explain that away. And besides, despite just being the cook, he was the oldest and longest serving man on that ship.

No one knew the cook well, or could even describe the way he made them feel. However, anyone would have recounted his actions as bizarre. What one does not understand, one fears. The passing crews of the SS La Pampa grew to fear the old Huarpe man, so distantly withdrawn into the meager comfort of his stovetops, pantry, and worn-out bunk bed.

He sometimes wore a veneer of a smile during the day, insisted upon by many captains through the years. Nonetheless, this could not obfuscate the bitterness raining from the rest of his face.

The old Huarpe cook having a sudden, radical softening of his heart would have never been believed. The only true explanation was that, seeing himself in the eyes of that boy, he believed God had given him one last chance to save himself.

With the stowaway's effects in hand, he opened the door to the forward hold. He dropped everything at the sight of the boy, lying in a pool of sweet smelling blood.

DIASPORA

5

The Storm

Foaming clouds shrouded the night sky. Lightning took the moon's place as the SS La Pampa's sole guiding light through the sea. The ship pounded her way above, through, and below the bubbling waves, the lashing spray, and the swirling rain. As the swells lifted her screws above the waterline, her mains gave a desperate cry.

Meir, on the verge of death, sweating, with his breath slow, deliriously wandered within an uneasy dream. As his mind came into a blurry focus, he found himself sitting at his dinner table, talking with his mother and father, his brand new motorcycle outside, still warm from his first ride back from Kalinasevka.

"So anyway, Ma, we don't *need* Miriam's eggs anymore. I can get the best eggs all the way from—" Meir began, digging a fork into his matzah balls.

"—Why did you leave us, Meir?" his mother asked.

"Oh ma, I thought we were past that. I was only gone for a few hours! Anyway, the ride from Kalinasevka isn't even forty-five minutes, now," Meir laughed.

"You left us, Meir," his father said, somberly. "Your mother just wants to know why."

Meir felt a bead of sweat on his temple.

"What do you mean?" Meir asked.

The room began to dim.

Feeling the ground become soft beneath his feet, Meir stood up, pushed his chair in, and ran outside. Watching his buckwheat crop sway in the wind, he took a seat behind his kitchen, caught his breath, and felt calm. His family was wrong, he told himself. He did not leave them.

His violin and bow sat in the dirt before him. He picked it up, preparing to play a simple tune.

When he looked at his hand, he found he was holding onto his mother's arm. He tried to, but could not scream.

His mother—in her simple, brown, Sabbath dress—sat supplicant by his feet. She grasped at his pant legs, his shirt buttons, and his collar, trying to lift herself onto his lap. But his worn, threadbare textiles flaked away like dry leaves. Ripping them to shreds, she sank back towards the Earth. Jumping up desperately, she took hold of him tightly, her arms wide around his shoulders, and pressed her warm face against his cheek.

Meir looked at her face, and trying to console her, reached for her rosy, tear moistened cheek. But when he touched her face, he felt nothing, as if his fingers had fallen asleep.

"I'm sorry, Mama, I'll be back." Meir said gently, looking into her imploring, gray eyes. Though he gazed directly into her eyes, he noticed she looked distantly through his.

She fell to the ground, and with her head down, cried horribly. He tried to pick her up; he tried to tell her that, whatever troubled her, it would pass. But reaching to her shoulder, his hand went right through. Crying into her palms, his mother slowly faded into the gentle breeze.

Raising his gaze above her, Meir surveyed the land where he, just moments ago, believed his family's buckwheat farm stood. In his delirious dream, he believed wholly in the reality he was seeing before him; a sprawling, glowing vineyard, with every shade of purple and blue, lovingly swaying for a hundred acres around him.

He stepped over the stratified ghost of his mother, still weeping silently. Beneath the dusk's sunburnt clouds, the vineyard sparkled like a jewelry store with hanging topazes, opals, and emeralds glowing and glittering by candlelight. Far into the distance, an olive tree sat in the center, taller than any tree Meir had ever seen.

Meir walked closer. With every step he took, the sun retreated further behind the horizon; the verdant greens and sparkling blues melted away like running paint; and the towering tree began to lose its leaves, silently blowing away, one after another.

Meir's walk turned into a run. As if in anger, the vines rapidly shriveled up. By the time he had stepped foot into the vineyard, ever retreating as he approached it, the last fiber of green vine had died, the vines' grapes had shriveled into dust, and the sun burnt out like a bedside candle in the wind.

Meir kept running towards the tree. Its leaves poured down like rain; its thick, brown branches turned red; and by the time Meir had reached its trunk, only rotting twigs swayed in the icy breeze overhead. The tree had seemingly long been dead.

Meir looked down; a sea of blood rapidly washed over the field, raised to his ankles, and drained back into the dry, rocky field. Like a shipwreck from an ancient time, his mother lay by his feet, contorted in the dirt. Her head, torn open by bullets, trickled out with purple wine.

Feeling weak, with his lip quivering, Meir fell to his knees. He grabbed her shoulder, now solid, and tried to lift up her wet body, warm like a hearth. She could not be moved, laying in the dirt, with an endless weight she never had while alive.

While holding her, Meir heard a whisper from the darkness behind him. He turned around. Staring at him vacantly, less than a nose width away, Meir again saw the pockmarked face that had appeared to him just before. He wore a dirty pair of cotton overalls and a simple, clean, white shirt. His skin was deathly gray. But cutting harshly through the darkness, his glowing eyes, face, and body lit his mother, the tree, and the dry ground on which he stood.

"Why did you leave them, Meir," the angel asked.

Staring into his eyes, Meir seemed to preternaturally understand who the man was.

"Why did I leave them? Why did *you* leave them? When all of this happened, where were you?" Meir asked the man. He stood up and tried to grab him. But the man stayed his distance at Meir's every move, as if Meir had been reaching up toward the moon.

"You did this!" Meir shouted.

At that moment, the ancient man quickly reached his arms out to Meir. Meir fell silent, in a trance, as the man traced his way down Meir's shoulders, his arms, and his hands. Meir's vision blurred. His thoughts obscured. The ground and horizon blended into one.

The ancient man pulled him close; feeling the limitless warmth of his skin, Meir's sadness drained from his heart. Under his warm breath, Meir felt the man blowing away the last of his anguish, his memories, and his pain. But before the angel could touch his glowing lips against Meir's forehead; before he could bring Meir fully into the warmth waiting in his breast; he paused, moved Meir back, and tilted his head in thought.

"What's wrong?" Meir asked, drunk in his all-encompassing love. The angel did not answer him, but having briefly conferred with God, slowly released his grip.

With a gentle push, the man let Meir out of his grasp. Meir's awareness of the world began to come back into focus, and he plummeted into a deeper despair than any he had ever known.

Arresting his fall, Meir crashed into the core of the Earth. As if given an electric shock, he violently sat upright, breathed in a tremendous gasp of cool air, and in a feverish sweat, flung off the blankets tightly tucked up to his chin.

Meir frantically looked around. A weak table lamp lit a small, dark sickbay, scantly larger than the thin bunk he lay on.

The door to a plyboard cabinet swung side to side. He saw stacks of towels, glass pill bottles, and opened rolls of gauze precariously by its edge.

He shivered feeling the air-vent overhead and wet sheets beneath him. As he tried to stand up, he felt a throbbing pain behind his eyes. He touched the thick, gauze bandage on his forehead, cold and wet from sweat and blood.

A tall canteen of water sat by his bedside. He eagerly took a drink. The memory of the dream clouding over as he awoke, he understood only one thing at the moment—he was hurt, but alive.

The door creaked open. The light from the passageway shone in. The dark silhouette of his rescuer, the cook, with the SS La Pampa's captain in tow, entered the sickbay.

DIASPORA

6

Puchero de Morcilla

Deep into the night, the sea had calmed. the SS La Pampa had plowed the evening storm off her bow; sailed north from the western edge of the Baltic Sea; slid through the German blockade across the strait of Skagerrak; and steamed into the Atlantic effortlessly, silently, leaving behind a smooth wake under the bright moonlight. Every soul on board but Meir, the cook, the captain, and one mate steering the ship, were in deep sleep.

When the cook delicately opened the sickbay door, Meir stood up, aware that that door was his only egress from that musty room he had inexplicably found himself in. But with his head pounding and his vision blurring, he nearly collapsed. The cook rushed to him and caught him under his arms, helped him back down, and filled him a fresh glass of water.

"*Pobrecito*. It's a serious gash," the cook said to the captain. Meir laid still as the cook replaced his bandage with a cool, wet rag.

"He'll be alright. He just needs more rest," he added, dabbing away Meir's dried blood, still sticky from the molasses in his hair.

The captain pulled the cook aside. Meir watched them attentively. He could recognize many languages; Yiddish, the language of his home; Hebrew, the language of God; Polish and Russian, the languages of the market; and English, the languages of magazines, and the rare BBC broadcasts he seldom overheard on radios.

However, the language of these men was a mystery, sounding to Meir like the words of a sorcerer's spell.

The captain eventually addressed Meir directly. Calmly, and with little emotion, he asked him his name. Meir stared blankly. The old, steely eyed man, receiving no answer, let out a defeated sigh. He cocked his head in thought.

Captain D'allasio was visibly tired, generally and from lack of sleep. He carried the air of a man whose mind may have been everywhere but in the present. Moreover, nothing could happen aboard a ship that he had not experienced before. The old captain had learned many lessons that only time could teach, and above all, excitement drained him; though he had lorded over many men in the merchant fleet in his younger years, he had since lost all inclination for contention.

Adding to Meir's benefit, the new Great War, much in the likeness of the last, had spread across the sea as fast as a gunboat's rounds could fly. Battleships prowled the coasts as u-boats scoured the deep. Forced to navigate through the German's war-time shipping blockades, one unplanned passenger, for the captain, was hardly worth a mention in the ship's daily log.

Meir, listening to the verbose dialogue of his apparent caregivers, gathered he was not in immediate danger. Nonetheless, he maintained his suspicion; he instinctively decided that saying anything in Yiddish would be *nischt gut farn die Yidden;* certainly, it could do him no good. Despite a few more half-hearted entreaties from the captain and cook, he had made up his mind to stay mute. Coupled with the fact that, despite growing a scraggly beard, he had never grown payot, Meir successfully avoided any overt indication of his being a Jew.

His instinct may have been for the best. What the captain would have done if he knew, no one could have known; in truth, he may have not known himself. Under the circumstances of the time, he could have been justifiably anxious if he discovered the spindly stowaway found in a molasses barrel was a Jew hiding from the Germans. In fact, quite a perceptive man, the thought crossed his mind.

The cook, understanding where the captain's mind was going, stopped him in his tracks. Fully out of character, he volunteered to see to the silent boy's berthing, employment in the galley, and to take full responsibility for his actions. The captain assented with a nod, and with no further thought, left back to his helm.

The cook zealously saw to the boy's permanent berth in his own stateroom, clearing off the top bunk he used for storage. Knowing the boy had nothing but the sticky shirt he found him in, he fished out some of his old shirts which ended up fitting Meir not too terribly. A pair of engineer's pants, found hanging in a recess of the windlass room, proved shriveled enough to stay above his waist with a drawstring. One of the cook's countless old rags, folded and held together with a safety pin, sufficed for Meir's new cap.

Once the stowaway had thoroughly washed off the last of the dried sugar, the cook helped him down to the galley. The rest of the crew had eaten hours before. He warmed Meir a bowl of red, oily soup with green leaves, floating pieces of bread, and chunks of unknown meat. Meir smelled the garlicky broth. Feeling the pain in his stomach where no food had been in days, he took a large gulp.

A stew similar to this, the cook remembered well, served as his own first meal aboard the SS La Pampa, many long years ago. As his years passed, this red stew never failed to elicit in him the same simple relief of a Huarpe boy, worlds away from his home. In his mind, that bowl of red puchero would mark the beginning of the new stowaway's own long life at sea, just as it did for him. Questions swirled in his mind regarding the circumstances of this boy's arrival; did he, as well, leave his home to find the resting place of the Sun? Likely not. But perhaps—no, without a doubt—the boy would relate enough to his kindred story if, in a short enough time, he could learn to speak. In this enthusiastic fantasy, the cook began to arrange the boy's first language lesson.

Meir, who could have never imagined half of what was preoccupying the cook, nearly coughed up his first spoonful of stew. As if it were caster oil, he tilted his head back and drank as much he could stomach in one go. The hot soup burned his throat, and the dark morcilla recalled images of rotten meat the butcher would give his father to mix into chicken feed. After a few more arduous spoonfuls, with his hunger somewhat abated, he looked up from his bowl. The cook's over-interested gaze hovered above him. Though bewildered by the unexpected attentiveness paid to him by a Goy, with enough sense to respond politely, Meir smiled, nodded, and—*Ribono Shel Oylom*—tried to think how he was ever going to get back to Tolevoste now.

Sooner than Meir thought, and perhaps in no small part to the mysterious potions he scarfed down twice per day, he gained back his health and his strength. The gash on his forehead healed over, leaving only a thin scar. On his fourth day on the ship, standing on his feet without help, Meir rose at the same time as the cook, followed him down to the galley, and made himself available for whatever chores the old man wanted to give him. Though not fully understanding the cook's intentions, Meir gathered well enough he should work, and would do so to the best of his ability.

As the voyage progressed, the new galley hand could no longer be cloistered; Meir piqued the curiosity of the other seaman on the ship. The bosun, ever in need of new hands, inquired to the captain as to why such an able-bodied young man pounded flank steak in the galley instead of rust on the forepeak. The oilers and stokers sought to occupy the boy with a scrub brush, bucket, or shovel; after all, if he could load potatoes into the oven, then why not coal into the furnace?

The captain scowled at such remarks. It did not concern him what occupation the boy took for his passage; to him, the drama of the crew grated his ears and rattled his mind.

To reach the boy, one had to accost the cook. Having once been a young man on the same ship, the cook must have known the crew's advances were reasonable. In fact, he had never set foot in the galley on his *own* first voyage, and hardly during his first year at sea. Despite all reason, the cook guarded Meir on his daily journey from their shared stateroom, to the galley, and back.

Meir, ever perceptive, gathered that chopping vegetables for the small crew with the dark, overly attentive old man was among the less strenuous jobs available on that ship. On stormy nights, after the cook went to sleep, he often gazed out their small shared porthole over the deck; seaman in dark jackets, shouting and signing to one another through the rain, strained their backs over chains and binders striding across great pallets. The wind raised tarps into thrashing billows, and the heaving sea wrestled odd deck-cargo loose from their lashings.

The feeling of his dry shirt on his skin, with the oddly comforting smell of the galley's grease, showed him God's grace. In the deepest whisper, he sounded out the Ma'ariv, just as he had done every night with his father since before his bar mitzvah. He made sure to thank God for the cook, who undeniably had played no small part in his safety, and found a modicum of quiet in his heart.

In truth, in the rarest moments, Meir did find small elements of peace during his silent days with the old cook. Ignorant of where he was going and how long it would take to get there, what more could Meir do? While washing his potatoes, slicing his carrots, and scrubbing his trays, his violin's melodies came back in simple phrases and heartfelt notes. He released them in momentary whistles or hums. Keeping watch on the broiler, sitting in the Huarpe man's own chair, he occasionally

DIASPORA

allowed his legs to swing. More than once, he shared a genuine smile with the old man; he liked when his potatoes came out of the oven with the perfect crisp.

But Meir's pain and sadness hung onto his shoulders; tears flowed just behind his eyes like the Jeżyna River through Tolevoste and the Rio Rosario behind the cook's childhood home. Thoughts of his mother and father tormented him as he slept and encompassed his prayers while awake. As gently as fleeting peace entered his mind, violent waves of guilt inundated his heart like the Atlantic squalls around him.

Meir would not truly allow his guard to fall. His yarmulke stayed in his pocket and his boots laced tight. The moment the SS La Pampa pressed back to land, he would run, wherever he may be.

In total, twenty six days at sea continued in this way. The end of the voyage neared as all ends must.

The SS La Pampa, on a warm, humid night, one hour after sunset, saw a thin band of city lights cut the darkness. Meir, having finished his duties in the galley, sat alone in his stateroom, resting his back against the bulkhead, patching a hole in his sock. The cook, as he often did on such nights, stood wide awake on the bridge wing, feeling the salty wind thicken his hair, smoking one of his precious Guatemalan cigars. He felt happy.

Many leagues behind their stern, deep into the misty Atlantic, a single cannon flashed. The deck crew of the SS La Pampa heard the faintest din of a faraway battleship sinking a French freighter.

The SS La Pampa, known well among Buenos Aires' aging bulk fleet, had its Argentinian flag to thank for its safe passage across that bloody sea. With a series of codes hastily scrawled into an address book, and an iron signal lamp in hand, the captain's third mate stood on the forepeak. He sent bursts of Morse Code to the Argentinian cutters patrolling the shore. A scant few nautical miles ahead lay the first range buoys of Rio

De La Plata, the wide mouth to Puerto La Boca in Buenos Aires, the SS La Pampa's port of call.

Crossing the naval buffer and in the lee of the land, the SS La Pampa had returned from sea. She glided quietly against the river's gentle flow. The engines throttled down; a lone tugboat up ahead gave fire to its boilers to build up steam.

Meir, lying awake in his bunk, had thus far not recognized the tranquil bearing of a ship nearing port. But smelling the muddy scent of the river in his stateroom's stuffy air, he got up, turned on the light, and peered outside.

He gasped. The banks of the Rio De La Plata surrounded the SS La Pampa in a great bowl of yellow and white city lights. Tears welled in his eyes. He never knew such beauty existed on God's Earth. He could have no doubt, then, that he had traveled farther from Tolevoste than he had ever imagined. But in the faintest sense, the eternal sentiment of a seafarer returning to land, felt by all the crew of the SS La Pampa, danced sweetly with his soul. The slightest drop of salt water had infiltrated his blood. However, it would not be enough to make him stay.

The sound of a watertight door, opening in the passageway, jolted Meir back to the present. He closed his porthole, turned off the light, and jumped back into his bed. Seconds later, careful to not wake up the sleeping boy, the cook delicately turned the stateroom door handle. Meir pretended to be asleep.

The cook smiled. Within the hour, the SS La Pampa would be moored in La Boca. Once the seamen stowed the ship's rigging, their work for the night would be done. Most of the crew would head straight into the village. Local *estibadores* would rise from their cots to begin unloading the ship's breakbulk cargo.

The cook seldom stepped foot off the ship in port anymore with the rest. But under the circumstances, he decided he would go along with the boy who, so diligently devoted to his shipboard tasks, deserved the respite. Surely, the boy had never seen a tango bar, ate a parrillada, or seen a market the likes of the one on the multicolored Caminito Street.

He had a suspicion that captain D'Alessio would delay their next voyage back through the Atlantic. For one, the captain had long intended to visit his sister, convalescing from a bout of pneumonia in their Lake Chascomus *estancia*; and furthermore, the guns off their stern only continued to fire. With no urgency, he crawled into his bottom bunk, closed his eyes, and faded into sleep. The thoughts of their next day in the bright port of La Boca swirled around his mind.

The SS La Pampa pressed against the dock, longshoremen caught the crew's heaving-lines, and her boilers relaxed. Great stores of steam vented into the night. The ship sat at rest. As the crew went ashore; as the captain and port officials discussed bills-of-lading in the wheelhouse; as the cook slept deeply in his bunk, Meir lay deathly still. The cook's heavy snoring signaled to the boy it was time.

He lowered himself from his top bunk, opened the cook's cabinet, and delicately removed the cook's canvas seabag. Reaching to the bottom, he confirmed the cook's wallet lay there. He felt several old banknotes and coins.

After quietly piling in his own socks, underwear, and shirts, he pulled out from his own stowage a handful of apples, tins of sardines, corned beef, and two bars of chocolate, all incrementally pilfered from the galley stores over several weeks.

The cook coughed. Meir shot his head around, saw he stayed asleep, and continued on. On his tiptoes, he walked to the door, delicately closing the latch behind him.

Meir had failed to see that the cook would have given him everything he needed, and more, if only Meir had known how to ask. Through the red-lit passageways and down to the cargo deck, Meir left the SS La Pampa into the brightly lit port of La Boca, with no evidence of his ever being there or having left—that is, except for the stolen goods he carried with him, discovered missing when the aging Huarpe man woke up to nature's call.

Immediately seeing the young man was gone, hours later, with his effects evidently plundered, the cook felt a dreadful pain in his chest. He did not care about the stolen money—the boy deserved payment, after all. For a moment, he wanted to go find him, which surely would not have proven too difficult. He knew all the places in La Boca a foreign boy was bound to hide. But the futility of finding him was clear. A heavy cloud set over the old man's eyes. A pain he had not felt in weeks returned to his back. His lungs, worn from repeated bouts of pneumonia, could not catch a good breath.

"Why would he stay on this old ship, for an old man, with a tired crew, anyway," the cook said to himself. *"The boy wasn't a fool—like me."*

Having relieved himself, he laid down in his tired, worn-out bed, closed his eyes, folded his hands on his chest, and let a deep scowl harden into his stoney face. He would have cried so easily if he believed there was just one person who cared.

DIASPORA

PART 3

1

Thieves

DIASPORA

In the city of Buenos Aires, on the banks of the Riachuelo, in the port of La Boca, thick, colorful, marine paint—from the same cans used by sailors off the ships at port—covered the corrugated steel panels of stores, homes, and cafes lining the riverfront streets. But in the not too distant past, even the pier that first greeted Meir—then as colorful as a Quinquela painting—languished no brighter than a rusty nail.

Decades ago, a young Italian immigrant sailor, home in Buenos Aires from a long voyage, plundered three cans of colored paint from his ship. His daring plan to misappropriate just enough to coat the roof of his two room house on a dirt road—or rather, his panicked response to a problem of his own making—would serve as the inspiration for a community's lasting identity, countless years into the future.

This sailor, with no home in the world, once disembarked in Buenos Aires from a nine month voyage. He sought no more than a spot to lay his head, ideally with a roof to cover it. But in that period, thirty years before he would find Meir sleeping by his doorstep, with droves of immigrants and wealthy investors driving up rent prices in Buenos Aires, several months of his wages could hardly buy him a few weeks of the modest privilege he sought.

Along with a growing number of other seamen, longshoremen, ironworkers, and the like, he took his housing into his own hands. On the outer fringes of the port of La Boca, a short walk to where his ship docked, he built a crudely framed shack beside other shacks on an abandoned patch of dirt—in this particular case, once occupied by an iron foundry, long torn down. Scrap sheet metal served as his roof and walls. Timber from cargo pallets sufficed for a simple, sturdy frame. In this small, two-room house, he would sleep soundly, undisturbed, returning to it from sea over the course of several voyages.

As years went by, the families of these growing shanties organized for their mutual benefit. Together, they leveled and swept the rocky dirt at their doorsteps into distinguishable streets. Old rubber hoses from their ships and warehouses diverted water into each home from a municipal main. Stolen copper wire brought them light from the city's power lines. Women taught children in their own schools, and even mailmen, though not officially obliged to deliver into the neighborhood, made rounds through their streets when they found the time. Naming it "the neighborhood of La Boca," a community had risen from the dirt.

Years passed for the sailor in relative peace. Through seasonal storms and heavy winds, his house stood bolt upright.

However, on one spring day, returning from a voyage, he found that his metal roof had corroded in several small spots, allowing for both rain and sun to penetrate. Finding a new roof would not be a problem; in fact, with money in his pocket, he considered purchasing the supplies outright. But for the sailor, the price for the paint cost forty five pesos too much.

He had an idea. His ship, with weeks before it would go out to sea again, sat unguarded. The very next day, at high noon, just after the longshoremen still loading her left for lunch, he boarded her unseen. Below deck, he hastily scoured through the paint locker.

Keen not to get caught, he thought about what would be least missed if gone. The deck's gray, the bulkhead's white, and the hull's heavy, anti-fouling black—the ships most frequently used colors—were off limits, he decided. But a myriad of pipes, hatches, valves, and tanks were painted with other, uncommon colors; red went on fire-monitors, blue on potable water pipes, yellow on emergency hatches, and so on. An over-supply of these pigments had sat untouched in the paint locker for years.

DIASPORA

Unconventional colors for a roof, no doubt—but with their labels fading and their lids rusting in dark, out of reach corners, he decided they were the perfect cans to misappropriate. Colors be damned—paint was paint.

He carried three cans back to his home, ensuring he would have to pull off his risky caper only once. But to his surprise, just one gallon of red sufficed to completely cover his new roof with two coats. With his other two gallons, blue and yellow, he happily painted his front door, the eaves above his windows, his window frames, and eventually, having barely used a quart of either, all four sides of his home. By the time he finished all three cans, his two-room shack could have been spotted by a ship's searchlight two miles out to sea.

Laying down his paint roller, he took a few steps back from his front door to admire his work. He was pleased. The sun had nearly set. His stomach ached for the mollejas he had waiting inside. But with his hand reaching for his door, an intrusive thought disquieted him. He backed up again, eyed his house up and down, and surveyed his neighbor's houses around him.

His brightly painted house, surrounded by rusted steel shacks, stood out on the dirt road like a peacock among feral chickens. He was confident that his ship would be no worse for wear without the three cans he took. But he could not deny the fact that no good could come from the attention.

"This might be a problem," the sailor thought.

He began to sweat.

Yes, the colors on his house were stolen goods. But everything in La Boca, from the planks, to the water, to the lights, was stolen. When the neighbors of the La Boca shanties wanted water, they hooked up whole streets in one night. When they wanted light, they strung together every rooftop before turning on the first switch. He had a realization; the more they had acted as one, the less the *policía* could act to counter them.

With this in mind, his solution out of his painted corner was simple, though potentially difficult; to lower his personal culpability, the rest of the houses would have to have paint on their walls as well.

The sailor put off his mollejas. Though tired, he could not yet lay in his bed. Watching his clock, at the strike of one in the morning, the sailor put on a dark coat, walked back to the port, and snuck aboard the SS Corrientes for a second time.

Below deck, he stacked up all the colored cans he could find, totaling a healthy seventeen. In several trips, he loaded an old wheelbarrow from the port, covered it with a tarp, and swiftly made his way across the train tracks to his house. After neatly stacking them all on the inside of his wall, he ran the wheelbarrow back to the spot where he found it, returned home, ate one molleja, threw off his coat, switched off his light, and fell into a deep sleep the moment his head hit his pillow.

This sailor, during his time away from sea, rarely rose from his bed before his stomach commanded him, when the smells of his neighbor's midday *asados* of whole chicken and flank steak drew him out the door. But that next morning, Paolo, still wearing his trousers from the previous day, woke up at sunrise. Lighting his stove for his Maté, he played in his head how he could execute his plan. He would buy six pounds of the *carnicero's* morcillas, a bag of medialunas, and several bottles of *el vasquito tinto*. Next, he would invite a few families around La Boca to an asado, and get the men of the families as drunk as they could possibly be. Lastly, in that instant, he would send each one off in laughter, paint cans and brushes in their hands. With any luck, by the time they slept off their wine, they would have plastered too much paint on their houses to change their minds.

A bold plan—but it was the best he could think of at the time. Gulping down his maté, he took a deep breath, and swung open his door. As his eyes adjusted to the clear sky's light, he saw his entire street, and half of La Boca, silently staring at his house around his doorstep.

He cautiously stepped out. People shuffled back and forth, some on their tiptoes, extending their heads over each other's shoulders. Fathers put their children on their backs. Mothers with babies pointed at the astonishing colors they wanted them to see.

"We—we deserve nice things, too, don't we?" Paolo said, breaking the silence. Whispers passed through the crowd.

"Right, and nice things don't fall from the sky…" said a sailor, suspiciously eyeing the engine-room colors.

"Well, we built our houses together, strung our lights together, and piped in water together. So, why then" Paolo said, reaching for the first of many cans behind his wall, "shouldn't we paint together?"

People looked at one another, scratched their beards, nodded, and smiled. As simple as that, the crowd walked forward. One by one, he handed out his paint cans. Seconds later, he had none. The paint cans dispersed in all directions as the crowd, young and old, from toddlers to grandmothers, hurried to paint their homes in the same fashion as the sailor's colorful shack. Within hours, walls, doors, roofs—even flower pots—all across La Boca, took on the striking colors of a bulk cargo ship's unseen engine room machinery.

More neighbors, those waking up, and those who weren't quick enough to Paolo's door, gathered around these new centers of color erupting on every street. With inspiration and envy, many had the same idea Paolo had just the day before. Scores of seamen, with their families in tow, paraded up their own docked ships' gangways, in the full light of day, carrying as many cans of colorful paint as they could lift in two hands. A few captains, still in their wheelhouses inspecting their logbooks, cleaned off their spectacles, unsure if they could believe their eyes.

Watching it all unfold, Paolo, with a tinge of disappointment, decided to light his parilla anyway.

"I thought, at least, we would have been a little drunk by now," he reflected, uncorking a bottle of wine for himself.

He laid back in his street-side chair. The day passed. By the evening, his coals sat smoldering, grease slowly dripping over the ash; the last of his wine bottles sat dry; and with each house in the shanties of La Boca painted more extravagantly than the next, all of his culpability vanished like his parilla's savory smoke, rising in the air.

DIASPORA

2

Choripán

The people of La Boca, long infamous throughout Buenos Aires, crowned their lawlessness in color; marking their walls and their doors, they warned God and man alike: "move along, for here lay thieves." But how people may excuse what lies beneath a beautiful face! Did the citizens of Buenos Aires heed the warning? Did they take the advice of the police, who rightfully feared for their own lives if their captains ordered them to make a show of force within her limits? La Boca's aposematism worked to repel others as well as that of a Monarch Butterfly, who must run from children chasing her beauty with nets, trapping her in jars, and pressing her into picture frames.

In truth, no one could blame those attracted to her; in some places, beauty can be hard to find. The prey of an angler fish hypnotically swims through the hadal sea to the light. So too did the citizens of Buenos Aires draw near that small impoverished neighborhood of bright colors. Even God took notice, if God could ever notice one thing more than another.

It must be said, nonetheless, that the people of La Boca were not a danger to anyone. Yes, they had robbed many ships, foundries, and mills. But in all the years passed since their houses were scarcely more than tarps held aloft by sticks, none could say a man there had ever stolen another's purse, necklace, or watch.

Many weeks passed uneventfully. On the east side of the tracks, stevedores and sailors hauled barrels up gangways, blocks and tackles hoisted pallets in the air, and the familiar steam whistles of the iron foundry and steel mill sounded in time like the church bells of industry. The people in the shanties to the west carried on with their lives much the same, relatively unbothered by the occasional strangers seen perusing through their colorful streets.

But under the watch of God, nothing can stay the same for long. On one Friday morning, Paolo, like the rest of his neighbors, woke up to find a team of journalists on his street. With tripods, film reels, and boxes of flashbulbs stacked in the beds of their Fords, a handful of men in ties, brown coats, and checkered flat caps captured scores of photographs in black and white. Their story spread in newspapers across the city:

NEIGHBORHOOD OF COLOR!

THE CITY OF YELLOW AND BLUE!

The next morning, on Saturday, businessmen in corduroy jackets, arm in arm with their wives in floral print dresses, promenaded through the well-buzzed-about shanty as if vacationing by the Costanera Sur. They admired the community's bold display of modern art.

"Charming. An expressionist statement," a stately gentleman said to his wife.

"I'm not sure, dear. It's a clear rejection of French Realism, quite garish I'd say, though."

Such discourse, and worse, continued into the twilight. The talk increased in fervor after the city had left church the next morning. The residents, with their streets suddenly overrun, watched and listened on, stupefied, holed up in their houses, as if bracing an incoming flood. Some preached to their neighbors that the Lord had, at last, found the way to punish them for their sins. With illness and privation already well known among them, God had sent them the only disease that could ruin them yet—an infestation of the bourgeoisie.

Paolo had not left his house in days. With wax plugs in his ears, holding a pillow tightly over his head, he let his frustration boil in silence. The chatter from the street echoed through his corrugated steel walls, into his sheets, and violated his mind. It was clear to him that he set in motion a deep and unexpected change in his neighborhood.

"God, why do the rich wake up so early on Sundays?" he lamented. He checked his watch, sighed, and tried to fall back asleep. Eventually, his eternal tiredness overcame him.

He drifted off into sleep. The furrows on his brow faded away. But just as he fell into a dream, a child, not tall enough to see through his window, knocked on his door. Paolo's eyes shot open.

"Sweetie, come back here!"

"Listen to your mother, Santi. Let's go. Oh but dear, look inside here. It's appalling!"

"Oh my. Are they all like that? Why do they leave the inside looking like that?"

Paolo raised his head and looked out his window. A husband and wife, holding their child up to see, stared at him through the glass. Their three faces pressed against one another. The boy tapped on the window.

"Que carajo!" Paolo shouted.

"Is he talking to us, dear?"

"Mama, what did the man say?"

"Sir, we can't hear you. Are you saying something to us?" the husband asked, fogging up the window with his breath. Paolo starred in utter amazement. He could hardly believe it had come to this. There could be no worse offense; *they woke him up.*

"Bueno. That's enough," he said.

Calmly getting up, he picked up his pants off the floor. He had not signed on to any upcoming voyages, but he could not stay there another minute; there must have been some vessel preparing to embark that day in need of a hand. His will hardened. He would take any position; a stoker, a steward—

DIASPORA

padre santisimo, he would crew up on a pirate ship—so long as they offered a quiet room to sleep in, the one pleasure he could no longer find at home.

He hastily threw together a sea bag. After taking a sip of cold tea, he left out his door just as the oblivious family moved to the next house, gazing through its window as if it were an exhibit at the Museo Nacional. Paolo walked briskly in the direction of the pier.

Avoiding eye contact with the tourists, he fell into a state of mind that overcame him in certain moments of his life. In truth, Paolo hardly ever went to sea in a different state of mind. In times of boredom, pain, or indignant frustration, Paolo had learned no other way to calm his soul. Perhaps, the rocking of a ship calmed a turbulence in his brain.

If his neighbors, seeing him abandon his home of five years over a nuisance not three days old, tried to dissuade him, to show him reason, their appeals would have fallen on deaf ears. Only God understood Paolo in that moment, listening in on his thoughts attentively, as Paolo waxed poetic in the following vein:

"The lord punishes me day in and day out! All the worse for the peace he had given me, now I must watch it be taken away. Nothing which is easy is true. As easy as we raised La Boca from the dirt, so too it must fall. And yet, just as I find a moment of quiet, of comfort, at that very moment, and not a second later, he decides it had been too much, too much for Paolo! Had he knocked my walls down in the wind, I could have rebuilt them. Had he sent a flood, I could have swam. But for the crime of painting my house, he decides to send an army to push me away!

I must accept that. Peace isn't my lot and will never be. I was born on this Earth tired. I learned to run before I could walk. I've suffered since before I knew the meaning of sin. Every *man has a home, but where is mine? Is my only true home the waves?"*

At that moment, as was his routine in such melancholic bouts, he recalled his troubled childhood in a sort of co-rumination with his present self and his past. He told that story often and when he could, usually taking the length of a whole evening, and longer still if his Fernet Branca was in reach. God had heard his story many times before, but He permitted Paolo to let it flow. To summarize Paolo's major points, it went along these lines:

His memories began at the age of three. His young mother had suffered the humiliation of paying his late father's unpayable debts until the end of her short life. Two days after a tragic accident and three days before her wake, the mafiosos of Portofino seized her small stucco house; her three acres, overlooking the seaside; her beloved original Benvenuti, a portrait of Count Ugolino, gray and tired, imprisoned, abandoned, and starved in the Torre de Gualandi; and her pearl earrings, straight from the cold body that had worn them since her marriage day.

His sisters carried their few clothes and little brother Paolo through the countryside for weeks, sleeping in barns and stealing nights in the bowers of inns. But the *Polizei* caught up; his sisters scattered to the east and the west while Paolo, the orphan, fell into the care of the state.

From there, his story continued just as tragically, if uninterrupted, until that present day. But God, having heard enough, whispered into Paolo's soul:

"Cease, Paolo! Your story grows old! Why torture yourself? You are no longer a child, running from abandoned house to house, gutter to gutter. At what point does your life become your own? Will you only act from sadness, from

anger, from fear, from pain? If only you would look around, perhaps the world isn't as bad as you say! Come, raise your head, and tell me what you see!"

Paolo bumped shoulders with someone and snapped out of his internal soliloquy. He scratched his face and looked around. Clouds drifted off his eyes. Hastily lighting a cigarette, he took a deep breath. Somehow, he felt better. His ruminations paused.

Nonetheless, he continued on his way. Still wading through the crowd, he thought he saw his next door neighbor up ahead.

"Cacho? Ey, Cacho!" Paolo shouted. He seemed to not hear him.

"He must be on his way out as well," he said to himself.

Knowing his neighbor to be quite the recluse, he imagined the noisy crowd had grated on him even more than himself. He hurried ahead, but just as he got closer, he stopped in his tracks. The elderly Mr. Francisco—a stocky, dark skinned, taciturn steel worker—paraded up and down the street in a new striped shirt. With a rickety wooden cart beside him, he sang out in great, bellowing belts:

"*Garrapiñada, Garrapiñada dulce!*"

Children tugged at their mother's dresses to look. Fathers fished out centavos from their pockets.

"Yes, little girl, here you are! Enjoy! Garrapiñada!"

"Ay dios mios," Paolo said aloud. "Señor Cacho, are you —are you hawking sweets to these people?"

"Ah, Paolo! So good to see you!" he said, not answering him. "It is such a lovely day! Would you like some Garrapiñada? Garrapiñada!"

More tourists with open purses walked closer.

"Oh my friend, we shall talk later, life is good, eh? Garrapiñada!"

Paolo stood for a moment in confusion, then hurriedly continued on his way. If Cacho was not leaving, Paolo considered, he was only making things worse. Does one feed the ants at their door?

"What has gotten into him? Poor old man, the fumes of the mill must have gotten to his head."

The fumes of the steel mill could not explain it because, just ahead, he saw another neighbor—a young woman in a bright, multicolored, Peruvian dress—accosting passersby in much the same fashion.

"Panchuker y Morcillas! Fresh Morcillas!"

"Is that Maria, the seamstress? And what is that dress?"

Maria waved as Paolo approached, but Paolo walked passed, pretending to not see her.

"Something has gotten in the water supply," he said. Determined more than ever to leave that accursed place, he hurried ahead, rounded a corner, shouted in alarm, and nearly threw his sea bag over his shoulder. An entire festival market, three streets long, completely blocked the rail crossing.

Visitors crowded around artists by easels with full pallets in their hands, clamoring for freshly painted pictures of the colored streets.

"Impossible! Since when do the Alfredo brothers paint?" Paolo said in exasperation.

More of his neighbors stood behind hastily piled stands selling maté cups, ash trays, tapestries, and other knick knacks—all cheap and innocuous—but with "La Boca," in blue and yellow, freshly painted or sewn on.

"Ave Maria purisima, Mr. And Mrs. Osvaldo, Señora Carmen, Diego Delucia, why are you entertaining these people?"

Men he had never seen before with bandeñeons played songs they had just written, their cases filled with coins, as men from the shanty held hands with wine bottles and women, dancing Tango and Cumbia in the dirt. Above it all, a continuous cacophony of *"Mollejas, Morcillas, Garrapiñada deliciosa!"* blended with the chatter of the hundreds of exuberant people milling around.

"Two pesos please, Sí señor!"
"¡Mamá, yo lo quiero!"
"Will you do three for ten?"
"Sí señorita, come again!"

As Paolo watched it all in silence, God whispered to him again:

> *"Can you now see the fruits of your own labor—the blessings which you have brought to your sisters and brothers beside you? You have given your neighborhood life and color, and from this, your neighbors can now earn their bread for themselves and their children into the future. You have unwittingly done good for your people; so, answer me, why must you leave them now?"*

Paolo shook his head as if he had just been slapped. A fresh understanding filled his heart. Tears came to his eyes. He gathered his thoughts, nodded his head decisively, smiled, and turned around. His walk turned into a run. The crowd around him blurred as he passed. He collected his centavos from his pockets, stopped at the *carniceria,* the *panaderia,* threw his seabag onto his bed, and pulled out his cleanest blue shirt from his pile of clothes.

Under the eave of his front door, he dragged out his grill, piled his coals high, lit the flame, laid eight large links of fresh chorizo over the coals, and tore open the loaf of Pan Francés he had just bought.

The meat started to sizzle. The smell filled the air. Several visitors of the neighborhood approached. He took a deep breath, and sang out as loud as his heart could sing:

"*Choripán. Fresh, hot choripán!*" People turned to see. Families gathered around. Fathers opened up their wallets. Children walked up to him, smiling.

"Hello, little girl! Solamente un peso, Gracias!" Paolo said.

"Yes, very fresh! Here little boy, would you like Choripán? The famous Choripán de La Boca. *Choripán, fresco y caliente!*"

And God, seeing it was good, whispered into his heart with a great, eternal laugh:

"*See, Paolo? That wasn't so hard.*"

DIASPORA

3

Padre Santino

A few weeks passed. A middle aged man in a dark hat and gray jacket walked into a two story colonial building on Lavardén street, in the neighborhood of Barracas, three blocks west from the port of La Boca. A young lady in a black, tailored dress approached him. He whispered something in her ear, making her blush; hung his coat on his chair; sat down at his desk at the end of the office; and as people with documents and folders crossed back and forth with intention, casually enjoyed the coffee his young lady assistant placed at his desk.

For a moment, he looked out his window. Lively and deliberate men and women, with arms crossed and faces turned, hurried down the clean, cool, breezy street. Dry cleaning, briefcases, and frigid paper bags of fruits and vegetables hung from their hands.

The winter, to Captain Vargas, carried with it a vivacity like no other time of year. On cold mornings, he woke up next to his wife with a light heart. He would walk briskly through the streets, loving the feeling of cool air permeating through his lungs, cooling his chest, cooling his mind. At lunchtime, the scent of *Case de Rosario's* charcoaled chicken and beef, across the street from the police station, filled his nose. For his walks home, a delicate, pink glow faded across his sky.

Turning to his papers, he arranged his assignments across his desk, from one side to the other, according to their urgency and perceived importance. Captain Vargas was late to work that day, as he often was, but in his position, this was not considered much of a transgression. Most of his work was delegatory, and having just passed thirty years with the *Policía Bonaerense*— Buenos Aires' federal police—he handled his workload with quiet precision. He took another sip of his coffee, scanned through his papers, and began ordering and assigning jobs and tasks to different people in his mind.

One document on the top of his pile, with the commissioner's seal stamped on its manila envelope, gave him pause. He scanned it carefully, checked his calendar, double checked the date, and dialed the number on the bottom with his telephone. Listening carefully to the other end, he uttered only a few words of understanding during the short call. Scratching his beard, he sat for a moment in thought, bit his nail, read the letter again, and put his coat right back on.

"Emilia," he called to his assistant. "If anyone is looking for me, I'm off to the Puerto Madero precinct on the order of Commissioner Valentino."

"I'll let them know, Captain," she said, lifting his coat over his shoulders, allowing her hands to linger on his back. "Is everything alright?"

"More than alright," Captain Vargas said, turning around. "Valentino is being vague right now, but I understand that the military police, from Paraná and Sante Fe, are arriving on rail. We might have *quite* the show tomorrow."

His young assistant gasped, understanding what he was insinuating.

"From what it sounds like, this time will be different," he said, grabbing her arm.

Captain Vargas was more right than he knew. Arriving at the Puerto Madero precinct by the river side, just north of La Boca, he found he was already late. Six garrisons of military police from the surrounding provinces, with the assistance of the more reliable men of the federal police, inspected, harnessed, and adjusted rifles, batons, and leather vests from wagons in the street. Other federal police captains spoke with army lieutenants, holding up maps, sharing notes, and providing insight into the streets and corridors their soldiers would soon march.

Captain Vargas pushed his way into the precinct and walked up to Commissioner Valentino's desk. Valentino smiled, stood up, shook Captain Vargas' hand, and took him aside.

"So, I'm the last to know, it seems!" Captain Vargas said, with a hearty laugh. "Are you keeping this a secret in Barracas?"

"A secret? No! A simple oversight, Captain Vargas! I assumed for days my deputy had already informed you," he said. "But no matter, you're here now, and tomorrow, I'd like to see you here again at dawn. You'll be right by my side."

Valentino instructed him to follow a sergeant of the military police just then walking by.

"Hey, you! Introduce the captain to the others!" He said.

He watched the two of them round the corner. Just when he was sure Captain Vargas was well out of earshot, he dialed a number on his phone.

"Vargas is here, go ahead," he said quietly, and hung up.

At that signal, several of Valentino's men, waiting on the other side of the city, pushed their way through the doors of Captain Vargas' Barracas precinct. Before dismissing Emilia for the day, they demanded Vargas' secretary provide a list of every junior officer who had grown up in the neighborhood of Baraccas. Valentino's men ordered that, the next morning, the entire Barracas squadron board the first northbound train to Paraná for a "training day." Silent glances passed around the precinct, but no one resisted the order.

None of those boys were in actual trouble. Most of them would end up enjoying their trip to the outskirts of Paraná, kicking up rocks, polishing their boots, or doing anything else that suited their fancy. Cloistered in the barracks of the military police that had just crossed their path south, Valentino only cared that they would be nowhere near La Boca the next morning.

Valentino was a realistic man. He considered who those boys were. The majority volunteered for the federal police, freshly out of school, only in an effort to avoid conscription into the army; most earned a salary marginally sufficient to afford their own boots; and few had anything more on their minds than to put in their ten hours standing on a street corner, kiss their girls back at home, and spend the night in the dirt soccer fields they grew up on. Valentino knew that, under the threat of a fight, Vargas' boys might realize their allegiances lied more with the families they were sent to arrest. For this same reason, he had dismissed his own boys on an early holiday. He needed to be sure no one would interfere with the work of the military police. Vargas—raised in Recolleta, a far wealthier neighborhood—was no threat, he decided.

Meanwhile, with affected seriousness, Captain Vargas shook hands with every officer he was introduced to. He delineated to the army officers, clearly and calmly, the names, locations, and family ties of the most prominent of the lawless vagrants whom he expected would cause them the most trouble. But of course, they all agreed, *every* man, woman, and child from the *so-called* neighborhood of La Boca should be considered a threat to the peace.

By sunrise the next day, down the cool and breezy Avenida Belgrano, the light gray facades of the stout, stone buildings reflected the sun in great canyons of sharp, blue light; mothers and young children fed pigeons in the Plaza de Mayo, curiously quiet and free from police; tall, pulsing columns of steam rose into the westerly winds across the Rio de la Plata; and two hundred and fifty military police, trained and armed, flanked by fifty federal police, crossed the Puente Balcarse into the Port of La Boca.

In truth, no man in that army believed they would meet the disjointed confusion their commanders expected. In past raids on the neighborhood, the people of La boca, bats and bottles in their hands, had famously been known to swarm any officer who set foot on their land, like honey bees defending their hive from a wasp. Eyes and ears, in all corners of Buenos

Aires, could alert their comrades of approaching danger with preternatural speed. But despite everything, even La Boca could not withstand the bullets of two hundred and fifty guns, no matter how far away they spotted their barrels glinting under the sunlight. With this in mind, the men of that army marched forward.

Yes, they expected to meet some resistance—they would not have trained so well otherwise. But what they did not expect was how well the people of La Boca had been preparing for that day, with the building of fortifications underway long before Commissioner Valentino had first sought approval from the Mayor for his grand raid. They were not the only men to load their rifles and shield their chests in leather that morning. Forming a barricade at the main entrance to La Boca on Suarez street, an improbable three hundred men stood waiting, shoulder to shoulder, three columns deep. Rows of heavy barrels, grain bags, makeshift barbed mooring lines, and battlements of corrugated tin and steel protected their vanguard. Following the example of *El Libertador General San Martín,* the Grand Captain, before his victory for Argentina against the Spaniards in San Lorenzo, the people of La Boca allowed not one pang of fear to enter their hearts.

Sailors and iron workers with breech loader rifles kneeled on the parapets of their homes; mothers with frying pans, bats, and pots of boiling oil guarded their doors; their young children hid their faces in the folds of their dresses; and boys with crates of glass bottles, sharp stones, and powerful firecrackers stood behind their fathers at the front. At the very front, behind the first fortification of grain bags, Paolo stood beside twenty of the neighborhood's most prominent men. Each held their preferred weapon in hand.

Nothing but the sound of their breath and the wind filled the street. Not even a dog wandered west of the tracks. Only the thrum of the police's footsteps, kicking up light clouds of dust into the air, interrupted their silence.

In the center column, a smirking Commissioner Valentino, with Captain Vargas and several more high ranking men, followed behind Colonel Longano. Outranking them all, he would be the day's commander. Leading his combined army within twenty meters of La Boca's vanguard barricade, they stopped.

Many of the police glanced side to side, the fastidiousness of La Boca's defenses catching them by surprise. A furrow fell over Commissioner Valentino's brows; a drop of sweat condensed on Captain Vargas' temple.

Colonel Longano, allowing Commissioner Valentino to address his *Porteños* first, nodded to him to begin. Tamping down the fear of a bloodbath rising in his mind, Commissioner Valentino unbuttoned his pocket, unfolded a piece of paper, and cleared his throat.

"By warrant of the *Suprema Corte de Justicia,* the occupants of the unsanctioned settlement of the Port of La Boca are under arrest for the harassment, vandalism, and burglary of twenty seven separate businesses, port warehouses, and shipping lines; the unlicensed engagement in vending and commerce; the unlawful redirection of municipal water and electricity; and the battery of three federal officers of the peace on the fifteenth of December, 1904, and the second of March of this year."

He put his paper back in his pocket.

"In my capacity as Commissioner of the Federal Police of Buenos Aires, I order you to lay down your arms. Vacate your dwellings and barricades. This shall be your only and final warning!" Commissioner Valentino said, his voice echoing down the line.

A moment passed in silence. Paolo wiped the sweat from his hands, grasping the seaman's pike at his side. The riflemen in the parapets slowed their breath. No man, woman, or child flinched. Through the ranks of the police, the young, uniformed conscripts looked at one another with nervous glances. Captain Vargas placed his hand on his pistol. Having received no response, Commissioner Valentino flushed red, his mustache quivering.

"The Argentinian Army is standing by my side!" Commissioner Valentino shouted indignantly. "We are clearing this land whether you comply or not!"

His voice rang through the street like a starling's cry. The Commissioner looked to Colonel Longano, flustered, having thoroughly failed to instill any fear in the hearts of the men he addressed.

Colonel Longano gestured for him to step aside, cleared his throat, and called out a terse command. An entire column of the police's rifles fixed their muzzles onto the barricades; the silence of death hung across the entire expanse of the port; and God Himself, fearing even a gust of wind could trigger the release of thousands of rounds of lead, held His ever flowing breath.

Colonel Longano held the command to fire on his tongue. But just as he prepared to release their guns, an old *cura*, evidently struggling to make his way, crossed from behind the people of La Boca's grain barricade. Paolo had thus far allowed nothing to disquiet his steady heart. But watching *this* man pass him and his compatriots, a tinge of panic shot through his chest. They pleaded as one for him to stop; without saying a word, he paused, raised his hand, turned around, and looked them all deeply in the eye. As they fell silent, he continued forward.

Colonel Longano, generally pragmatic and immune to undue emotion, indicated to his men to lower their guns; it appeared to him that an envoy of theirs intended to negotiate. If this was true, he saw no harm in hearing their terms. The quiet, old priest continued his forward march, solemnly hanging his head, as if already in mourning for a loss too heavy for him to carry. He stopped precisely halfway between his men and the police before him. Colonel Longano frowned, astutely sensing that the man's intentions may not have been what he first hoped.

The old man lifted a rosary and wooden cross into the air. He drew his breath and called out to Colonel Longano:

"I am Padre Santino, *cura villero* of La Boca, ordained by Padre Juan, archbishop of the archdiocese of Buenos Aires. In your hands are the tools of Satan; on your shoulders, his evil hand is resting. You are marching yourselves into Hell! In the name of our Lord, lay down your arms and embrace God's light. Scorn Him and you will be damned!"

Colonel Longano scoffed. "This is your statement? Padre Santino, you are mistaken; the army's guns are no tools of Satan! Our Springfield rifles shine under God's light. You doubt their righteous cause, and yet, you must remember that our Bishop, Padre Juan, has blessed every gun which my men carry! For at this port, May of 1901, he stood beside me, blessing their pallets and the ships off which they were unloaded. Rest assured, each soldier behind me has been baptized by our church. Their allegiance is to God and their country. They aim their guns at evil with righteousness in their hearts. You, on the other hand, raise your cross in defense of the devil. The devil is standing behind you, all around you, with contraband rifles in his hands! You enable their crimes! We may ask the pope himself how a man who has been ordained could have had the darkness of Hell cast over his eyes; but we know," Colonel Longano said, turning to his men around him, "that as long as the kingdom of heaven hangs above the Earth, even a priest may stray from the light of God, no matter how brightly it shines over us all!"

Padre Santino, listening carefully to Colonel Longano speak, felt great sadness upon hearing his answer. After a moment in thought, Padre Santino responded:

"If you allow me to speak for the Most Reverend Padre Juan, he has blessed these guns and your soldiers to *defend* this country and its people—not to point their barrels at their fellow citizens! They only remain blessed so long as they are used for the purposes they were blessed for," he explained. "But beyond this, any man of God should be well aware that all of creation is the blessed word of God. The ships, the guns, and the army Padre Juan once blessed would not so much as be dust if He had not imbued them with the properties that allow them to sail, to fire, and to walk. Withholding a blessing from any man, army or not, would be denying them the right of God's light, free and endless to all since the creation of time.

And yet, you are correct, my son," Padre Santino continued, "in your assumption that whoever or whatever has once been blessed can subsequently fall into sin! For how could a murderer confess his crimes and receive the sacrament, only to commit the same deadly sin upon his release from prison years later? Yes, if sin did not rest on our shoulders, then your army would have no purpose; the pope may levy a blessing on all of Buenos Aires, and surely, we would live in paradise on Earth! You know very well that the world does not work this way, and yet, you fail to apply your knowledge to yourself! Do you believe, as a man whose duty it is to uphold our laws, that the words of the bishop have freed *you* from the eternal temptations of the devil which God has made you susceptible to? If so, you have fallen as low as a man can go, wallowing in stupidity, vanity, and pride!" Padre Santino declared.

The men behind him cheered. Many marked the sign of the cross on their chests. Apprehensive whispers were heard through Colonel Longano's ranks.

"You must choose at every moment between the paths of righteousness and sin," Padre Santino concluded, "for the influences of the devil never cease. In this moment, God is watching you, and he is watching you lead yourself and your army of police to damnation!"

"Blasphemous old man!" Colonel Longano shouted. "Your trick tongue spins my own words around, and tragically, is giving the men behind you false hope in their evil cause. But let this be my answer to you, *Santino*," he called out to the men of La Boca behind him, "lower your guns and surrender from your fortifications now. If any of you believe in his words, you will meet God and learn of His judgment presently! Forward ranks, prepare to fire!"

Obeying his command, the forward ranks of the military police raised their guns once more. Paolo and several more men called to Padre Santino to return to them behind their fortification. Several women, looking from their windows, were heard crying for him. Colonel Longano pursed his lips, sweating, privately hoping that the old cura would step aside. He did not want his men to hear him give the order to fire on a priest. But Padre Santino did not move. Instead, he clutched his rosary, held his cross high, and looked above the police and their guns. He saw the white sea birds above flying east, and felt the cool sea breeze through his wispy hair. A single tear fell down his cheek.

"Forgive them, Father!" he yelled into the sky. "And forgive me…" he added, with a whisper.

He reached into his pocket to pull out a Colt Revolver. Before Colonel Longano could gasp, Padre Santino, holding it at hip level, fired one round at the Colonel. Having held a gun just once before in his life, his shot only hit the Colonel's abdomen. Captain Vargas, standing by his side, rushed to catch the injured Longano in his arms. In shock, just as Paolo and the other men could dive behind their barricade, Colonel Longano roared the command to fire. In an instant, a thunderous volley of bullets pounded their grain bags, their corrugated walls, and the body of Padre Santino. Five police carried the bleeding Colonel Longango away.

With their ears ringing, Paolo and the other men cautiously stood back up. The corpse of Padre Santino was barely recognizable, laying on the ground in a pool of his own blood. A fire erupted in the souls of each and every man and woman behind that barricade. The men in their corrugated parapets instantly returned fire, striking scores of the police with lethal efficiency. A bullet grazed Captain Vargas' right shoulder; the police haphazardly reloaded their guns; women ran from their houses with wooden bats and iron pans towards their enemy; and through the police's next volley of fire, a furious cry of hundreds of men and women rose into the sky as if the foghorns and steam whistles of every merchant ship, train, and steel mill at that dock had sounded in unison.

As Paolo ran forward with his seaman's pike, aiming towards the breast of Commissioner Valentino; as children and teenagers threw glass bottles and improvised grenades in great batteries over the police's head; as wives and daughters charged beside their husbands and fathers; as the staccato ringing of breech loader rifles levied salvos of lead, back and forth, through that chaotic sea of men and women; the military police stumbled back, step by step, tripping on their own bloodied reinforcements behind them.

Captain Vargas had already taken it upon himself to levy commands in Colonel Longano's absence. Paolo's pike came within an arm's reach of Commissioner Valentino. Captain Vargas, seeing the commissioner—fumbling for his pistol, too sweaty to take hold of his bullets, and seemingly unsure of which way he was supposed to be charging through the fray—cut Paolo down with a bullet to his hip just before he could pierce the Commissioner's heart.

A comrade pulled Paolo aside as several more of La Boca's men fell to the ground. Two columns of the military police, finding their footing behind the experienced Captain Vargas, frantically organized, making an effort to follow in his command. In turns, they reloaded and released volleys of lead into the crowd. The men carrying Paolo atop their shoulders took rounds to their necks. Scores more men and women took the police's bullets to their bodies, collapsing into the street, their life drained into the dirt. Pressing back their line, with the handles of their pistols, the federal police bludgeoned wives and daughters across their faces, breaking their jaws, splitting their skulls, and releasing their bullets into their husbands and fathers beside them. The riflemen of La Boca in their parapets, one after another, took the military police's bullets to their faces. They fell from their rooftops like cargo breaking free from a ship's high tackle. La Boca's line collapsed, their barricades rapidly overrun.

Boys continued to lob bottles, explosives, and rocks at the police, but as the soldiers marched forward behind Captain Vargas, the boys retreated. Some took new positions from behind the broken windows and jagged corners of their once-beautiful homes. In disarray, those still standing in the crowd dragged their loved ones out of the line of fire. Many were bleeding. More were dead. The police trained their rifles and pistols down every corner, firing at any man or woman who did not run fast enough in a different direction.

Captain Vargas, with rage in his heart, had released all six shots of his revolver into the stratified crowd. With shaking hands, he paused to reload his cylinder. He cocked his hammer, and with his finger resting snugly on his trigger, raised his gun.

Just as he rounded a corner, he saw a young woman lying in the street, her floral print dress stained in blood, unable to walk, with a bullet in her calf. With tears on her face, she pleaded to Captain Vargas for her life. Her husband lay dead on the street beside her. She raised her arms, asking a human to spare her in her suffering. But after a lifetime of cold cruelty towards the most destitute of his fellow porteños in Barracas, Vargas could see nothing but another criminal, justly cut down from their lawlessness.

As he raised his gun to her, the woman's son, possibly just out of diapers, ran from his open door to her. The woman shook her head at him, desperately trying to compel him to return inside. Captain Vargas commanded him to return inside as well, but too inconsolable to understand, the boy clutched onto Vargas' leg.

"Fine, stay there!" Vargas said. He fixed the young woman between his iron sights, still calling for mercy, and shot her dead. Adding to the indelible colors of death painting Suarez street, the woman's blood-spattered the front door of the child's multicolored home.

As the thunderous clap of the shot faded away, captain Vargas vacantly looked around him, gazed at the corpse of the mother, and saw the crying child, still clutching his leg. For the first time in his life, he felt a dark, harrowing terror rushing deep into his soul. The end result of his remorseless and prideful life lay before him, the anguished image of an orphan, crying on his leg besides the corpses of his parents. He understood the magnitude of what he had done.

God, seeing the tragedy that had come to pass, could no longer restrain His tears. The ocean breeze carried one lone cloud from the Rio De la Plata, veiled the neighborhood of La Boca, and released a soft, mournful drizzle over the soldiers, the wounded, and the dead.

The police marched past Captain Vargas, still staring vacantly at the street. As if mocking God in his sorrow, they continued leveling the barrels of their guns on whoever was within striking distance. God saw this. His sadness burned into rage. A great, heavenly gust flew west across the Rio de la Plata. Docked ships blew their foghorns and rang their bells. The strands of their mooring lines popped and parted in the wind. Vessels nearing the port furled their sails, dropped their anchors, and reversed their engines, their captains aware of a great tide drawing them inexorably towards the land.

DIASPORA

Within a moment, the river effortlessly breached the dock's pilings and pier. The port of La Boca sank beneath a frothy, wild sea. Grain pallets, oil barrels, and train cars heavily laden with cargo rolled and overturned. Horrible flashes of lightning cracked over the sky.

The police turned around, seeing the wall of chest-high water carving its way towards Suarez street, chasing them with supernatural intention. Most of the residents of La Boca had already taken shelter in whatever homes they stood near. The police, profoundly unwelcome where they stood, recognized God's frightful anger being levied upon them.

Commissioner Valentino, still of no use to anyone and at the very back of his men, was the first to run. Even Captain Vargas, snapping out of his delirious blur, followed suit. The rest of the conscripts ran as one. God, having no desire to see another person die in La Boca that day, reigned in the flood's speed just enough for the cold water to ride on the heels of the slowest conscripts trailing in the back. Chasing them out of Suarez street, the water rose as high as their necks. Though the flooding stopped at the edge of the port, none had dared to look back until far from the neighborhood, across the puente Balcarce.

Those of La Boca still alive, for hours more, sat on their beds and tables. Rain and sea water battered the corrugated panels of their homes. Though sea water soaked through the creases under their doors, God made sure that not one house's thin steel walls fell under the weight of the chest-high flood.

Meanwhile, Paolo, in the care of his neighbor Maria, lay on his back, breathing slowly, listening to the melodic thumping of the wind and rain against her roof. At times, he felt his bed rising and falling, as if riding atop an Atlantic swell. He smelled the salty sea foam bubbling through her door. Maria worked to stop his bleeding, adding rag after rag from her endless pile. His blood continued to drip to the ground like a foundered tanker, steadily leaking an endless stream of oil into the sea.

He tried to hear what she was saying to him, now and then reassuring him, calling his name, and insistently tapping on his bearded face. But his ears began to ring, his vision faded, and returning home from a voyage, he found himself lying in the grass on his mother's seaside, Portofino estate. He felt the sun's luxurious warmth on his skin. God did not permit him to die. However, He allowed Paolo to wander the rest of the night within his comforting dream.

At long last, the wind settled down over La Boca, the rain abated, and the Earth soaked the flood waters away.

With the day over, God relaxed, breathing a sigh of relief. A calm wind flowed through the neighborhood, once more permitted to rest in silence. But late into the night, word of the massacre began to filter through the streets of Buenos Aires. Priests, medics, and nurses, clutching their crosses in horror, poured into La Boca from their clergy houses, hospitals, and clinics.

The church, defying the orders of the police, commissioned horses and carts as ambulances. As medics tended to the wounded, the priests administered last rites to the dying and final absolutions for the dead. However, they arrived at La Boca unprepared to help the survivors in the ways they needed the most. Seeing the people freezing in their wet clothes, and having never imagined they should have prepared dry blankets, shirts, and beds, the priests and nurses looked at one another with stupefied glances. The evidence of water damage was clear, but none could honestly believe the story as the survivors counted it. It was only then that the people of La Boca discovered the astounding truth; despite the biblical flooding they had just seen at their doorsteps, the rest of Buenos Aires had not so much as a drop of rain all day.

***

Just a few days following the raid, when a convalescent Colonel Longano and still frazzled Commissioner Valentino presented their report to the mayor, they spoke of nothing but their "success." In truth, no raid in the past had ever been less of a "success." Above all, fifty-five of the neighborhood's leaders and troublemakers had been "arrested," and despite several "injuries" to their own, all were "recovering well." When the mayor asked where those fifty-five "arrested" were being held, they assured him they were in the competent custody of the military police. But as far as Colonel Longano's own military commanders claimed, those men were being held by the federal police in Buenos Aires.

For many police who were killed that day, medals and promotions were formally logged into their records. Eight months later, the Commissioner and the Colonel finally reported that those men had died from unrelated, sudden outbreaks of typhoid fever. Their medals were presented to their loved ones, in polished wooden cases, with sincere condolences that their bodies could not be preserved for their funerals.

Captain Vargas, never reconciling with what he had done, filed his retirement from the federal police. He, and many others, publicly scoffed at the idea that the raid had been "a complete success." The mayor eventually agreed, inspecting La Boca for himself. If any squatters had been arrested or dispersed from that parcel of industrial land, twice as many came to rebuild and replace them.

The borders of La Boca never fell, even three decades later, when Paolo and his wife, Maria, would welcome the young Meir into their home for a night. The children of the families that had risen their corrugated steel houses from that abandoned patch of dirt still called it home. Yes, the neighborhood's claim to that ground, undeniably, stood just as firmly as it did the night before the raid. But in the truest sense, the outcome of the raid was not so far from what the mayor, and the industry leaders from across the tracks of La Boca supporting him, had actually hoped for.

Was it better, they asked themselves, to grant hundreds of squatters the dirt plot of an abandoned steel mill next to the port, or have them resort to city corners, tram stops, and park benches the next day? Most of them worked at the port, too, and having to pay no utilities or rent, they appeared to tolerate their starvation wages better than any others could. All the city truly wanted, and had set out to do, was to instill fear; to remind them that their lives were tolerated, that their continued existence was a privilege—not a right. In exchange for granting them their right to exist, the city made clear they would receive no support, protection, or official municipal services of any kind. While their lives endured in La Boca, they would always be as fragile as the thin, steel walls of their homes.

The message was understood well. Every man's head hung just a little lower; every child quieter in the streets, where they used to organize boisterous games of soccer in the nights. Just two days after the massacre, those with jobs in the port returned to work. The few scores of men who had been killed had their positions filled without delay. Their names were memorialized only as scrawls on one concrete wall on the port.

With the spirit of the neighborhood sufficiently broken, one matter still remained to be settled; what would happen to the markets of food, art, and music that had attracted so much attention and prosperity to the neighborhood? Though the people never held another market day again, the answer to this question came from the owners of the river-facing warehouses. Despite all that happened, they came around to the idea of a colorful La Boca. They happily painted their own facades, licensed stands for food vendors, and employed musicians from all around the city to entertain the visitors who had become accustomed to patronizing La Boca's weekend markets.

DIASPORA

The plan worked without a single hitch. To the west of the tracks, the neighborhood of La Boca steadily fell into disrepair, eventually losing nearly every flake of paint the sailors and warehouse workers once adorned their homes with. To the east of the tracks, through an industrial thoroughfare soon renamed "Caminito street," a *new* colorful market for food, art, and music, sanctioned by both the city and the business owners of the port, thrived.

As decades passed, the children of the survivors of the battle doubted their parents' fantastical story. As less and less people remained who had seen it in person, what had once been fact steadily devolved into a myth. Nonetheless, to the elderly survivors of that night—and the retired Colonel Longano, Commissioner Valentino, Captain Vargas, and their aging conscripts—the memory of God's flood would endure, carved as deeply in their minds as the rust on the hulls of the merchant ships at port.

4

Judío

DIASPORA

Lying awake on a humid, summer night, a gray, heavy-set Paolo quietly left his bed. Maria soundly slept. Ever since he was a teenager, when he first worked the night watch on a steam tugboat in Portofino, his sleeping habits had been truncated into sporadic late morning and early afternoon naps. But now an old man, he hardly slept at all. He crawled under his blankets beside his wife only for her to feel his steady heart long enough to fall asleep on his chest. His heart beat like the rhythmic pulse of an idling tugboat engine, and since the day of the flood, thirty five years ago, it had not once deviated from its gentle cadence.

He opened his door, lit a cigarette, and while looking up at the full moon, exhaled its smoke into the wind. Smoldering away quickly, he might have gone back inside without seeing Meir. But in his troubled sleep, Meir mumbled a few incoherent words, alerting Paolo to the small teenage boy curled up against his wall. He noticed the tattered canvas sea bag under his head.

He gently kicked Meir awake. A scent of salt in his hair, with the wild eye of a man who did not trust the solid ground he stood on, Paolo quickly recognized a boy arriving on land from sea. He had seen cases not too dissimilar before, where either from drunkenness or wages gambled away, a sailor had failed to secure dockside lodging the same evening he left his ship's berth. But the case of Meir was peculiar. Paolo, guiding the boy inside, quickly learned the boy lacked documents. Though they scarcely could communicate, Paolo surmised that the boy did not even know where he was. The words Argentina and Buenos Aires elicited not one spark of recognition in his eyes.

Meir, in contrast to his taciturn countenance aboard the SS La Pampa, had no strength left to hold anything in. The moment Paolo laid out a pallet for him to sleep, all of Meir's love, so wrenchingly sequestered in his heart, flowed out from his chest. What swirled in his mind would have been ineffable even if he had a shared language to speak it; but with his words meaningless, his home inconceivably distant, and the grace he had just been shown utterly beyond his belief, Meir could do nothing but fall on the warm, steady old man's shoulder. He allowed his tears to freely soak into his sleeve.

When Maria woke early in the morning and found Paolo was not by her side, she accepted without almost any surprise the sight of her husband at their kitchen table, sitting beside an unfamiliar teenage boy. Meir slowly sipped from her husband's maté cup. A small pallet was already set up by their door as a makeshift bed, cushioned with rags and Paolo's own winter jacket. Clearly, much had happened while she slept.

Maria sat down beside her husband and the boy. Meir grasped for any way to communicate, if only to offer his name. With Paolo clearly having judged him trustworthy, Maria embraced him with no reservation; she placed her head on his hair, thick and clean, and in doing so, felt his tremendous warmth radiating into her skin. To Maria, there seemed to be a hidden power in him—an energy greater than what God allotted to every man. But having never had children, she had not felt too different towards every boy and girl.

Maria set out to warm for them a serving of arroz con pollo for lunch. Paolo sat in thought beside Meir. There was no question that the boy could keep his pallet on the indoor side of his steel walls, but this solved only the most basic of his problems. He was not a dog; he had to be able to talk. But despite trying several times to sound out the most basic of Spanish words, Meir just shook his head, staring at him as if they were babbling in tongues. Paolo searched his memory, through all of the distant countries he had sailed to and bizarre people he had met throughout his life. The language that Meir spoke was vaguely familiar, but the name of it eluded him. Perhaps, he considered, someone would have the answer at the University of Palermo. However, if the security at the door so much as asked for his identification, Meir would invariably end up detained. He could safely bring him to the church in La Boca, but if he could not recall this language, what were the odds the priest could translate it? If nothing else, he could try and ask his neighbors, but would parading a likely stowaway from house to house—at the *port*, of all places—be a good idea?

Paolo sighed.

Meir, too, searched for a way to communicate with Paolo. With so much on his mind to say, he would have struggled to begin even if Paolo spoke perfect Yiddish, let alone the bizarre language of ports, ships, and friendly cooks. He decided, as he had no fear of the kind old man and his wife, he would pray. At last, putting on the yarmulka he had kept hidden in his pocket, he closed his eyes. He briefly, humbly asked for God's guidance in the matter.

As Paolo and Maria watched him, they noticed his strange head covering. A spark of recognition flashed into Paolo's eyes. He stood up, raising his hands in gratitude, and nearly knocked over the bowl of arroz con pollo Maria had just set before him.

"Of course! *Un Judío!* Maria, the boy is a Jew!"

Before Meir could open his eyes, Paolo put on his hat, grabbed him by the arm, and rushed out the door with Meir. The Zinkov Synagogue, completed only a few years prior, was just a ten minute walk west of La Boca. Hardly releasing his grip until just footsteps from the tall shrubs bordering the door, he looked anxiously at Meir, gestured into the air at the building, and raised his eyebrows as if to ask, "I was right, no?"

Meir gasped at the sight. Countless countries and seas away from Tolevoste, in a world he did not know existed a month before, a blue, finely painted Magen David proudly crowned the two great, hardwood doors of that tall, granite-walled shul. Though that single-story building on Rocha street was nothing more than the most economically viable property the congregation could afford, Meir looked up at its doors as if he stood before the Second Temple.

An early Wednesday morning, the shul seemed quiet from the outside. Paolo could not have been sure it was open and had never been inside, but Meir did not hesitate to enter. He pushed its heavy door open; a scent of oak, old books, and Turkish coffee filled Paolo's nose. The blue stained glass windows, with depictions of Mount Sinai, the Ten Commandments, and strange golden candleholders, cast iridescent bands of light across the empty pews. If that house had been built in honor of the same God as his, Paolo reflected, they had his respect.

The *shacharit*—the morning prayer—had already been recited. The pews sat empty, but a few men lingered by the bimah in quiet, serious discussion. Though Paolo hung back as Meir approached them, he felt from the tone of their voices their worry. The young rabbi, looking down and scratching his short beard, was the first to see Meir approaching.

With sunken faces, the three men at the bimah looked at the overly excited young man, with an oily shirt and a crumpled yarmulke.

"Stare at me any longer, child," the rabbi jested in Yiddish, "and I'll have to tell my wife. Out with it, boy."

"Baruch Hashem!" Meir said, rushing to embrace the rabbi around his waist. "Rabbi, listen to me. I'm from a small shtetl in Poland, by the border of Slovakia, called Tolevoste..."

Though the order of events did not flow linearly from his mind, Meir elaborated on everything that had happened to him, to the best of his ability—from his stolen motorcycle, to hiding in a barrel of molasses at a Polish port. Their three jaws dropped to the floor.

While he had recounted seeing the planes, the bombs, and the bullets fly with his own eyes, Meir had never connected that singular event with the great tear in the fabric of the world that followed. Listening to him speak, the men glanced at one another incredulously. Could a teenager who had traveled halfway around the globe have no idea the world had erupted in war?

Perhaps Meir had chosen not to see it, and perhaps he truly did not—and could not—have known. After all, his village had withstood the Great War. Despite what may have been happening above its skies or abreast its fields, Meir rightfully figured Tolevoste had nothing to do with the world's problems. He had fled out of fear. He had been swept across the sea by a series of implausible mistakes—but now, he explained to them, he had to get back home to his family at once.

As the two men behind him covered their mouths in shock, the Rabbi, imperceptibly abating his tears, stepped within inches of Meir's face. He placed his right hand on Meir's shoulder.

"Sweet child," the rabbi said in a severe yet loving tone. "If there's one thing which I can say for certain, it's that there is no Tolevoste for you to go back to."

Within a moment, the rabbi ensured Meir had no misunderstanding about what he had seen unfolding near his village. Meir's heart beat fast. His breathing escaped him. Dark vignettes of his worst nightmares, for weeks past accosting him, erupted before his eyes. Meir fainted to the ground.

The two other men beside the rabbi, watching carefully, rushed to lift him. Paolo came forward as well. As the rabbi gently tapped his face, trying to wake him, Paolo frantically asked the men in Spanish what they had just told the boy.
While the rabbi instructed the men to get help, he calmly explained to Paolo a story that he, and every Jew, knew so well. There once was a family that had lived and died, for a thousand

years, on a small, cold parcel of farmland in Poland. Now, in the year 1939, this one boy had the privilege to learn of the *Churban* of his family—the annihilation of his village, everyone he had ever loved, and everything he had ever known.

DIASPORA

5

Churban

At the moment Meir learned of the fate of Tolevoste and his family, a part of him died as well. In its stead, a walking shadow of a man carried on his life. Obligated by the Talmud, he married a Jewish girl, Yael, fathering his only son, Uri, after the war. Within three years of his marriage, Paolo's niece, Rocío, gave birth to his second. She remained a mystery to Yael until just after the birth of Martína. Though each woman knew bitterly of the other, Rocío died in a drunken car crash, ending their feud, distraught over her lover's unwillingness to love her back. With a deep discontent which only time would allay, Yael agreed to raise her husband's illegitimate, *non-Jewish* daughter—renamed Delilah from Martína—beside her own. They decided to withhold this secret from their children. However, questions over Delilah's identity would rise again in her life.

Though the spirit of Meir had died, the shadow behind his eyes endured long enough to see a new world unfold. The state of Israel was founded in 1948; at that time, a patriotic identity rose within many Jewish people from the ashes of their lives. However, the morning Yael came to him the news, excitedly showing him the headline in La Nacíon, he barely glanced her way.

"Aren't you happy, love?" she asked, letting the paper fall to her side. Drinking his coffee, he paid her no mind.

He could not have responded, even if he wanted to. A dark cloud had perennially settled over his mind. He felt an everlasting ghost swirling in his belly—not bad, not good, not threatening, nor comforting—just a ghost, which seemed to quietly fill the void of a guardian angel. On sleepless nights, he found this ghost rose from inside him and floated before his face, staring at him with cold, white, vacant eyes.

DIASPORA

At the beginning of the *Guerra Sucia* in 1974, drinking his Maté at his dinner table one evening, Meir found Uri and Delilah came home from public school crying, with bruises to their faces and mud smeared on their shirts. Their teachers had watched, they said between their tears, as the other kids stole their backpacks and forced their faces into the soccer field's dirt. Even Uri's best friend, Santiago, kept his back turned, kicking his ball with the other kids across the field.

That very same week, Meir came home one late night to find Yael crying at their kitchen table, their shattered window broken by a brick, the words *Judíos Bolches* painted on in white. Pale, with his children cloistered in their room, he walked through the halls of his *conventillo*. Hearing the sound of crying, he learned his neighbor, a professor at the University of Palermo, had his door broken down by a death squad just hours before; the man's college-aged children had been "disappeared" while he slept soundly in his bed.

At that moment, Meir realized he had not finished running. The next morning, in the height of Operation Condor, as Videla's troops marched down his street, he left his sorry Buenos Aires apartment for the last time. Through streets of broken glass, with his family's two meager suitcases in his hands —passed crying mothers in frantic search for their missing children—Meir led his family to the Israeli embassy of Buenos Aires. Beside them, he boarded a plane for the first and last time in his life. In Jerusalem, he tried to let his shadow rest in the holy city of a sacred land, though still just as lost, as if never having left the SS La Pampa, still plowing through stormy seas.

Years passed. On those clear, dark nights, as Yael and their teenage children slept soundly in their beds, rest eluded Meir. He gazed down from his porch across the hills of Jerusalem, seeing the glass windows of the sandy, stone buildings, shining like lanterns on ancient cavern walls. When Meir *did* sleep, in his dreams, recurring images of that young girl he had scorned and forgotten the name of—mixed with the faces of his mother, his father, his sister, an old Huarpe cook, a kind Argentinian man, and countless more—flowed into a dark, red river, swirling around his head, drowning him in waves of unending guilt. He would wake up more tired than when he closed his eyes; no, he preferred not to sleep at all. But though his mind could not rest while asleep, he could find no peace while awake.

He understood why. Ever since he first stepped foot off that Boeing jet, the ghost in his belly had darted side to side like a young fish in a glass bowl. This lost ghost had followed him to La Boca, and with seemingly nowhere else to turn, clung to the warmth and comfort it found inside its host. But in Jerusalem, as Meir looked over those lantern-lit hills, this ghost rose up inside him, saying, "Meir, I am dying in here. You know you cannot be the only one from Tolevoste who survived."

What this implied terrified him. If he met someone from Tolevoste, he would have to face all the horror that passed him by the day he boarded the SS La Pampa, and feel the unbearable shame and guilt of leaving his family behind to suffer and die alone.

In those panicked moments, in defiance of his ghost, he rushed back inside to wallow in the dark—as if by depriving the ghost of the sights which had stirred it, it could be pacified. But his ghost refused to let him be; the more Meir cloistered it inside the darkness of his home, the more angrily it twisted and gnawed at his insides. He would shut his curtains, close his eyes, hold in his tears, and try to play the grade-school violin he had bought for twenty shekels at the shul. But despite drawing his bow across his strings, his violin would not sing the faintest tone.

Meir could not deny the untenable truth: He could not continue on with a ghost from Tolevoste within him—nor could he bear to let it out.

DIASPORA

PART 4

DIASPORA

1

Uri

Four years having passed since emigrating from Argentina as a teenager, Uri—Meir's son—leaned back in his small, wooden chair. With his feet on his desk, he tried to overlook his discomfort long enough to finish a chapter in his book. He shifted his weight to different parts of his back, crossed his legs one way and then the other, and flexed the muscles in his feet. Despite his effort, he had to accept that if one part of his body were to be comfortable, another part would have to strain.

He knocked his knee against his desk, his paperwork fell to the floor, and his flickering lamp went out. He jiggled the wire in just the right way to get it to work again. This happened all the time. He had a spare bulb, but like he tried to tell his commander, the lamp itself was the problem. No one listened to him ever—least of all his commanding officer. That lamp—his one precarious source of light on those cold Be'er Sheva nights —would never get fixed.

A *refusenik* since basic training, his army record had not earned him any favors. Having gone to jail just after high school for ignoring his orders to report for entrance processing, and again in basic training for refusing to fire his gun, Uri had earned credibility among his pacifist and dissident friends—but none whatsoever with anyone who had control over his life.

To his great fortune, after being driven from one position to another, he had finally landed the most perfect station in, perhaps, all of the army—the guard shack at the end of his base. Sitting alone, listening to his radio, and reading whatever book he had asked his parents to send him that month, Uri cherished his guard shack. He made a modest effort to perform his job well. But even in his private box—in the still hours of the night, with a fifty meter view of anyone approaching in all directions—

he still could not avoid getting himself into trouble. Having been caught twice sleeping at his desk that week, drooling over a copy of Jorge Luis Borges' collected works, Uri landed himself on thin ice. His sergeant, one year younger and generally affable, warned him that he would be forced to send him back to jail if he caught him sleeping at his desk again.

Regarding his radio, Uri had specially requested it, insisting that it would help him stay awake. Satisfied enough if Uri remained where he was placed for one complete watch, his sergeant acquiesced. But listening to his radio singing, Uri's mind always drifted away. Closing his eyes, tapping his foot, letting the songs swirl in his head, he saw himself driving his father's convertible Citroen. Tracing the high hills of Jerusalem, he rode along the ridges of Ramat Rachel, his car swaying in Jerusalem's gentle breeze. He saw the sun reflecting against the burning hills, spun in circles with the sweet melodies flowing from Arik Einstein's guitar, felt the warm glow of his lamp behind his eyelids, and drifted into sleep.

Will you hear my voice, my distant one…
Will you hear my voice, wherever you are…
Hatishma koli… rechoki sheli…

A car horn blipped twice. Uri sat bolt upright. His book jumped from his lap. He quickly shut off his radio, got his lamp working again, and an officer rolled down the window of his car to show him his ID.

Just as he drove away and Uri bent down to collect his papers off the floor, his Sergeant surprised him from behind. The door to the guard shack swung open.

"Ah, Vostęvskie, awake I see!"

Uri jumped up in fright.

"At ease! This is good—I was sent to check up on you. I heard you got leave for your birthday tomorrow? Good for you," his sergeant said.

Uri responded with polite formality, thanked him, and sighed in relief as he walked away.

Watching his sergeant rounding the far corner of the barracks, he relaxed, confident he would not be bothered again for the night. He put his feet back up, turned his radio on low, and tried to pick up where he left off in his book. However, a few thoughts floated through his mind; his sergeant remembered his birthday, surprisingly. In truth, Uri would have been happy to forget it. Unlike most other men soon to turn twenty one, Uri did not like getting older. He believed he saw life for what it was—rare, irreplaceable—and watched the passing of it in the minutes counting down on his guard-shack clock. But to actually use his gun—or just as awfully, have a gun used against him—would have been the greatest possible poison to his ephemeral soul. His job could have been worse. Death was not worth a blue star or stripe.

This is not to say he felt no patriotic inclinations. After all, if it were not for leaving high school in Argentina when he did, he could have been dead. He would have publicly spoken out against the military dictatorship, and likely would have received an answer back. Seeing the Israeli flag on the base's main field, eternally lit and gently fluttering, filled him with a degree of pride. A *degree*, to be sure, for in that flag, he saw that some part of himself—perhaps his best part—was not there.

But how could he say such a thing to his comrades? How could he express to them that the Hebrew language—the unifying glue of a young nation and an ancient people—felt like a foreign language on his tongue? His language instructors, three years ago when his family had made *Aliyah*, assured him he would know Hebrew had become his own when he would dream in it. But though he learned it fast, saw beauty in its sounds, and enjoyed having an entire new language to read in, he never dreamt in any language but Castellano.

Nevertheless, Uri thought the sandy hills and green valleys of Israel were gorgeous; he looked forward to completing his compulsory conscription if for no other reason than to finally have the chance to explore them. Having been issued his identity documents just months after his seventeenth birthday, he had hardly spent a year in Israel in civilian clothes. His upcoming leave would allow him much needed room to breathe. He hoped that his father and mother had taken time off from work like they said they would. They promised to pull his sister out of school so they all could drive together to the Dead Sea.

At the thought of seeing his mother and father in the early afternoon the next day—the two of them waiting for him in his father's car, with his favorite sufganiyot in a cardboard box —Uri felt content. He turned up his radio, put his book down, closed his eyes, and swung his foot to the rhythm of Arik Einstein once again. He painted memories in his mind of places he had not yet been, and times he hoped would come to pass. Once more, Uri fell asleep.

Rounding the corner of the barracks again, Uri's sergeant, with his commanding officer beside him, carried a small piece of chocolate cake on a paper plate. In honor of Uri's birthday, and in mostly humorous recognition of his staying awake for three watches in a row, the two felt in high enough spirits to share a gesture of good will with their "favorite" private.

When they opened the door to the guard shack, the sergeant dropped his cake; the commanding officer shouted so loud that the coyotes in the Negev ran the other way; and Uri, with his head tilted back in his chair, snoring louder than his radio, jumped up so fast he nearly kicked his desk in two. His commander grabbed his arm, dragged him halfway across the base, and threw him into a holding cell. His radio still softly played back in his guard shack.

Following a very brief hearing in the military court, it was ruled that a fourteen-day sentence was appropriate. Uri's watch relief had the privilege of welcoming Uri's parents the very next morning. They wished Uri a happy birthday from behind a panel of glass, leaving his donuts in the hands of the holding cell guards.

Uri spent four days without saying a word to any of his cell mates. He ate a few bites of eggs at breakfast, drank a few spoonfuls of soup at dinner, and sat in his cell. In some moments, a hairline fracture seemed to form in his soul; he felt his spirit beginning to crack. But just as fast as tears came to his eyes, he wiped them away. He had been behind bars twice before and had learned a lesson that only experience could teach: *This too shall pass.* He laid down with his hands behind his head, looked up at the ceiling, and envisioned visiting the Dead Sea with his family, whenever he might get the chance.

One night, echoing within the small, group cell, Uri heard two of his fellow inmates whispering in the corner. He saw them cross legged, unusually awake at a late hour. Something in their tone of voice had a different weight to it; Uri could tell they were not talking about the guards, cigarettes, or the falafel the cook had burnt for lunch. Listening carefully, to his great surprise, he heard them talking about *Yitzhak Leibush Peretz.* Peretz, the prized writer!

Uri listened closely, raising his head to hear. He was able to ascertain one of them asking the other if he understood a specific quote which Uri knew well. Could that imply they had a book of his in their hands? A spark alighted in Uri. Having loved Peretz since he was a teenager, he quietly lifted his blankets, rose from his cot, and approached the two young men in the corner. They quickly glanced up at him, tucking their contraband book in one of their pillowcases.

DIASPORA

"It's a fantastic thought, you know?" Uri whispered, crouching down on the floor as if they were old friends. "I love *Yitzhak Leibush Peretz*."

Without hesitation, Uri repeated himself, explaining the context of his thinking. Casually, he reached out his hand and gestured for them to give it to him—their book—so he could explain further.

Glancing left and right, the young soldier pulled his book back out and handed it to Uri.

"Be careful with it," the soldier said.

With familiarity, Uri flipped to the right page showing them the idea in one section which related to their question in another. In soft whispers, as others slept on, he soliloquized not only about Peretz, but Borges, Buber, and Frankl, referencing lines from each by memory. The boys smiled. They found a new friend.

As the days went by, other boys overheard the bizarre discussions happening in the far corner. By day eleven, a modest group of seven sat around Uri, discussing philosophy and poetry through the night. They rotated through different subjects, debating with one another about what they gathered from the writings, looking to Uri for confirmation that their interpretations were correct. If his time in his jail cell was not in addition to his total compulsory conscription, Uri mused, jail may have been his ideal station. *Holding cell discussion detail*—yes, Uri liked the sound of that.

On the twelfth night, after many of his group had already been released, and others had gone to sleep, Uri stared up at the ceiling. Half lit by a street lamp through a small window in the concrete wall, Uri reflected on novel thoughts. The wisdom of Peretz hit him with a gravity beyond what he felt before. He fell into peaceful sleep, philosophy and poetry floating in his mind. Just as he began to dream, he saw blue and yellow butterflies circling La Boca stadium, back in his childhood home of Barracas.

Early in the morning, while the dark sky blanketed the desert and the rest of the base peacefully slept, Uri's commanding officer arrived at his cell. Waking him up himself, Uri was almost concerned he was being let out early. The commanding officer put a hand on Uri's shoulder.

"Uri, I'm sorry to tell you. Your father has died," his commanding officer told him. "There's a car waiting for you. You're released."

Uri stared straight through him as if he were no more solid than the air. A deep, horrible pain struck his heart.

"How," he asked with a short breath.

"*Sorry, chaver*—I don't know."

DIASPORA

2

Delilah

That same day, finishing up her classes, Uri's sister, Delilah, collected her results from her proctor—a perfect score. She concealed her smile from her classmates behind her, aware that the majority of them had a hard enough time passing the standardized exams, let alone excelling at them.

She walked down the hill from her high school, stopping to mail letters for her mother, buy malawach and tomatoes for breakfast, and feed the cats that waited for her in the park across the street. Nearing the end of spring, the days were long; she knew she would be done with her homework in an hour. She thought about how else she would fill her day.

She already could run in the top percentile of her grade, had credit for volunteering three days per week, and had aced each of her practice tests for admittance into the Mossad; all she had left to do was bide her time until the end of the school year.

In Argentina, Delilah lived her life in much the same way. With her head to her books, she impressed her parents and teachers with her devotion to her studies and her community. She ate well, did not smoke, avoided the boys, and never drank alcohol, except for the sip of wine her parents gave her at the Sabbath meal. She seemed to live for something greater than herself—though exactly what, few could say. As a young girl, she extracted meaning from the rabbi's teachings at the shul, staying after the *derasha* to study Hebrew with him. On the weekends, she shopped with her mother at the kosher grocer while her father and brother ate choripán from the street vendors. Other children from the *Chabad* befriended her, keeping her company on the evenings her family spent at La Boca Stadium. While her father made a modicum of an effort to keep the Sabbath, and her mother, for a short while, sent her and her brother to Hebrew school, she had found the Jewish spirit deep within herself. She sought to understand it and fulfill it wherever and whenever she could. During the Yom Kippur War, just two years before her family made Aliyah, the mythology of the unconquerable state of Israel crystallized in her mind.

Three years having passed since the day of her Aliyah, she had only a half year of school left before she would receive her *Tzav Rishon,* the first step of her drafting into the IDF. Countless practice tests over the preceding years had assured her she would not only qualify for service in the Mossad, but would likely be specially selected for it. Every time she saw the Israeli flag flying over Jerusalem's Central Command, riding in the back of her father's Citroen on their way to the hot springs on the weekends, she felt her own spirit fluttering in the wind.

At that time of day when she came home from school, her father was normally out working. He sold t-shirts and socks produced in a factory in Ramallah below the hills of Jerusalem, and was often out of the house in his Citroen until sunset. Her mother, meanwhile, worked in a typewriter supply store in the mornings. She could have easily been back home by the time school was over. But between the store and her house there were no less than three liquor stores, a billiards hall, and an open air hookah lounge. On most nights, Yael came home just soon enough to warm some couscous before Meir stepped inside, the scent of tobacco and wine still on her breath. Meir would kiss her forehead and sit down beside her. Listening to their radio softly sing, the two would spend the rest of the evening looking at one another, sometimes in each other's arms. On some days, a smile could break through Meir's lips. On others, a few sweet tears could leak from Yael's eyes.

Her parents were not old—each was over ten years away from retirement—but Delilah noticed a marked difference in their strength. Yes, they could no longer carry her—she was, in fact, taller than both and just as tall as her brother—but it seemed that daily tasks tired them. She had the subtle intuition that her mother brought less and less home from the grocery store for no other reason than the bags tired her thin arms. She saw her father come home later and later, but with the same income, gathering that he slowed down his drive on the fast, busy roads below the city.

She loved both her parents immensely, but perhaps not directly. She held an all-encompassing love for everything in her life; her parents, her brother, her teachers, her city, her country, her flag—all pieces forming a private universe of which no one could understand the beauty but herself. In truth, if one stepped back from this picture, one could see the cracks, stains, and peeling glue. Her parents loved her, truly, but Yael always looked at Delilah with a sadness that Delilah could not account for. Her teachers, her country, and even her flag, all shining and fluttering for their pupil, hid pockets of discord from her eyes. No one had ever taken Delilah to the West Bank, where the Israeli flag and all its people were held in contempt. Whispers of war amounted to abstract ideas to Delilah, as if the *Israeli State* would execute and finish it. To her, the people *of* the state, only fifty kilometers from hostile borders in every direction, would somehow not be a part. But no secret could have ripped apart Delilah's worldview and identity more than the most fundamental secret, painstakingly withheld from her, for her entire life.

Delilah unlocked her door, finished her homework, sat alone at the dinner table, and sighed. The nights only grew quieter as the months passed by. Usually, she could settle her mind by exercising her own will, breathing deeply, closing her eyes, and fixating on the sounds of the chirping cicadas and the steady drone of the freeway far down the hill. But despite her efforts, something disturbed her peace. She stepped out to their porch, scented in herbs and covered in vines, and saw how the sun had rapidly descended since she came home. Although the season was changing, it seemed to her that the night had come too fast. She looked up at the sky. Bands of woody, orange light shot through the stratified clouds, as if a barrage of artillery lit the sky in smokey, red fire. The gentle breeze picked up; it must have been the first chill of Fall. Her skin shivered; her nose itched; and something in the air drew tears from her eyes. A sudden awareness of her own impermanence tugged at her soul.

A sad, eternal ghost lost its host. It wandered on. With cold, white eyes, it saw Delilah from atop the hill, permeated into her belly, filled her lungs, and stared deeply, inquiringly, into her unfamiliar mind.

Staring back, Delilah sat on her porch the rest of the evening, ruminating over dark thoughts that had not once troubled her before. She heard her front door open. Her mother, with dried tears on her face, walked onto the porch.

"Your father was in a crash..." she whispered, her lips quivering.

"What do you mean?" Delilah asked.

The green vines and herbs behind her dried and withered away. The stars in the night sky dimmed, turned red, and fell to Earth like droplets of blood. Her mother wept, drew her daughter close, and cried, burying her face into Delilah's shoulder. The hills of Jerusalem shattered into billions of cold shards of glass; their small apartment's walls crumbled to dust; and the solid ground beneath their feet melted into a cold, dark, fathomless sea. Without another word, Delilah understood her father was dead.

3

War

DIASPORA

Uri and Delilah searched for their father anywhere they could find him. Wherever they looked, Nothing stood in his place. Nothing sat at their breakfast table; Nothing wore his suede jacket and corduroy pants; Nothing behind searching eyes, on a taciturn face, in small, sepia photographs, on their shelf. When they looked into their photos, Nothing stared back.

As most do, Uri and Delilah averted their gaze. Like a soldier staring at the passing road behind them, their truck and their comrades driving towards the front, so too did they fixate on the road already flown by beneath their feet. They gazed at days long gone, when they were small enough to sit on their father's shoulders or rest in their mother's arms. They saw a bright, wintery night in Buenos Aires, when their father came home from hawking socks after dark, with a tired smile, his jacket smelling of cold leather and sweat. They saw a man glowing like an angel, with endless warmth, endless love, and endless sadness emanating from his dark, glassy eyes.

On random days, at different times, Uri would think to ask his father a question or share an idea. A second later, he would remember he could not. In his barracks, at the mess hall, or at his station, Uri would silently cry.

What could Yael do? If she knew of a comfort, she would have given it to them. But she had suffered long ago in the same vein, continued suffering up to the day her husband died, and would never cease suffering until the day she died. She had no answer, and was too tired to tell any more lies.

When Delilah returned to school after sitting for her father's *Shiva*, the color in her face, red and tanned, had taken on a sallow hue. The fire behind her eyes had dimmed. She gazed upward and out the window, her glassy eyes fixating on wispy clouds. For three months, Delilah did not say a word to anyone, as if by keeping her mouth shut, she could restrain her tears from flowing.

A boy, in time, found his way through the cracks that Meir's death had left in Delilah's life. He sat behind her in math class with a soft, narrow face; thin arms, delicately hanging by his side; dark, wavy hair, brushed behind his ears; and deep-set, searching eyes. Living just a few blocks past her with his father, he frequently saw Delilah just one block ahead of him on his way home from school, striding with a long, deliberate gait. Her long hair bounced behind her with her every step. He had watched her from the back of their classes, never with longing, but with curiosity. The few times she spoke to answer the teacher's questions, he felt captivated by her raspy, Spanish-inflected Hebrew. She possessed something different in her; something new.

He watched how she changed over the past few months. He wondered if he had anything he could say. On one windy, Friday evening, just one month before the last day of school, he watched her from afar as she walked home. Ariel took a deep breath and caught up to her side. She turned to see him, and though locking eyes, her mind remained elsewhere. He saw how distantly she stared through him; the way her eyes seemed to sparkle beneath her tense, dark eyebrows; he liked the smart, subtle scowl on the corner of her lip; and he felt his heart melt like warm honey.

He said something to her that she would recall, later on, had made her blush—and for the first time in months, smile. He could never remember what it was, and when she asked him again months later, he could only recall that smile. In that moment, Delilah would say she had fallen in love, though she would always deny that the young man stood in the likeness of her late father.

DIASPORA

He thought about her all the next day at school, studying her from the back of the classroom, feeling his heart skip a beat when she answered the teacher's questions. Seeing an opportunity to connect with her, he anxiously thought over things he could say in response. Rushing to catch up to Delilah after school, he gathered the perfect points on his tongue. She stood just outside the doors of the school, her books in her hands, scanning pensively around her.

"*Is she waiting for me?*" Ariel wondered. He walked right up to her, seeing the diamond like glint of her gray eyes soften upon seeing him. For her part, she had hoped all day that he would find her after school again. Seeing him standing in front of her, she gained the confidence to believe that the gorgeous boy who had made her smile the day before was not a figment of her imagination. Ariel forgot everything he planned to say. On their way home, they slowed to a crawl as they neared her apartment. Talking about nothing important, they danced and circled around ideas each could not be sure the other wanted to hear.

For the rest of the week, every day after school, Delilah waited by the door, her books in her hands. Ariel would rush out of class to find her, nervous as to whether or not she had waited; the two would feel their cheeks flush, their hearts beating loudly, and as each was in no rush to get home, meander through the streets of Delilah's neighborhood. On Friday, gathering her own courage, Delilah decided they were acting silly. She invited Ariel inside. They did homework, played chess, drank lemonade, picked herbs, and anything else Delilah normally occupied herself with on those warm, bright evenings.

Having had such a beautiful, brilliant girl invite him into her home, sharing with him her inner thoughts, her private space —not to mention *alone*, while her mother was out—filled Ariel with waves of excitement. Nonetheless, he desired nothing from her, enjoying every second of her hidden life that she shared. He watched, mesmerized, as Delilah—that striking, distant girl from class—glided from one corner of her apartment to the other in her socks and pajamas, To Ariel's joy, he found that she loved to shout, gasp, and laugh over board games until she turned red in the face, covered her mouth, and stared at him with her sharp, smiling eyes.

She would grab his arm and pull him one way or another when she wanted him here or there. She showed him her stuffed animals, drawings, favorite clothes, and the pictures of her family on the walls. In one photo from a few years passed, her whole family stood around Meir as a birthday cake lit his kind face. The dark, red walls of his favorite Puerto Madero parrilla blended into shadows around his birthday candles' glow. Laughing, she recalled how Uri, smoking and drinking past his limit, fumbled onto the table, knocked over a glass, and sang one of Mercedes Sosa's most popular songs for the whole restaurant to hear. His mother, horrified, shouted at Meir, arguing he should not have let him drink at all. Meir answered only by firmly placing one hand on Uri's shoulder, pulling out his cigarette with the other.

While she showed those rare few photos, a single, sweet tear fell down her cheek. Ariel's eyes darted across her face, her eyes, and her quivering lips, but he collected himself before she looked up. A pattern like this continued. Delilah would lean within an inch of him on her bedside, showing him something dear to her; Ariel would feel the heat of her skin, her shoulders, and her arms; and before she could notice his wandering glances, he would bring himself back to the present.

She saw his eyes, heard his breath, and felt her own heat. Her eyes lingered on him as well. She had rarely gotten so physically close to a boy before. Ariel's scent arrested her breath; an inexplicable urge to lean towards his neck almost overcame her many times. But in what way did she want to touch him? Could she tuck her head under a boy's chin, put her hand against his chest, press her nose against his neck, and stay there to feel nothing but his warmth?

Delilah could not help herself for long. While doing homework together after school one evening, the two of them enjoying the easy silence between them, she let her head fall on his shoulder. Ariel, feeling the blood rush to his face, slowly inched his hand behind her head. Delilah pressed her ear against his neck, closed her eyes, and listened to his heartbeat.

From then on, they could scarcely wait to be alone after school—whether with Delilah head in Ariel's lap, him playing with her hair; with their legs crossed on their couch; or, as it happened one time, when the two feigned needing a nap, and Delilah curled up onto his chest. But despite their affection, neither felt sure enough to make the intractable next move—going in for a kiss.

As a matter of habit, Delilah did not want Yael to know about Ariel; she had never spoken to her about boys before. In some irrational way, she feared disappointing her. For weeks, she made sure that Ariel left before Yael would come home, or if they went over to his father's small apartment, to leave after a short while. But one night, laying in bed, waiting until the next day when she would see Ariel again, she had a realization—what did she have to fear? She was seventeen, after all; she had the right to have a friend over at her house—even if he was a boy. And if she *liked* him—well, then she liked him!

She decided to settle it the next day. Sitting on their couch, when five o'clock came, and Ariel knew he should pick up his things to go, Delilah stopped him.

"Stay for a little while longer, won't you? We could watch a movie," she said, tracing her finger up his arm.

They shut off their lights, put their feet up on the ottoman, and curled up together on her living room couch. Her VHS tape of *Dizengoff 99,* almost two hours long, would surely keep Ariel there long enough for her mother to come home.

Fifteen minutes before the movie ended, Yael proved Delilah right. She came through their front door with two bags of groceries, smelling of cigarettes, and still in her heels from her morning job. Delilah knew that her mother, veiled in the dark, could see them, lit by their small, gray television set. Delilah did not look at her when the door opened. But with her heart beating, she waited to see what her mother would say.

To her surprise, and somewhat disappointment, she said nothing. After audibly arresting her movements for a moment, Yael shrugged off her own surprise, put the groceries away, dropped her heels by the door, and went straight to her room.

"Hola, *linda*," she said in passing.

"Hi, mom," Delilah replied, astonished.

Ariel thought nothing of it, but Delilah's heart was beating out of her chest. Her mother saw her with a boy! Her confidence shot through the roof. Seemingly out of nowhere, she gave Ariel a huge hug. Finishing the rest of the movie with him, she played with the curls of his hair.

By the time the movie ended, Ariel had to go. He knew his father expected him earlier. While he stood at the door, Delilah squeezed his hand.

"So, I'll see you tomorrow?" she asked.

"Of course, *linda*," Ariel said, teasing her, but only to see the beautiful color of her flushed cheeks. "See you tomorrow."

Her mother, lying in her bed, exhausted, got up when she heard the boy had left. Delilah started a pot of boiling water for pasta. At dinner, as they ate silently, Yael spoke first.

"So, that was a nice boy," Yael said, lifting her eyes. "Why didn't he stay for dinner?"

Delilah immediately felt her heart pound, but without looking up, still casually twirling her pasta in her fork, shrugged.

"Well, I'll ask him to come over tomorrow," she said, unable to hide the color of her face, red like her pasta sauce. She quickly collected herself, rubbed her face, looked away, and finished her dinner.

Delilah had accomplished something she had never done before; she brought a boy home to her mother. But thus far, while at school, Delilah still waited until after classes to see Ariel. During lunch the next day, the tall, dark, gray-eyed Delilah walked straight up to Ariel's locker. His friends stood around. He turned around, met her eyes, and saw Delilah standing strikingly, awkwardly close. Feeling the heat of her skin, her face burned like a havdalah candle.

"He—hey, do you have any plans later?" she said, brushing her hair behind her ear, trying and failing to seem calm. "I'm asking because my mother—and *I*—want you over for dinner." Ariel's friends looked at one another in amazement.

"No—I mean, yes—I... I'd love to have dinner. And I don't have plans later!" Ariel said, flushed. Delilah exhaled, smiled, and concealing her excitement from the boys, turned away.

After school, Ariel sprinted to his house. Meanwhile, on her walk home from school, Delilah was unsure if the warmth she felt came from the sun or the heat in her own chest.

Delilah's mind swirled with questions she had never asked and feelings she had never had. A knot formed in her stomach. Fear gripped her; she was terrified of what could happen, what she should say, and what she would do at dinner. Secretly, she hoped that Ariel would get there before her mother. She needed, even for a moment, to be alone with him.

To Delilah's surprise, the moment she opened her door, she saw her mother standing at their kitchen countertop chopping carrots, potatoes, celery, and fresh herbs. A wave of disappointment hit her. She realized, as her palms sweated and her heart beat in her ears, that she enjoyed the feeling that had been building in her body. She wanted to let it flow.

"So, now she comes home early," Delilah said to herself.

She gathered her mother had come straight from work to cook for Ariel; something clearly had been stirring inside her since last night, as well. She had not chopped fresh vegetables in months, after all; her hands held the knife apprehensively. Delilah was thrilled that the thought of him coming over enlivened something in her mother—but how she wanted to skip dinner, and just hold Ariel in her arms already!

Waiting for him to arrive, she felt the heat in her face. Only thirty minutes later, Ariel knocked on the door. She scanned with approval his ironed slacks, buttoned shirt, and gelled hair, seemingly all borrowed from his father.

"Mom! *Ariel* is here," she said, presenting the charming young man to Yael.

Dinner came and went. Ariel survived all of Yael's prodding questions, speaking slowly and softly, aware that Hebrew was not either of their first languages. Delilah constantly blushed, smiled, and turned her head away in embarrassment. In a few instances, she scolded her mother for prying—*mama callate, no le molestas!*—but Ariel never needed her help. He had a simplicity and ruggedness to his character and mannerisms. His wisdom and tact seemed to transcend his place and time. When Yael asked him about his parents, he said nothing of his father, but explained how he lost his mother to a bus bombing when he was seven. With perfect grace, he gave his heartfelt condolences for the loss of Meir. Yael softly gasped. Delilah's eyes swelled with love.

They spent hours at the dinner table. Both Yael and Delilah explored the mind of this boy. Ariel allowed his thoughts and feelings to flow. They only realized the time of the night when they noticed the room dimming from the setting sun.

Stretching her legs, Yael left to pull a package of rugelach from the refrigerator.

"This old woman is done being a pest," she said, winking to her daughter, handing her the dessert. "You children have fun."

Yael opened her porch door, gestured for them to go outside, and happily left to her dishes.

Delilah felt the ghost inside her come alive. After counting down the seconds for her mother to be far enough away, she reached for Ariel's hand. The two looked over the hill. The answers to questions they had both been afraid to ask sparkled in their eyes like the stars, the hills' glowing apartments, and the headlights of the highway's passing cars. The ghost in her belly felt a modicum of happiness.

Hours passed. The two never realized they had stopped talking. Their fingers played with one another's. They had nothing left they needed to say. Ariel pulled a packet of tobacco out of his pocket and rolled a cigarette. Delilah watched his peaceful face, his skilled fingers, and his tongue wetting the gum on the paper. She let her lips open. Ariel lit his cigarette with a match, exhaled its smoke into the air, and passed it to Delilah. Having never smoked before, she was not sure what to do. But when she put it to her lips, Ariel leaned towards her, lifted his hand, blocked the wind, and saw Delilah's smokey eyes glow like the moon. She dropped the cigarette from her mouth, raised her hand to grab his, and kissed him.

The last day of school came and went. Delilah passed her exams for the Mossad. Ariel would soon enlist in the infantry. With an entire world behind them, and many more in front, they saw the time ahead as mysterious and magical. Together, they had nothing left to do but pass their last few weeks as civilians. They decided to take Delilah's Citroen to Kiryat Shmona, near the Lebanese border, both to enjoy the trails of the city's quiet, sandy hills, and to visit Ariel's grandmother. Yael had no issue with the idea, and in a change of heart, felt she might enjoy her alone time.

Descending into the valley beneath Jerusalem, they rode north, passing a hundred kilometers of lush, green fields; passed chalky hills, sand swirling in their car's eddies; through modest, clean towns, blending into the color of the dirt beneath them; and eventually arrived to Kiryat Shmona. The sun was setting, rich like an egg yolk. The side of Ariel's grandmother's house shone with a bright, orange glow.

The small, dark, wrinkled woman took Delilah into her open arms. Warm shakshuka sat on the table, along with jars of schug, za'atar, tahini, and a pitcher of mint lemonade.

As with most people, Safta Altie nearly lost her breath at the sight of Delilah's bright, gray eyes, reflecting and refracting the low lamp light in her small house. Altie had already heard much about her—nearly every night, in fact, when Ariel would call home.

Born in Beirut to a Turkish mother and Iraqi father, Altie had made Aliyah shortly before the war of independence. Her husband left his well-paying job at the *Al-Alam al-Israeli* daily newspaper to volunteer for the newly formed IDF. Though it scandalized her parents, her siblings, and her cousins, she followed him in the defense of Israel, leaving her fourteen-year-old daughter in her parents' care. Yaakov Dori had personally awarded Altie the Hero of Israel medal for her service as a nurse throughout the war. Notably, on the 19th of June, 1948, Altie dragged a young radio operator through the dirt, bleeding to death, two thousand meters past combat lines in Galilee, back to a defensive position. Through an enemy barrage, with his instructions, Altie used the equipment to provide coordinates of enemy movements to a battered platoon of IDF Sherman tanks, anxiously waiting in silence one kilometer to the rear. Her other bloody hand stymied the man's hemorrhaging thigh. The Jerusalem Post partially attributed that day's victory, and four thousand men's successful advance the next day, to her bravery.

DIASPORA

One month later, a Syrian battery against Israeli positions in the Golan Heights killed her husband. But Altie worked on, ignorant of his death, for four months; she only suspected something had happened after all one hundred and twenty of her nightly letters went unanswered. No body was ever recovered.

Altie lost her husband in 1948 and her daughter, twelve years later, in just as violent a fashion. She recognized the same sadness in the creases framing Delilah's eyes. Delilah had suffered immensely. But how her eyes remained so bright with such horrible sadness weighing on them! Altie had to grab her own chest; she saw, in an instant, how Delilah had fettered her grandson's heart.

After they finished their meal, they spent the rest of the evening cleaning up Altie's modest kitchen. They set out their individual pallets, separated by a hair. Once his grandmother had gone to sleep, Ariel and Delilah quietly left through the rear sliding door, closed it gently behind them, and rolled two cigarettes. Sitting in her wild garden, lit by starlight, fireflies, and their smoldering tobacco, they listened to the cicadas, the light wind, and Ariel's radio playing melancholy melodies on its lowest setting. Delilah kissed Ariel on the cheek.

Ariel tilted his head back, staring at the constellations, and thought about how many other people, in that moment, gazed in the same direction.

Delilah asked him what he was thinking about. He told her nothing in particular. He grabbed her hand and kissed it; took one last draw on his cigarette, nearly smoldered to his fingertips; crushed it between his fingers; and threw it past his grandmother's brick wall.

Suddenly, as they sat quietly, they heard their radio shut off. Ariel picked it up, checked its batteries, and realizing nothing was wrong with it, shrugged it off. But following a brief moment of silence, Delilah and Ariel heard a mix of static and pops, as if radio frequencies were being manipulated.

The garbled voice of an old man came through. He calmly read from a list of numbers and words, seemingly nonsensical—*188th Lightning, Lamed Mem Lamed, First Golani 743-821*—before falling back into static.

Delilah felt a cold sweat break out from her neck. Ariel looked at her confused. Though she could not be sure, she had studied enough of the IDF military structure to understand one thing—those were division codes, commands, and likely locations, broadcast over public radio waves. She contemplated if it could have been a drill—but any drills or equipment tests should have been preceded with a warning. She leaned in closer to the radio, gripping Ariel's hand, aware that its silence had already lasted a moment too long.

"*Military operations are underway. All civilians remain indoors,*" the radio cut in. Delilah gasped. God, listening in, regretted that Arik Einstein's ethereal melodies had been silenced for the night.

Not a moment later—forty kilometers to the west, guided by radar, night vision optics, and the glittering stars—missile boats, naval cruisers, landing crafts, and paratroopers stormed Lebanon's misty, Mediterranean coast. Sixty kilometers northeast, Israeli AH-1 Cobra attack helicopters fanned across the outskirts of Lebanon's fertile Beqaa Valley. Like a drumbeat's crescendo, the crack of mortar fire echoed from just past the hills of Kiryat Shmona.

A flight of A4 Skyhawk attack aircraft broke the sound barrier above Kiryat Shmona's stratified clouds. Heavy artillery, camouflaged east and west of the city, shot ear-shattering volleys of hardened steel at Lebanese defensive positions. Infantry fighting vehicles, Sho't Meteor tanks, and M113 armored personnel carriers charged forward at high speed. Great plumes of dust rose across the horizon, lifted into the sky by the prevailing winds. Just beyond the hills that overlooked the Israeli State, the awakened residents of Kiryat Shmona, and one

DIASPORA

Delilah Vostęvskie, heard Yasser Arafat's enraged army levy their first sporadic shots of return fire.

Amidst the blasts, Ariel ran inside to check on his grandmother, shuffling around in the dark for her light switch, shouting for her grandson. Delilah, stupefied, looked up at the sky, seeing the aircraft's contrails dissipate into the wind. She listened to the rolling fire over the hills, like fire crackers on Independence Day, and felt her heart fill with dread. She would be joining the IDF in only four more weeks, and as far as she could tell, in the midst of war.

4

Hero

DIASPORA

Tens of thousands of soldiers flooded into Lebanon every day by land, air, and sea. Eighteen days after the initial invasion, as the PLO began to fall under the heel of the IDF, the Northern Command called for every division—from the *366th Amud HaEsh* camped in the south, to the *256th Sinai* guarding borders to the west—to help press forward the bombardment of Beirut. Sleeping in their cots, Uri's battalion, the *33rd Karakal*, woke to the shouts of their commanding officers. Within twenty minutes, under the moonlight, through the cold desert air, Uri and eight hundred more rode north to the front.

By the first light, his convoy had crossed the Lebanese border. Uri listened to the steady drone of his truck's diesel engine, its squeaking leaf springs, and the blood pumping in his ears. For one last, quiet moment, Uri closed his eyes, letting his body sway with the bumpy road.

Just across the IDF's thin pontoon bridge over the Litani River, an improvised mine—likely from a Lebanese militia—exploded under their wheels. The driver and two more died instantly. Heavy fire followed from a western tree line, perforating the thin walls of their truck. By the time Uri fumbled out the back, several more of his comrades had bled out into the dirt.

Crouching behind his truck's flat tire, Uri held his rifle to his chest. His mind raced with questions he had long sought answers for. He realized that he might not be the one to answer them. A heavy weight settled over his mind. His eyes welled up. He did not mourn for himself; rather, he saw the death of the universe within him, endlessly stretching as far, wide, and deep as any other under God's domain.

He switched off the safety of his gun, checked his magazine, and stood up. The world around him fell into silence. Uri trained his rifle towards the enemy, unloading his Galil's magazine into the woods.

Just after stepping out of the truck's cover, a young recruit, firing by his side, took a bullet to the stomach. Uri did not see him fall. A radio man, taking cover behind the flattened tire of their truck, shouted bombardment coordinates into his microphone, but Uri could not hear a word. Hellfire erupted in his eyes. Uri locked a new magazine into his receiver. He allowed his lead to fly.

He took his two grenades from his belt, pulled their pins with his teeth, lobbed them in the direction of the enemy fire, and fell down in the dirt; just as he lifted his head, he saw the tall, thick trees explode in volcanic flame. For a moment, it seemed as if his two grenades had lit the forest ablaze—but moments later, the crack of IDF attack aircraft ripped across the sky.

In a trance, he felt the fire's heat on his face. He smiled. Warmth pulsed through his veins. He rolled onto his back, letting out a deep sigh; put his hand on his head, feeling something tugging at his ear; and felt his blood dripping down his face, soaking his shirt, and soaking his sleeve. A bullet had torn his ear. He felt calm. He shut his eyes.

At that moment, God whispered something in his ear; Uri only heard ringing. He shouted like thunder into his face; Uri's eyebrow twitched. Not even God could rouse a man in such deep sleep. Uri stayed silent as ancient blood drained into the dirt, cleaving itself free from his body and his mind. Uri felt himself rising into the air, the hands of angels cradling his legs, his back, his arms, and his head.

Uri tumbled further into the deepest sleep a man can know. He fell into a thick, black sea, shining under celestial light. His boots, his bullets, and his gun weighed him down.

Through the water column, he tumbled in the wake of passing hadal creatures. He settled gently onto the dusty bottom.

He opened his eyes, looked around him, and screamed, but his voice made no noise. He thrashed left and right, choking for air, and woke up in his hospital bed, soaked deep in sweat.

Panting, he looked around. Three rows of twenty beds each filled the tent. Two dim lanterns cut the darkness. Most everyone lay asleep. He looked to the floor beside him and found a canteen. The water cooled his throat. He wiped the sweat from his forehead, took a deep breath, and touched his head—a large, damp bandage had been secured to his left ear.

For a moment, Uri's mind went blank; he gazed far into the distance in front of him. He did not feel any fear, nor did he feel relief. Like a record needle tracing the runout, spinning but making no noise, Uri's mind swirled in a static haze. With some clarity, he surmised he may have been under the influence of a drug. But another part of him suspected his brain was as sober as the day he was born.

He laid his head back down on his pillow, feeling—in some dark way, even enjoying—his mind swimming blankly from side to side. But a sense of dread suddenly overcame him. He felt his bed rocking, as if he were on a small boat at sea; noticed a sick feeling rising up from his stomach; quickly searched under the hospital tray table beside him; and found a plastic bag. He lost control of his stomach. A wave of relief hit him. The ceiling fan above him cooled the sweat off his forehead. He fell asleep once more the instant he closed his eyes, dreaming of little. Blue and yellow butterflies crossed his eyes, as if tumbling in a strong breeze.

The sun set.

Meanwhile, Yael, in her lonely apartment, sat in darkness. Much had happened in her own life while her son was at war.

The phone rang for the third time that evening as Uri's division attempted to reach his next of kin, but she would not answer it. Her head rested in her hands. Wave after wave of guilt, confusion and shame—all encompassing, uncompromising shame—inundated her, silencing the world around her, ensnaring her within her own shivering mind. All this, and she had not even yet heard her son had seen the precipice of death.

As the hours passed into the night, she tried to steady her breathing, much the same as when she was a kid and her parents would fight. But every time she thought she caught her breath, her lips would begin to quiver, she would cover her face from God, and she would resume crying quiet tears outside of His gaze. She asked Meir in her heart what he would do, but heard no answer. As she learned many times, she feared there was no answer. All she could do was look at her daughter's red, angry face, burning behind her closed eyes.

She ran through the day in her mind; was there anything she could have done differently? She wondered if she should have lied. But Delilah was too smart. Since she was a small child, she had been nearly immune to any deception; she knew if you were lying just from the flicker in your eye.

For many young women, that day would have been the greatest of their lives. At 9:30 a.m., Delilah and Ariel stood in line at the Jerusalem Magistrate Court, their identity documents and two hundred shekels in their hands, to apply for their marriage license.

Ariel's father and grandmother stood with Yael behind them, waiting to embrace the two of them. Yael subconsciously held her breath.

With war raging on the northern border, and conscription paperwork filed for both Ariel and Delilah, one may have thought the time inopportune to begin a marriage. In fact, if it were not for Delilah having already been accepted into the

Mossad, marriage would have been impossible, as women could not be ordinary soldiers and wives at the same time.

Delilah handed her identification card to the clerk. Their appointment that morning had been scheduled two weeks in advance, and all their necessary corroborating documents and forms had already been submitted. However, upon taking her ID, the clerk appeared to cross reference the name on the card with a note, scribbled on a page, on the corner of her desk. Something gave her pause. Delilah noticed this, leaning over the counter slightly to see.

The clerk made a quiet phone call. Within a minute, a young rabbi came from around the corner of the office, introduced himself to the families, and pulled the parents aside.

He smiled and put his hand on Ariel's father's shoulder. Before anyone else could speak, he assured them all that, *B'ezrat HaShem*, all would be well. A few clerical documents, he explained, were not in order. To no surprise of Yael, the rabbi made clear that Delilah's birth certificate appeared to have a discrepancy. Blood drained from Yael's face.

Clerical verification of documents, he continued, could be needed for any number of innocuous reasons, but whatever the reasons were, the court had ascertained that the signature of the doctor could not have matched with the date of birth as listed. Likely—without a doubt, in fact—the hospital had made a typographical error. But in matters as serious as a Jewish marriage before God, the rabbi had to be sure that both parties were, indeed, *Jewish*. It all would be fine, he explained; the hospital of Delilah's birth had a phone number listed in the international telephone directory in the courthouse. *Undoubtedly*, the hospital would be able to send them a corrected version of Delilah's birth certificate by fax. With his reassurance, he instructed the office secretary to make the necessary requests on their behalf, and to call him again when things were in order.

Yael froze, maintaining a strong front. But in her head, she rapidly considered all of her options. Everything lead to a dead end. She only wished she could disappear. As the rabbi walked away, Yael grabbed Delilah's hand, and nearing a complete panic, rushed her outside through the revolving door.

Ariel, his father, and his grandmother watched them in silence. They looked at one another with bewildered glances.

"What did he say to you, Safta?" Ariel asked.

Altie, reading further into the Rabbi's words, feared letting her grandson know what she surmised.

"I'm sure it's nothing," she said, pulling her grandson to her side.

Knowing the rabbi would discover the truth regarding her daughter's doctored birth certificate any moment, Yael allowed it to fumble out. In the span of seconds, Delilah learned Yael was not her biological mother; her true mother, Rocío, long deceased, was not Jewish; and by the rigors of halachic law, Delilah could not be considered Jewish either. At any moment, she warned her daughter that the rabbi would come out from his office and inform them all that she was not eligible to marry a Jewish boy.

Delilah said nothing. She anxiously laughed. But seeing her mother's shattered expression, her smile melted away. Tears quickly came to her eyes. For the second time in her life, the solid ground beneath her feet shattered into glass.

She wanted someone to hold her. She wanted to cry. She looked at her only parent. But like a figurine melting under the sun, the image of her mother glazed over in her eyes. She could not recognize the woman standing before her. Yael held back her own tears, waiting in pain for her daughter—yes, *her daughter*—to speak, but Delilah would not. She could not. Confusion stirred in Delilah's belly, blending with fear, hardening into anger, burning into rage. She caught her shallow breath. Yael stepped forward. Delilah took one step back.

"Don't—" Delilah said, her voice shaking.

"Bubbale, please—" Yael said, reaching her arm out towards her.

"*Mom*—I need you to leave me alone right now."

"If you would just—"

"Get away from me!"

People around began to look. Delilah backed away, turned, and ran to her car, parked just across the street. She frantically drove away. The mortar binding the pieces of her mind began to crumble. Her tears poured down her face like warm rain. Immediately entering her home, she packed her suitcase, left a short message on Ariel's answering machine, and just before she could step outside, met her mother at the front door, panting. Yael saw the suitcase in Delilah's hand.

"Get out of my way," Delilah said, but her mother would not move.

"Delilah, linda, *tiere kinderle,* Stop this now. I know you're in shock, but don't act like a fool. You're being crazy!"

"You can't tell me anything, *Yael*—I'm *not* your daughter. You're *not* my mother! You don't even know, you—you ruined my life!"

Delilah ripped the Mezuzah from the door frame and threw it at her mother's chest. As Yael gave out a cry of pain, Delilah slammed the door shut behind her. She walked to her car, opened the door, and felt a tap on her shoulder that she recognized was from God. For the briefest moment, Delilah paused. But even He could not reach her.

Now both of Delilah's parents were dead.

5

Undone

DIASPORA

In the following weeks, Delilah wrote a letter—one letter—to Uri during his convalescence. Regarding his injuries, she expressed her sadness, her prayers—and to some small degree, her surprise—upon hearing of his uncharacteristic actions in battle. With dry humor, and to Uri's amusement, she assumed that, hearing of her brother's heroism through her mother's messages on her answering machine, the army must have confused her brother with another Uri of the same rank and age. But she quickly turned to her own news, starting with the most astonishing; she had learned their mother was not her own.

Uri read this part of the letter several times over, as if unconvinced that the meaning he extracted from it matched the words written on the page. That night, after dinner, as the wounded and sick men around him fed themselves of the hospital's meal, he read it again. After the lights went out and he stared at the ceiling fan in troubled thought, he returned to his sister's letter with his flashlight one more time, ensuring he had not just had a delirious dream.

The story she recounted seemed too impossible to believe. But if he had any doubt of the content's veracity, he could not deny the metamorphosis his sister had undergone, evidenced by the page. Where she once spoke with a certain stilted, preoccupied anxiousness that often caused Uri to roll his eyes, her words read poetic, unfiltered, and electric. Bright, fanatic ideas seemed to be erupting in her mind, like a geyser steaming through a fracture in the earth's crust. Whether or not, in the cold light of day, she would stand by all she had confided in him and all she had planned, he would see. But in a certain dark, scandalous way, as she divulged her private thoughts and daring plans, he felt closer to his *half-sister* than ever before.

On the day Uri was discharged with a small box of painkillers, a red and purple ribbon pinned to his shirt, and a signed and stamped letter of honorable discharge, Uri met his mother outside the hospital. Waiting by the entrance in her idling car, she kissed his head.

"My darling child!" she said. "All is okay now!"

"Thank you, mom," Uri said coldly. He hugged her back, but gave her a vacant smile. They rode back home saying little.

Glancing to her side, she understood Uri's silence. Without a doubt, he had heard from Delilah already. Realizing Uri's opinion of her had likely never been lower, and hearing Delilah's hurtful words ringing through her head, a dim, cold, and indelibly lonely vignette of an aging widow played out in her heart. Yael felt a deep pit in her stomach. Yes, she had no more secrets to weigh on her. But if a person has outlived the love the world has for them, what is the purpose of their life? As her son sat distantly beside her, dark thoughts such as these pounded within her mind.

And yet, God's love, as Yael had been told as a small child, would outlast the water in the oceans and the stars in the sky. Through the faint, wispy wind, blowing in between the panel gaps and her window, God spoke to her:

> Yael, do not fret over your son's silence. You have done all right.

Knowing Yael well, God knew He had no more He needed to say. His words stirred in her soul. The turbulence and thrashing in her mind slowed into a gentle river. The faintest smile played on her lips.

Yael could admit she may not have loved her daughter as fully as she should have in the earliest days of her life. In fact, during the most difficult days of raising a young girl, in a dark recess of her mind, Yael could not decide if she had one child or two. But as years went by, her children rose off the ground, and Yael's roots took on their first silvery tones. She saw, in panoramic view, how she had steadily loved her daughter more and more with each passing day. On the front steps of the court house, as she tried and failed to give her daughter a worthy explanation, and Delilah stared at her in disbelief, she saw Delilah glow with the same unmistakable spirit she recognized only two times before; once, when she met Meir at shul as a teenage girl, and once more after Uri was born. She loved her fully.

Yes, her son did not seem to want to talk to her. But that was okay, she told herself. She would be there if he changed his mind.

As years would go by, in her dreams, she would still see Delilah the day she left her. However, God spared Yael from torment. In Yael's visions, there would be no scowl on her daughter's face. She he would see Delilah approaching her at her front door, saying that she loved her, taking her hands in hers, and kissing her on the cheek.

Delilah did, to Uri's surprise, follow through with the plan she laid out in her letter. On the day she had disowned her mother, Delilah spent the night at Ariel's house. The two sat awake in fanatic discussion, ostensibly to plan. However, seeing the state of his fiancé, Ariel had no choice but to agree to anything and everything that Delilah desired. Despite Ariel's initial call for temperance—he even insisted *he* did not care whether she was Jewish or not—Delilah resolutely declared she would be on the very next plane back to Buenos Aires that she could board. Interrupting Ariel's train of thought, she knew she had already been drafted to the Mossad—after all, the IDF did not care if she was Jewish or not *either*. But she would not serve the country of Israel anymore; she would get discharged one way or another.

This did not prove difficult. During her appointment with a military psychologist, she threatened to cut her own veins. Justifying her state of mind with the death of her father, the failure of her wedding, and the unfortunate way in which she learned she was not her mother's daughter, the IDF granted her dismissal without delay. On the day of her flight, as she hugged Ariel goodbye at the airport gate, Ariel promised her what he knew he had no choice but to say: in three years, after his military service, he would join her in Argentina. They would marry in Buenos Aires, he told her, where the magistrate courts —say what one will about them—would not be concerned with religious matters. She smiled and kissed him. But Ariel's voice hesitated.

After a thirteen hour flight, arriving in Buenos Aires after midnight, Delilah was delirious. Two hours and three buses later, she banged on the door to, what she was sure was, a distant cousin's apartment. In reality, this cousin had moved ten years prior. An old woman, yawning in her night shirt, cautiously opened her door. Extending her hand, Delilah briefly introduced herself as her Israeli cousin, picked up her bag, and walked right past her. For a moment, the shaking woman was not sure which one of them had lost their mind.

"*A cousin from... where? From what side?*" the woman asked herself.

Delilah laid out her belongings with a psychotic presupposition of familiarity. The woman made a few more meek entreaties. Delilah, ignoring them, kissed her on the cheek, laid her head down on the couch's pillow, and before the old woman's eyes could jump from her skull, fell asleep.

If the old woman's eyes did not deceive her, it appeared that, within the span of two minutes, a strange young lady had just taken lodging in her living room. After standing entranced for a moment, she scoffed, sighed, shook her head, and went to find a blanket. She laid her quilt on top of the strange girl, turned off her lights, clutched the cross on her neck, and said a prayer.

"I suppose I'll sort this out in the morning," she said, shuffling away to her room. But satisfied enough in her knowledge that every man and woman was a brother and sister in God's eyes—or a cousin, perhaps—she fell soundly asleep.

Delilah slept long, deeply, and quietly. She breathed low, melodic, meditative breaths. But tossing within her, a ghost, quietly resting for some time, stirred with uneasy dreams. It opened its vacant eyes, looked around, and could not understand. It tried to wake her, but Delilah would not move. It made a quiet, pitiful call, but she could not hear it. And for the days that would follow, the ghost would not abate its cries. Delilah could not—or perhaps pretended not to—hear them.

Delilah began her life again with her same vivacity. She profusely apologized to her magnanimous host, found work teaching kindergarten, looked for her own apartment, and took classes at the University of Palermo on the weekends. She smiled during the day. She may have seemed to thrive. But the ghost within her, or just the sharpness of her mind, made it clear to her that *a place* could not right what troubled her. Only during quiet and lonely nights, when her belly would endlessly tumble and stir, and she searched her cabinets for the medicines her doctor had given her, was she forced to accept a fearful thought —her soul ached in a way no medicine could cure.

She and Ariel maintained contact through letters. With no subtlety, Delilah allowed him and only him to know the quiet unhappiness she had found herself in; she looked forward to nothing except the day he would come to be with her. But after just one year had passed, Ariel's patience grew thin. He waited in vain for her to accept that her desperation was by her own design.

The once passionate letters that flew between Delilah and Ariel became fewer, shorter, and bare of their warmth. When a month elapsed from Ariel's last response, Delilah made a long-distance phone call to both his father's house and his grandmother's. Her messages on their answering machines never received a reply. Only by chance, when Uri made one of his occasional long-distance phone calls to his sister, did they each surprise the other; for Delilah, it was the news of Ariel's engagement with another girl, and for Uri, the discovery that she had not already known. Delilah hung up the phone. She sat on her bed, held her legs to her chest, and realized fully the darkness surrounding her. The last remnants of her former world had collapsed. She barely had family, she had walked away from her dream of serving in the Mossad, and her fiancé had walked away from her. But rather than allowing herself to cry, she thoroughly hardened her heart. She had one more name, she told herself, which she would never utter again during her life.

From that night on, Delilah allowed her years to fly under her feet. She married a laborer; had three children of her own, each with Christian names; in due time, saw each one leave her in succession; and in her later years, realized she had never loved, or even known, the man she had spent her life with. God had watched it all, but there was little He could do; shortly after Delilah lost the ability to speak Hebrew, she had altogether lost any interest in prayer.

On one of her quiet, dark nights—with her children long gone, her husband distant, and decades having passed since she had even seen her brother Uri, his wife Donna, or her three estranged nephews—Delilah stared deeply into her mirror. She noticed her gray hair, gray eyes, and gray, dusty skin. For the first time, she cried out for the ghost, still twirling in her belly. With one brush, it floated out from her; stared at her with cold, white eyes; and accosted her with merciless, angry, and blinding clarity. From there, it flew from her body, never to turn back to Delilah again.

DIASPORA

She finally accepted that, the day she scorned her mother and abandoned her, her brother, her fiancé, and God, she had made every possible mistake.

PART 5

DIASPORA

1

The Lamp, or The Allegory

In the town of Scarsdale, New York, a small park—with three benches, two paved walkways, and one old, tarnished, Victorian lamp—filled the empty space between a gas station to the east and the Metro north railroad to the west. Uri's third child Yuval passed by that park every weekday afternoon, laying on his back in the backseat of his mother's car. His mother, noticing the beauty of its lush grass, its wooden benches, and its old, quaint lamp, looked in her rearview mirror. She noticed Yuval's eyes, glazed over, staring into the black headliner of their Subaru.

"Honey, Yuvi—why don't you ever look outside? It's a beautiful day."

Yuval shrugged.

Later that night, when Uri came home from work, Donna accosted him at the door.

"I'm worried about Yuval!" she said to Uri, dragging him into their living room to take a look at their son. Yuval sat motionless by their TV, not noticing—or caring—that his parents were standing over him.

"We didn't move to Scarsdale for Yuval to be a shut-in," she protested, as Uri shuffled away to brew his espresso, passively avoiding eye contact. She noticed he stared at his wilting Magnolia tree through his breakfast nook windows.

"See? It's so beautiful outside!" She added. "Judith and Yonatan never spent this much time in the house at his age."

Uri nodded in assent.

In the four years since they had moved to Scarsdale from their Bronx apartment, Donna had never noticed that everything that catalyzed her train of thought that evening—the park by the tracks, its wooden benches, that quaint Victorian lamp—were phantoms. But the young Yuval, on their first night in town, after having moved house for the entire day, noticed immediately. Driving home from dinner at a Chinese restaurant their first night, their kitchen still packed away in cardboard boxes, he saw that supposed "lamp" dark and cold under the snow. The park's only light came from the moon and the gas station's fluorescent glow.

At some point in the past, that lamp may have emitted light. But without it, the park was no worse for wear; why light a bench, Yuval reasoned with himself, that has never been sat on? Why illuminate a pathway that has never been of any use? Yuval understood why the lamp was never lit. What Yuval could not understand, however, was the purpose of the old, bronze lamp in the first place.

At the start of his first winter break, he decided to investigate the issue. Having never seen a single person step foot within the borders of its grass, he chanced to be the first. He cut through the soft layer of fresh snow, avoiding the shoveled pathway that crossed it perpendicularly, and put his hand on one of the benches—plastic, formed in the shape of wood. He squinted his eyes in thought. What was the purpose of designing a wooden bench to look like wood, but not be wood? Perplexed, he walked on.

In the center of the park, he came up to the lamp, took his gloves off, ran his fingers along its fluted post, and noticed something similarly peculiar. In his fingertips, he felt that what he saw was not as it seemed.

He gave the base of the lamp a hearty kick. To his shock, he kicked a hole straight through it. He hastily looked around, noticed there was no one nearby, and bent down to investigate it further. To his amazement, the entire form of the lamp's base was built from molded plastic, painted in the *likeness* of tarnished bronze. The entire design, from the base to the lantern's cap, rang with the hollow sound of a plastic toy, no different from the Halloween decorations he often saw for sale at the CVS.

His eyes lit up. He knew it! All this time, his mother had been badgering him to enjoy the outside—and all this time, he felt that *there was no outside to enjoy.* Now, he had proof! The lamp, the benches, and the park, in his mind, were all as hollow as the entire suburban town built around them.

The next day at school, he told all of his classmates about his discovery. He found evidence for a point he understood well but had found too difficult to articulate up until then. He told them *exactly* what had happened—the lamp broke under a soft kick! But to his utter shock, and in one of his earliest moments of great disappointment, they unanimously berated him.

"So, you broke the lamp in the park and you're proud of yourself?" one sneered.

"My lunchbox is plastic. You gonna kick that too?" another teased.

Yuval looked around, his mouth hanging wide, and responded indignantly. "Don't you understand? It's—it's not real!" he said, red in the face. "None of it is!"

"Your mom's not real!" a little girl said, as everyone erupted in laughter.

Bewildered, Yuval stood frozen. He nearly cried—had he said anything wrong? What had caused their vitriol? He spent the rest of the school day with a pit in his throat. He said nothing on his ride home from school once more. He stayed in his room with his door closed, his curtains down. His spirit hardened. He had said *nothing* wrong. Those kids were too stupid to see and understand, he told himself. He would just have to keep his distance—from that park, from his mother's questions, and above all, from those awful, dumb kids his mother wished he would befriend.

***

DIASPORA

Yuval, as a young man, still would hold this chip on his shoulder. In his most solitary, anxious moments, he would run up the water bill in his shower, arguing with this memory, practicing responses to his soap bottles aloud.

"How could you not care about this? This is our home! Don't you care about its quality? Don't you care about what's inside? Say you were to go on a long voyage at sea—you scale the gangway, step foot on deck, see its deck plates bonded with strong welds or thick rivets, and feel safe. But what if you knew that the welds were glue, the rivets plastic caps, and the deck itself no thicker than foil? Would you be happy knowing a child's kick could pierce its hull? You wouldn't cross the sea in a vessel of no quality or strength—why would you pass your ephemeral life in a world of no greater substance?

You may not see it now, but you will one day. On a dark, cold night, when you're days out to sea, you'll feel your ship's deck start to buckle; the heat from her engines will melt her thin deck plates, soften your boots, and burn your feet. That's when you'll list your home for sale. A young couple will walk up your driveway, looking at one another with a smile.

You'll see that blinking, white signal of a lifeboat approaching your sinking ship.

But as they get closer, you'll see them pause. Looking through your window, one of them will scowl, pull the other to the side, and gesture for them to turn around.

The ray of her searchlight, though scanning the horizon for a ship, will pass through you like the wind.

'Lost beneath the sea!' the coxswain shouts to his lifeboatman, holding his cap to his chest, letting the cold rain drip down his watch cap, his stoic face, and his hard weather gear.

'I'm not sure if this is the place for us, honey,' the wife says.

You'll see her swinging her running lights around, and you'll panic. As invisible as the wind? You'll need a sign of life —and fast!—but you'll be at a loss for anything to show. The bulbs in your mast light have all burnt out, the wires to your radios frayed, and the reflectors on your life rings worn by the bright sky. Digging through your chests, stores, and drawers, you'll lament that you have maintained *nothing* of serviceable value.

But then, and *only* then, will you remember you have something to show them. You have the park! And remembering that it had never been used—that it was still as *pristine* as the day you moved in—you'll rush out your door, give the buyers a wide smile, and offer to take them for lunch. They'll stop, glance at one another, and smile once more.

The coxswain sees the flicker of your light! He turns his vessel back around!

You'll take the buyers out for lunch, and during the drive, point out of your window at parks with lush, mowed grass; winding, quaint walkways; and old, charming lamps.

Like chasing an anglerfish's lure, the coxswain will follow your bright, flashing light. His crew will throw their lines to your cleats, climb your Jacob's Ladder, and fan through your decks.

As the coxswain's back is turned, after the last of his crew has climbed aboard, you'll jump into his lifeboat, cut the lines, and start their motor. Pulling away, you'll never look back. You may, however, wonder how long it'll take before he realizes, stranded behind, that your ship is empty, as hollow as the wind."

With thoughts like these, he would pace back and forth in his single bedroom apartment, day by day, late into the night, extracting novel responses from wisdom, experience, and bitterness.

DIASPORA

After hours would go by, Yuval would sigh, look at his watch, and see how long his ruminations had dragged into the night. In a vain attempt to get some rest, he would lay his head on his thin pillow.

2

משנה שם משנה מזל

DIASPORA

Meshane makom meshane mazal—change your place, change your fortune.

And when that does not work, *meshane shem meshane mazal*—change your name.

Uri and his wife Donna met under no remarkable circumstances. Sitting with a few friends on the small stone quadrangle of the Martin Buber School at the Hebrew University in Jerusalem, days after Uri had begun his fourth year studying philosophy, and weeks after Donna began her year abroad studying Sociology for Yeshiva University in New York, Uri noticed a pretty, quiet girl. Even without her Nikon Rangefinder hanging from her neck, Uri recognized that, from her pale skin and yellow gypsy skirt, she was not from Israel. He walked up to her, she smiled, he liked her accent, and she liked his scruffy beard. They started to date.

Uri had been with a few different girls through his first three years of college, and in this time, resulting from his varied experiences, had come to a realization: if he were to settle down with a girl, he'd prefer she not be an Israeli. If she must be, under no circumstances would they stay in Israel. When he told his mother of his vague intentions to move abroad, just months after beginning his studies, Yael listened, nodded, and said nothing. With her husband dead, her daughter estranged, and her son preparing to leave her as well, what more could she do? For the remainder of his college years, she would cook him breakfast and dinner, hug him every chance she got, and hope, if God and Uri pitied her, he would visit enough for her to not be alone on every holiday.

Nonetheless, she would have been surprised if he stayed. Uri came to feel that the discourse—of his classes, of the school parties, of the political parties, of the news, and of the State of Israel as a whole—followed a predictable, hopeless, and degenerating formula. His father had once told him, when Uri would vent about the military on his leave from the base, that he would meet like-minded people when he went to university. But by that point, having completed three years of studies, he had come to find his classmates far more insufferable than his comrades were from the barracks. When the boys answered their teachers' questions, their pretension and arrogance grated on him; when the girls cleared their throats, preparing to deliver their opinions in their articulate and affected manners, he could predict exactly what each one would say.

Uri asked himself, if every one of his classmates could confidently answer great questions of society—those of governance, justice, human rights—why did society remain in such disarray? The most educated students and professors around him spent their lives constructing algorithms, hypotheses, and well researched theses—and yet, when Uri looked outside, he saw nothing but escalating wars, dysfunctional social systems, economic instability, and polarized masses. He was confident that the problems Israel faced could not be solved by students in a classroom. When his professors asked him to speak, he said little. He had opinions. But to Uri, whoever shared them had already arrived—or would at some point arrive—at them by themselves.

Regarding social and political positions, any that a person could have, Uri maintained, if not stemming from ignorance, were clever pretexts to justify people's fears and selfish desires. Therefore, the more a person talked about politics, the more disinclined Uri was to trust them.

Donna, unlike the other girls in his classes, hardly ever said a word. Donna listened to every side of her classmates' debates with a smart and neutral expression. From there, Uri projected his own mental processes onto her like a canvas. Uri did not know that, though he and Donna shared a similar inclination for silence, their reasons were totally different. But at that time, Donna appeared, by all standards, to be quite the perfect girl for him; reserved, elegant, and—miracle of miracles—from the United States.

By the day of Donna's graduation, one semester after Uri's, they had been dating for ten months. Uri's impatience to leave coincided with the conclusion of Donna's program. They traveled to the US, got engaged, and with no great passion or dispassion, were married at a Brooklyn court house within three months of Uri's first visit to New York.

They hosted a small reception in the startlingly well furnished, two-bedroom apartment that Donna's father had given her. They invited Donna's parents, two sisters, and some of her University friends. To Uri's general ambivalence, Yael flew in to join them. After a brief introduction to Donna's father and mother, Yael spent most of her time alone, standing beside the breakfast table with the poundcake and Manischewitz.

They made many plans—and several would even come to fruition—regarding their continued education, housing, and employment. But before anything else, Uri made a point to start the process of naturalization with the US immigration office. He made an appointment for a green card on the same day of his marriage. After a three-week wait, at the Federal Plaza Immigration Court, Uri began filling out his thick packet of residency forms. Donna sat by his side, anxiously pressing her knees against his.

Page after page, the paperwork was tedious—the majority of the effort lay in preventing a cramp in his hand. Section thirty-four, *Application for Name Change,* gave him pause. An idea flashed through his mind. His pen momentarily hovering over the paper, he put it down to scribble his name—Vostęvksie.

"*Vost-ęv-skie...*" Uri sounded out in his mind. "*People could smell a Pole from a mile away with that name... Vost_____.*"

"Hey dear, what was the name of that—of the Batman actor? The funny one?" Uri suddenly asked in Hebrew.

"Hm? Adam—Adam West?"

"Yes, that's it!" Uri said, returning to the page with his pen.

"What's *it*?" Donna asked. Uri answered by handing her his paper. She noticed the name "West" on the name change line.

"...West?" Donna asked. "Are you—are you really that big of a Batman fan? I mean, I kind of preferred Robert Lowery's—"

"—No, Donna," he said, with a nervous laugh. "It's the name—like my name... but *American*."

"Oh! *West*! Of course! Well, if that's what you want, then I support it! We'll be the Wests," she said, and laughing, kissed him on the cheek.

"Are you sure?" he said, surprised at her nonchalance.

"Of course! It's whatever you want. I mean, it's just a name—It doesn't matter," she said, putting her hand on his back.

Uri was not sure if she understood what changing his name meant to him. But that was okay. He touched her other hand, resting on his thigh; put his head to hers, so their temples touched; looked at his new surname once more; and flipped to the next page in his application, satisfied with his decision.

The two of them smiled. But unbeknownst to him, the ghost still inside of him, seeing and listening through it all, was highly dissatisfied. Having heard Donna's words, and seeing what was about to come, it could no longer restrain itself. It ignited with rage.

A sharp feeling clutched Uri's belly. The ghost within him, having reserved indignity for the greatest of offenses, erupted in fury through Uri's mouth and eyes.

"What do you mean it doesn't matter? Of course it matters!" he snapped in a deep, rueful voice, foreign to both Donna and himself. Donna shuddered in surprise.

"Honey, I didn't mean anything—"

"My name! My identity! Does my past matter nothing to you?"

"But—but you're the one who wants to change it!" Donna answered, searching for the right words with her open palms. "I mean, you are *you,* and I love you. I'm just saying your *name* isn't important to me. But I can see that it's important to you."

The ghost inside of him came to its senses, saw what it had just done, and fearfully withdrew. Uri's own mind came back into focus. He rubbed his eyes, coughed, looked around him, and came to an awful realization; had he just yelled at his wife? His eyes glistened with shame.

"I'm sorry!" Uri said. "I don't know where that came from."

Donna stared at him, more concerned for him than for herself. She justified his outburst as being the product of neglected trauma from his time in the war. But she would have found a way to justify it even if there was none. She loved him so deeply and secretly; seeing the pain in his eyes constituted more of an apology than she wanted, and more than she could bear.

"It's okay!" she said, holding onto his hand. "I'm sorry. Don't be upset with me, please."

Uri knew she had said nothing wrong. But he also recognized that, something about what she said ignited a deep, perplexing, and dissociated agitation within him. Trying to explain to her what had caused it would accomplish nothing. Anything else she might say about it, no matter her good intentions, would invariably agitate him all the same. Uri realized a chasm had formed between parts of himself.

Meanwhile, with eyes gazing up, the ghost looked on to the chasm it had created; felt the pain it had just caused Uri, his wife, and itself; and resigned to sit aside, letting come what may.

"Go ahead, finish dear," Donna said, putting the pen back in Uri's hand. Uri, sweating from his temple, continued on, though a deep, unsettling murmur continued from his belly. When finally done, he handed the papers to the courthouse clerk. The clerk examined them carefully, pulled out Uri's name change application from the pile, scanned it over, and laid a pen in front of him.

"You forgot to sign and date—here, on the bottom right."

And so Uri did. Walking away to their car, they had nothing left to do but wait—and so did the ghost within Uri. For several weeks, while they furnished their new apartment, submitted their resumes to employers, and worked on their graduate school applications, the ghost sat still in quiet contemplation.

On one cold, December morning, just after the first snow had fallen, a bureaucrat in the immigration offices of Staten Island picked up a green card application, combed through it for errors, and raised her rubber stamp in the air. Pressing it down three times, Uri's applications had been approved. A man named West had been written, and a man named Vostęvskie had been erased.

Cooking breakfast beside Donna, Uri felt a sharp pain in his side. The ghost within him, having felt from afar what had been done, took a wide look around Uri's soul; it saw that the home it had found within him was no longer there. A stranger to his belly, it darkened, coalesced, and swirled like the cold eddies of an Atlantic storm. In small, invisible droplets, formed from distant places and forgotten times, it poured from Uri like cold rain.

DIASPORA

Donna rushed to grab Uri as he fainted for the second time in his life. But this time—as the arriving paramedics hastily checked his heart rate, his blood pressure, and his pupils—Uri had no visions, dreams, or angels coming to visit him. He laid still, breathing slow, as the blessings and curses of a thousand years dissolved away like the sweat from his skin.

For the first time in his life, and for the first time in two hundred years, a man born of a Vostęvskie carried no other spirit within him but his own.

3

Funeral Shawl

DIASPORA

Two years into their marriage, on a chilly autumn day, a secretary at Columbia University received a call from Beth Israel Medical Center. Within minutes, Uri West had gathered his papers, rushed from the lecture hall, and caught the A train heading south.

Eight months earlier, Uri and Donna had planned their first pregnancy, timing the conception for the greatest likelihood of a birth during Uri's winter break. With financial assistance from Donna's father, the CEO and founder of a private equity firm, her pregnancy passed relatively pain free. For one, neither Donna nor Uri had to worry about medical, prenatal, or generally any other living expenses. Donna's only obligations were to eat according to her dietician's regimented schedule, attend her twice-weekly Lamaze classes, and call her father regularly enough to keep it that way. Uri, for his part, could find no fault in this arrangement. Though he wholly welcomed the surprise of Donna's familial wealth—he had never imagined he could be a full-time student—he maintained a TA position during Donna's pregnancy and his Master's program. He took home six hundred dollars per month for, if nothing else, his own satisfaction.

The baby was not due for another five weeks. Though Uri had not yet begun his term paper, and the IKEA crib Donna's parents had bought them still sat in its box by their couch, Donna felt a sudden, sharp contraction in her abdomen.

In the midst of preparing dinner, she braced herself against the fridge, let the pain subside, shook her head, and continued chopping her cucumbers and tomatoes. She was told that, weeks before her due date approached, many women begin having contractions in preparation for the childbirth. The baby, too, would kick and turn to practice using its muscles and bones. She told herself she had nothing to worry about.

But not one minute later, as she reached for a mixing bowl, she felt a gnawing, wrenching pain in her abdomen again. She dropped her head to the counter, pushed the cutting board aside, and fumbled for the phone as a series of sharp pains rapidly shot down her spine. The ambulance arrived just as her water broke, thirty-five days before her due date.

Hours later, in the delivery room, Uri stood by Donna's bedside, holding her sweaty hand. Donna gave her final push. The doctor gently took hold of Judith's head with his forceps. Having been administered an epidural, Donna felt nothing but a tremendous pressure released from her lower back.

She sighed, laughed from profound relief, and laid her head back on her pillow. Judith was born. But not a moment later, Donna noticed something unexpected. The air felt heavy. The birthing room stood silent. She lifted her head in terror.

The doctor appeared to perform several rapid tests on the newborn, gave orders to one of his nurses, and gathered various things. Judith, as silent as the still air, left from the delivery room in the doctor's arms. Donna tried to throw off her blanket and stand up, but fell back. She desperately tried to get an answer as to what was going on, even just to know if her baby was alive, but the nurses demurred—in truth, they did not know. Imploring her to relax, the nurses explained that Judith was in the doctor's experienced care.

Donna, calming herself down, answered questions as the nurse checked her vitals—*apparently*, she answered them, because when asked about that night later on, she would insist that she had stopped hearing anything at all. Her mind shook like the static of their television. When Uri looked at her scared and vacant expression, he could see her searching his face for comfort. He could see her shocked that there was no comfort there. If either could have spoken at the time and distilled into words the turbulence of their minds, they may have recounted a similar sensation; though neither had ever truly seen, spoken to, or heard from God before, each thought that He should have been present. They felt, distinctly, that He was not there.

As to whether or not their sentiments were true, no one but He could have said. After all, if God's being anywhere was predicated on his perceptibility, then man would have concluded long ago that He was nowhere. God could have been everywhere around them, and within them, and if He chose, remain less visible than the air.

But though God can remove himself from anywhere, His absence can be noticed as well. In times when He is gone, idols and phantoms may fill the profound vacuum of his presence. Like warm air, faith condenses on His closest facsimiles.

To Judith's benefit, there existed less desperate facsimiles around her than the golden calves of long gone times. For in the year 1986, the healing shaman's regalia made way for the white coat and mask of the doctor; a stethoscope replaced his scepter; sterile air displaced incense; and Judith's NICU incubator replaced the midwife's loving arms. A hospital gown supplanted her funeral shawl.

An unaccountable miracle presented itself, whether God showed his face there or not; Judith survived. Taking her first breath moments after leaving the birthing room, to Uri and Donna's elation, her pediatrician concluded that the premature birth did not have a substantial impact on her prenatal development. Her weight, size, and muscle mass were within normal range. Judith's indisposition to crying could only be attributed to a simple disinclination. The doctors discharged her in her parent's arms the following week.

The newborn did not seem to mind her own premature birth very much, either. Held against her mother's chest while leaving the hospital, she gazed at her with a bright, well-rested expression. With an uncanny awareness, Judith looked deeply, intelligently, at both of her parents' faces.

"You see it?" Donna asked Uri, with an ethereal smile.

"I do," Uri said, stupefied. He stared back into his daughter's deep, purple eyes, like amethyst kaleidoscopes under the hospital's light. A moment later, tiredness overcame the baby girl. Forty five minutes later, she woke up when her mother carried her through the door of their apartment for the first time.

A few weeks passed for the family in relative peace. Donna and Uri took turns sleeping through the nights. Donna's parents visited their granddaughter on two consecutive Friday evenings, showing a modicum of warmth; her younger sisters, studying in Connecticut and Massachusetts, paid them a visit when they had the time too. In Judith's apparent precocious fashion, and much to her parent's relief, she had already learned to sleep most of the night by her fifth week.

One late night, with Judith atop Donna, both in deep and comfortable sleep, Uri finished assembling Judith's crib. Though Judith would continue to sleep in her bassinet by their bedside for the time being, Uri began planning Judith's room for the months and years ahead.

Their spare room had sufficed for his study since his semester began the previous Fall. He had just filled the cedar bookcase he found abandoned on the edge of the street outside their apartment; cleaned, sanded, and repaired his antique roll-top desk which he found in disrepair at an estate sale in Yonkers; and found the perfect spots to hang his three Chagal lithographs, brought over from Jerusalem. He loved the way the sun, reflecting off his green walls, softly illuminated them. But now, his desk would have to be dragged into the kitchen; his lithographs would take shelter in the closet; and his most precious books would seek refuge on the bookcase's top shelf.

Uri sat down at his kitchen table, looked out the small window overlooking the rooftops of the brownstones, and

DIASPORA

sighed. Judith had kept him awake the previous night, but he did not mind. Late nights calmed him. Morning rays of sunlight, shining through his windowpane, energized him enough.

He had every reason to smile. Logically, blessings showed themselves all around him; a loving wife, a healthy child, a comfortable home, and the education he had waited a lifetime for. At some point, he would need a bigger apartment—but he would get one soon enough. In the meantime, the entirety of New York sat at the edge of his door. Uri began to smile. But before he could, something stopped him.

Uri's life as a Vostęvskie had been punctuated with tragedy. From fleeing violence as a teenager in Argentina, to years wasted in idle military conscription, to the day his blood drained into the sand from a Lebanese bullet, a scowl hung heavy on his face. And he knew, from the indistinct stories of his father's life, and deeper allusions to an ethereal past, that few Vostęvskies before him had fared much better.

But what reason could a W*est* have to frown for? He shook his head at the thought of sadness, as if dismissing the mere suggestion. He ran through every one of his blessings in his mind once more—and then again, and a third time—until he could prove to himself that he had, in fact, reached a turning point. The fate of the Vostęvskies was behind him. Through a thoroughly dialectical, internal debate, he found no evidence of anything wrong in his life, cleared his mind, and looked out the window again. And yet, again, something still held him back from smiling.

One bead of sweat formed on his temple. He stood up to look at his wife and child, still in peaceful sleep, to calm him; he combed through his bookshelves, past the likes of Tolstoy and *Yitzhak Leibush Peretz*, in the hope that a great thinker's wisdom could reason with him. He looked deeply at his Chagall, as if the red and green fiddler, swaying through blue and yellow orchids and daffodils, could settle the turbulence in his brain. Not for the first time since he had moved in with Donna, the apartment's warm air suffocated him.

He pulled his leather jacket from the closet, silently closed their front door latch, and left for a walk

Down Greendale road, cool wind spun in small eddies, crossing between the brownstones, chilling his ears beneath his cap. A cobblestone park on the corner sat still and quiet. Dead leaves rested by its gate.

Uri sat down beneath an Elm tree, shading a great expanse of the park's short, brown grass. With the bench's cold steel against his faded jeans, he took a deep breath, letting the cold air invigorate his lungs; stretched his arms, resting his hands on the ridge of the backrest; and looked up at the bright, clear sky.

He knew from his time in the military that a cigarette would calm him down. A bright, cold, and quiet day satisfied him in a similar way. He had frequently begun taking walks, always at random hours, and never for the same amount of time. Donna, with her usual passivity, had no qualms with the habit; she even supported it, as he would tend to come home with greater vibrancy and color than when he left. But if the treatment of fresh air was a better one than cigarettes, his main problem still lay with his affliction. Uri was not happy. Nothing he had changed, gained, or accomplished, had made him any happier. And as far as he could divine, he had no reason for his unhappiness. He dropped his head in his hands. With the clarity of the cold sky, Uri contemplated his uncanny reality.

DIASPORA

4

The Mother

Uri was unhappy. But if unhappiness was an arresting force, then the Brooklyn-Queens Expressway would bake silently under the sun; ticking clocks would echo through Grand Central's halls; the rats would find the subway's tunnels too cold and dark to navigate; pilots and passengers would plummet indifferently from the sky; and all the ships crossing the Atlantic would lose their engines, fall into a trough, and drift under the command of the prevailing winds.

The world would come to a grinding halt. And yet, every evening and sunrise, the Brooklyn Bridge shines with brake lights like Christmas day at Rockefeller center, the L train beneath stays packed from door to door, and endless crowds wait under cloudy skies and fluorescent lights for their turn to board. With this primordial velocity, carried on since the day we wandered towards the grassy plains, Uri carried on his life. By all accounts, he carried it on well. Through various jobs in the financial services sector, he would maintain his family's reasonable standard of living; afford them a home in an affluent suburb north of the city; send the young Judith to Hebrew school, largely at Donna's behest; and father two more children, Yonatan and Yuval.

Outwardly, for nearly its entire expanse, Uri and Donna's marriage appeared to settle into a pleasant, stable symbiosis; they would dance around, through, and beside—though never quite *with*—the other, as part of their daily routines. One could see this dance in the most mundane aspects of their lives. rom their newly purchased home in Scarsdale, Uri would catch the Metro North train at the Scarsdale station at 8:28, ride it to 42nd street, and walk the rest of the way to the Lehman Brothers building on 7th avenue—nothing strange could be seen there.

DIASPORA

But Donna, meanwhile, would delay *precisely* long enough to catch the 8:56—despite the school bus coming at 7:30 and the nanny arriving at 8:00—to get off at 125th street, take the 1 train down to 103rd, and stop for a bagel and coffee at Stein's Deli just across the street. While Tuesdays and Thursdays became Donna's nights to watch the kids, giving Uri the time to attend lectures at Pace University, Monday's and Wednesday's were his, allowing Donna time to work on her Master's degree at NYU.

In some ways, at some times, and largely for their children's benefit, they made a modicum of an effort to integrate their lives. And yet, for years of their marriage, they routinely tried and failed to cook together on a regular basis, share the house cleaning, or find family activities outside of PTA meetings, medical appointments, and late night television. As their obligations in work and research grew, they quietly dropped their pretenses of trying. Their apologetic, late night phone calls home increased only in frequency, brevity, and indifference. Chinese and pizza delivery gradually replaced their home cooked dinners of Israeli salads, couscous, and braised lamb shanks; maids replaced Donna's floral sticky notes of laundry duty and chore divisions; and tutors, coaches, and GameBoys filled the roles which Uri and Donna could not.

Their children could see that, though their parents' routines were similar, each maintained distinctly divergent inward lives. Uri's earliest experiences and painfully acquired wisdom had taught him to separate himself from his ever present ruminations, see them from a distance, and let them freely pass. He found contentment and inner silence through deep dives into philosophical literature, explorations of Eastern thought, and an immoderate taste for expensive whiskey and wine. For better or for worse, he demurred at his own discontent; at the very least, he allowed his time to pass with grace.

Donna, on the other hand, steadily permitted her dissatisfaction to grow, evidenced by the ever present furrow over her brow at work, in her bed, and at the dinner table. Her protracted unhappiness accosted her—even *surprised* her—more and more each day. Her career progressed, the family wealth grew, and her children grew older. But all the while, Donna felt as if she—still a young girl herself, still smitten with an enigmatic philosophy undergrad, still trading glances with him from across the classroom—had somehow been left behind, betrayed by everyone in her life.

To her children, their mother's internal mental processes produced a distinctly unpleasant outward effect; during their silent dinners and beneath her hollow questions, they sensed her intensity—she *wanted more* from them. As it happens when someone seeks to take, her children pulled away. Her feigned composure crumbled in the face of their growing distance. If for no other reason than his appropriately measured detachment, the children, one after the other, steadily drifted closer to their father.

One Saturday morning, Donna walked into their living room in her bathrobe, looking to pour herself some coffee. She saw the teenage Judith and Uri's feet up together, as if they were brother and sister; saw what was undoubtedly not Uri's first snifter of McAllister twelve, twirling in his hand; saw Yonatan on the rug, holding the toddler Yuval in his arms; saw one of Uri's favorite kung-fu movies playing on their CRT TV, the volume too loud for children's ears; and saw the same expression of polite—yet impatient—inquiry on each of their faces. Uri turned down the TV, as if it was obvious she had not come to join them; the children adjusted their posture, as if their teacher had just walked by; and even Yuval, feeling the warmth of the room drain away, became restive in his brother's arms.

DIASPORA

Donna felt a chill down her spine. She turned around, ran up the stairs, locked herself in her bathroom, turned on the shower, and cried.

"*What have I done to deserve this?*" she asked herself, staring into her foggy mirror, searching for the answer in the reflection of her eyes.

She could accept that her babies were growing up; after all, she was no stranger to developmental psychology, having minored in the field during college. She knew that any child would, at certain stages, push their mother away. But what she could not account for was their icy indifference. If only they showed her anger or derision, like normal children, she would know that they loved her! The worst thing they could do to her was nothing at all.

Donna collected herself, got dressed, and took a walk. The cool January air calmed her. And yet, she could not shake the sting of her tears on her cheeks.

Deciding that her *personal connections* were suffering, over the next few days, she paid visits to her sisters and her parents, called old friends for coffee, signed up for fitness classes at the YMCA, and booked therapy sessions for herself near her work. But despite surrounding herself with anyone and everyone she believed could *give* her the comfort she needed, no one could give her what she sought.

Donna turned to reality TV, self-help books, the ice-cream in their freezer, and the baked sweets on the grocery store shelves she had stoically passed by for so many years. She spent most of her late evenings with moist eyes—either in her bathrobe, on her bed, watching television alone—or on her side, staring into the darkness, waiting for the night to pass, and listening to her husband gently snore.

Several years passed, as all years do—her eldest left for college, her husband began teaching his own classes, and her other two adolescent children thoroughly cloistered themselves in their rooms and out of her life. One evening, as she drove to her parents' house, she saw the wrinkles around her eyes in the rearview mirror of her Subaru; saw the gray hairs piled up in her old hairbrush, sticking out from her handbag; saw the first of many spots that would come to speckle her delicate hands; and came to a simple realization. Not one person—not her parents, her sisters, her husband, her kids, or any other in her life—had ever hated her. She was not, and had never been, unworthy of love. No—it was quite to the contrary; she was as worthy of love as anything in creation. She was just simply, innocently, ordinary. Seeing reality more clearly than the brightly lit highway in front of her, she looked back at her four decades of passive inertia. At every junction, little more than passing thoughts stood at her life's forks.

DIASPORA

5

Punishment

Judith grew up with no fear of violence and war. Nor was she persecuted by the ghosts of places and times long gone. She had never hid under the canopy of dark forests or within the break-bulk cargo of merchant ships. Neither did hunger or winter ice mean anything more to her than an uncomfortable rumbling between her breakfast and the lunch bell, and an opportunity to wake up late, earn money shoveling snow, and enjoy a day off from school.

In these ways, Judith's life differed little from her classmates and friends. On the soccer field, in the classroom, or during her Pokemon tournaments on the playground, she showed no greater or worse skill, intelligence, or luck than any other. She may have had the seed of *something* inside of her—something that could have made her greater than the sum of her apparent parts; a few of her teachers would recall their astonishment when, after first meeting her, her radiant, purple eyes betrayed a confounding cognizance and maturity. But fostering that seed—to try and find that greater sum—would have asked from the adults in her life just a little more than they had the strength, time, or acumen to give. Her teachers were content to let her play with her Rubik's Cubes when she finished her class work early. They watched her read her science fiction novels on the attendant's bench at recess when she was bored; her mother chose to leave the responsibility of her Hebrew exposure to her after school classes; and as for her Spanish, her father found no purpose, or even desire, for her to learn it at all. They looked at her test scores, her lap times, her general affability, and shrugged. For better or for worse, everyone agreed that Judith was, pretty much, doing just fine.

DIASPORA

And so Judith grew up no faster, nor slower, not more anxious, nor more confident, than any other young woman in her school. Her straight brown hair grew to be no more or less long; her young boyfriend Theo, no more or no less funny, cute, or kind. Options and opportunities naturally presented themselves to her as they did to any of her peers, and the system, designed for clear purposes, offered its clear answers to them all.

In just one way, Judith could have distinguished herself, if she wanted to, from the majority of her friends and classmates; she was a Jew, no more or no less than any of her ancestors before her. But to her, this represented little more than an annoyance, and no less a superstition, than her astrological sign, spirit animal, or birth stone. From an early age, her parents saw that well. She squirmed at Sabbath dinners when her mother would place her finger on the correct line of her siddur; she groaned on the high holidays when, from the bimah, the rabbi alluded to things she could not see, feel, or hear; and she mumbled her prayers beneath her breath, never bothering to remember the meaning of the Hebrew words as she spoke them.

By her teenage years, a novel realization took hold of her. She was fully convinced, and allowed it to be known freely, that there was not, and had never been, anything such as a God at all.

When God heard how Judith felt, and heard the same message coming from innumerable others, the loneliest person on Earth would have understood Him better than any other before. God looked back at His covenant, read the first of his ten commandments once more—*ani adonai elohecha, ani adonai echad*—and finally realized the agony of His position: *God is One.* He had been condemned to be eternally, hopelessly, and irreconcilably alone.

And yet, as He helplessly watched Judith from afar; as He listened in on the cartoons she diverted herself with after their classes; and as He observed, from above, her family's quiet, weekday dinners of various ethnic take-out; He smiled sweetly, shedding one, melancholic tear.

He had no issue with Judith's comfort. After all, since time immemorial, God had never wished for His children to suffer. During famine, He felt their same hunger, and through the winter ice, His soul had shivered beside them through it all.

Neither did God find Judith's life too boring; for Him, eternal wonder could be found everywhere, even within empty air. Nor were Judith's teachers or television shows too vapid to pique His interest—God could find endless depth within the minds of the starfishes on the ocean floor. No moment, place, or time within His creation had any less value to Him than any other. God only regretted one thing—He had created both suffering and loneliness, His children had felt it before, and now, suffering and loneliness were His to bear.

But God's loneliness could not be His only punishment. A great contradiction—a Father denied by His children—superseded a great cosmological shift around Him. He learned He had never any power but what *they* had given Him. The fabric of the universe shifted before His eyes. Though His soul wept—which at one point would have collapsed Heaven to Earth—nothing in creation, from the stars to His children, seemed to mind. The sun, which He had kept bright since the beginning of time, seemed to no longer need Him to illuminate the sky. On Earth, the rain fell no sooner or later than the weatherman—not He—divined it would.

God wiped away his tears. He looked away in thought. If the sun burnt apart from His will, would that mean He could no longer glow with His own light? If the rain fell when the weatherman foretold, would He have to wait for the weatherman's forecast before He could cry? An infinite fractal of questions and answers tormented Him. But despite His questions, God understood, from the depths of His internal soul, that one thing was clear; He was being punished for everything

He had done, for all that He had not, and by all that He would now have to bear.

    Every moment God spent in contemplation, eternities passed Him by. Judith, by the time she had advanced in the course of her life, tried to speak to God. At that point, however, it was far too late; God had fallen into too deep of a meditation to hear her. His silence may have been better than the truth. If God had answered Judith, and told her there were questions that even He struggled to answer, Judith would have realized that she had not the faintest chance of answering her own—not in a thousand lifetimes.

6

The Clove House

DIASPORA

The teenage Yuval watched with his father, recently divorced, passing his time in tranquil inebriation; watched his mother, on weekly visits, medicating away her dissatisfaction; saw his older sister and her friends, stumbling through the back door smelling of cigarettes and beer; watched his brother, Yonatan, asking for little more than what remained of the love his mother and father could spare; saw a nameless mass of students amble sleepily through the double doors of his school; and felt thoroughly unimpressed.

The morning after he graduated from high school, he got into one final argument with his father; told his mother to stop calling; put three pairs of underwear in a backpack; and filled his Geo Tracker's gas tank. For a short time, he wandered through various southern highways, worked odd labor jobs, paid for motels by the week, and subsisted on All-Star Breakfasts at the Waffle Houses along the way. That story may have continued little differently from the nameless and forgotten many more who had wandered similarly. But for various pragmatic, capricious, and possibly misguided reasons, he escaped that desolate path before he may not have had the chance. Taking a job as a deckhand on a Mississippi River tugboat, and with hardly enough cash for a sandwich and the gas to get there, Yuval, at the age of nineteen, began a long and varied life as a deckhand on rivers and seas.

Yuval spent five seasons hauling steel rigging on coal barges on the Tennessee River; passed four winters trawling for pollock through icy waters, on rusted factory trawlers, in the Bering Sea; and worked four summers on Mississippi River tugboats, passing the nights drunk from wine in hostel courtyards. If nothing else, he took satisfaction in his earned right to say he had seen the coldest of the sea's wind, the hottest of the southern sun, and the brightest of the starlit sky.

By his twenty-fifth birthday, a beard had covered his face. The sun creased his eyes, lightened his hair, and darkened his skin. Tattoos of anchors, hooks, roses, and pin-ups littered his arms and chest. On many days, Yuval could have said he would not have done anything differently. But on others, he recognized his old dissatisfaction in strange places and unexpected times.

As if blowing in the air, he caught glimpses of it everywhere; from the rakes of grain barges, silently plowing through southern rivers; in the hum of tugboat engines, rhythmically pulsing in time; in the scattered light of Alaska's summer sun, dipping below the horizon, rising sooner than the next day could begin; or while looking into the black void of windy, moonless, winter nights. He discovered that, no matter what corner of the Earth he may have wandered to, that thin, quiet, unmistakable feeling of discontent followed him.

For a while, his discontent periodically ebbed and returned. But as far as the magic and bright feeling of meeting unique people and traveling to exotic places—that left almost as soon as it came. Boarding his vessels on those cold mornings and warm nights, he carried strength in his gait and sharpness in his eye. But the progression of time had squelched the fire in his heart. Even when he would come home, sleep late into the mornings, and enjoy the spoils of his wage, happiness appeared more elusive with each passing job and each passing year.

One summer evening, another river tugboat job came to a close. Yuval threw his sea bag over his shoulder. He stepped foot off the M/V Liza Ann securely moored to her berth and found the city of New Orleans quiet beneath the heat. After a long streetcar ride and a short walk, he arrived at the steps to the Clove House Hostel; checked into his bunk, prepaid since he last left; walked past the staff, drinking whiskey, sweating away the night; and laid his sea bag at the foot of his dormitory door. Warm rain began to fall.

    The Clove House Hostel, he had discovered years before, had everything he needed and much of what he wanted. The drinks were cheap, the girls plentiful, and he could sleep there a week for less than a day's worth of deck pay. As he lay in his bunk, soaking in the dormitory's air conditioning, he heard the travelers in the beds around him softly snoring. Bumping against the bunk above him and the stucco wall beside him, he noticed, through an adjacent window, one of the hostel's garden-side private rooms, glowing through the soft drizzle. He got up, paid the difference at the front desk, and indulged himself in the rare pleasure of a private, queen-sized bed.

    He opened the door and looked around the room. Painted stick-men covered the red walls. Sharpie-written hearts overlapped each other on the hardwood boards of the bed. He listened to the clicking of the ceiling fan, the buzzing of the old, yellow lamp, and the fountain outside the door. The gentle laughter of girls, running for cover, splashing through the puddles, fluttered by.

    He faded into sleep with the hum of the air conditioning filling the void left by the M/V Liza Ann's rhythmically pulsating engines. He felt his body gently swaying side to side, like a tugboat crossing a tanker ship's gentle wakes; and felt warm behind his eyes, like a deckhand hours into his shift under the sun. As he routinely would when first arriving on land, he dreamt that he had never left the M/V Liza Ann, had been forced back on his vessel, and had been condemned to never leave.

    He mourned for himself, dreaming he was back on his vessel's thin cot. Unable to get any rest, he waited for nothing but to start another working day. The steel bulwarks constricted around him; the paint, flaking overhead, fell to just inches above his face.

He thought of a nameless girl's face. She had radiant red cheeks, a white smile, and smelled of flowers and sweat. He asked her if she would wait for him until the day he could come back. She answered that there was no need.

In his dream, Yuval saw her on top of him, her gray eyes smiling, the creases around her lips in deep relief. This dream faded away, but in doing so, carried away some degree of Yuval's pain and stress. He relaxed into a more restful sleep.

The smell of the hostel's bacon, frying on the grill, woke him late in the morning. A few moments passed before he could confirm the truth—he was back ashore. A vague sense of loss fell over him, but the visceral relief, sweetness, and complacency of a mind of a seaman awaking on land quickly overcame it. He ameliorated a subtle pulsing in his forehead with a few deep gulps of cool water; sat on the edge of his bed, thinking over his many shoreside obligations; and decided that he was, all things considered, doing okay. But if any of the darker realities of his position were to weigh on him, he found himself quickly preoccupied. Opening his door to the sunlight in the courtyard, he saw that suntanned girls in spaghetti straps and thin sandals had just begun pouring their first glasses of wine.

The girls who stayed at the Clove House were the type who could drink during the day without consequence. For Yuval, as long as it was measured and purposeful, damage was attractive, like tears on a pair of jeans. He particularly liked the ones who smoked for their visceral, effeminate cough. Everything they did was with style.

Yuval decided those girls would distract him. Walking into the courtyard, he lit a cigarette, and momentarily feigned disinterest in the girls sitting around. With a kind smile, he befriended them by seeing their beauty, not hiding that he saw it, and not wishing to take anything from it. He found that to be the best way to treat pretty girls. After nonchalantly asking if they had plans—knowing they always had none—the three of them left to get breakfast.

While riding the streetcar, talking with the two nymph-like creatures beside him, he learned they were not longtime best friends as he had believed from first sight. Though they were the same size and shape, each had a contrasting personality and beauty.

For the entire breakfast at Mandina's on Canal, their conversations danced around topics that meant nothing unless one handled them with confidence and joy. Yes, the day was beautiful, the restaurant was brilliant, the air was cool—but only because *they* were brilliant, beautiful, and cool, and were talking only to let the warmth of their voices fill the empty air between them. Yuval offered to pay the bill.

One of them, an Australian girl, perceptive and cautious, was happier listening than speaking during breakfast. Yuval believed he understood her; she was naturally blonde, wore the latest fashion, and had an air of perfection that Yuval had grown to find boring. She may have been looking for something, but Yuval did not know what, nor could he have noticed, at the time. He had kept his eye on the other girl, Maria. Luckily for him, the girl from Australia, either truthfully or as a lie, left them after lunch for some nebulous reason. Leaving the restaurant, Yuval and Maria walked side by side down the street.

Maria explained candidly that she came to the city just to explore, feel free, and for nothing else. The city was to her—and she to him—colorful, different, and unique, which satisfied them both well enough.

She had brown hair, dressed in dark purple, and characterized her opinion of people by the way she wore a scantily perceptible smile or frown on her open lips. Her neckline hung low, but she did not have the air of a girl wishing to reveal herself. To her, it was simple; the air was hot, and other people's gazes were irrelevant.

Their pace slowed as they walked through the Garden District. They quickly found themselves pulled into unexpectedly personal conversation. Despite her airy nonchalance, he piqued her interest with his stories of Alaskan ice, rusted tugboats, and rigging wires.

The sun fell to the golden hour of the day. They neared their hostel, passing the quiet coffee shops, Italian restaurants, and the vintage, single screen movie theater that played cowboy movies and cult classics in rotation. Virile, peaceful chatter flowed through the doors of the glowing entrance. Yuval looked up and read the Marquee.

"Oh my god, we just missed it!" Yuval exclaimed, putting his hand on Maria's shoulder. "One of my favorites. Have you seen *Mulholland Drive*? If you're not doing anything later, do you feel like watching it on the pay-per-view in my room?"

Maria stopped, looking at him with a wry smile.

"Calm down, I'm not trying anything," Yuval said cooly, gently grabbing her hand to come along. "I just like movies."

She playfully pressed her shoulder close to him; their fingers interlocked.

They ambled quietly, happily, to the hostel; sat down momentarily with the rest of the guests in the courtyard, bottles of whiskey and wine already scattered around; stood up, smiling at one another; walked past the rest of the guests; and gently closed the door to his private room.

Late into the night, they got out of bed, hungry. Hanging onto his hand, Maria jested that they still had to *watch* the film, like Yuval promised, when they got back. Yuval laughed.

They repeated their same walk from the morning, ate to their heart's content, had a few more drinks between them, and returned to his room. With the TV on, looking through the pay-per-view movies as he promised, Maria took the remote from his hands. They quickly found distraction in one another once more.

Early the next morning, Yuval laid peacefully asleep. But Maria, still laying her head on Yuval's chest, was wide awake. A knot pounded behind her eyes. She quietly lifted herself off of his bed, grabbed her scattered clothes, made sure that Yuval was still asleep, and checked her phone. She covered her eyes and refused to cry.

"*Shit. What have I done,*" Maria said to herself, silently leaving. Unable to bring herself to read her boyfriend's many text messages from the previous night, she slunk back to her own room, fell on her bed, covered her face, and cried.

Late in the day, when the sun shone onto his face, Yuval rolled out of his sheets. She was gone. He left his room, looked around the courtyard, did not see her, and shrugged; he would see her later in the day, he told himself.

With nothing better to do, he went to the Riverwalk to watch the boats. It was early Fall, when the breezes wafting across the river were becoming cool. The sun seemed to charge the city. Yuval bought a cheap, wine-dipped cigar. In the foregrounds of the passing tugboats and ships, he watched the girls, bright and airy, wearing the sundresses for sale in the French Quarter. The brisk, cool wind cut through his thick hair, a deep draw of his cigar filled his lungs, and his eyes took in the blue sky above him. He thought about Maria. He could not help but smile.

By sundown, he made it back to the hostel. A new group of travelers was just checking in as he arrived; four college girls in jean shorts, crop tops, and Abercrombie tennis shoes sat impatiently on their oversized suitcases while two tall, thin boys, in light shorts and polo t-shirts, quibbled at the desk over who would pay for what.

After briefly looking around for Maria, Yuval sat on the raised porch. He stretched his legs and rolled a cigarette. One of the girls saw him through the hostel's colonial style arched windows. She looked him up and down; liked his dark skin, his stained jeans, and leather boots; opened the creaking, wooden door to the outside; and introduced herself.

"I'm Emily," she said, extending her hand to Yuval, looking him in the eyes.

"Yuval," he replied, looking back into hers. Shaking her hand, he took her in as a whole—from her thin fingers, to her slender shape, to her skin's warmth, flushed from traveling all day in the backseat of her friend's Toyota.

"Would you like one?" he asked, lighting his cigarette.

"No thanks," she said, though she sat down beside him all the same. With her knees pointing to him, he restrained himself from acting on his impulses. He responded to her small talk and answered her questions politely, but his focus stayed on the street. His day apart from Maria had only increased her allure; he waited, against his more simple desires, to see that spectral girl again.

Emily quickly felt and saw Yuval's preoccupation. With a somewhat confused look, she turned to her friends, stood up, and politely told him goodbye.

Yuval fixed his attention fully on the street. The sun fell. He rolled a few more cigarettes, listened to the chirping cicadas, and heard the warm, rising laughter from the other side of the hostel's door. The night grew later. His heart grew more anxious. He knew Maria would have to come back at some point; she said nothing about leaving. He stayed fast.

Hours passed as droves of guests wandered in from the streets. The young man working the night shift at the desk silently checked on him. He saw him fixed to the front porch's cold, uncomfortable bench. By early morning, the last of the street musicians and drunken couples rambled their way through the front door. Yuval sat motionless on the bench as the first light of the sun rose above the oak trees lining the street. She was not coming back.

Yuval resented himself. He hated how much he cared.

DIASPORA

Twelve days passed. Yuval spent the majority of his time on land sleeping in his queen bed. The next person he would talk to would be his fleet dispatcher, calling him two days before his contract's renewal date, to confirm Yuval would be ready at the shipyard by crew change.

"Yes," Yuval answered dryly. He hung up.

Two days later, shortly before dawn, Yuval loaded his Geo Tracker with the extent of his possessions—one backpack of clothes, a spare pair of boots, and a winter jacket. He drove across the river to his shipyard with a furrow over his brow. Leaving land had stopped giving him any pleasure, but something else wrenched his heart—though he did not want to leave, he had failed to find any reason to stay.

Driving through the shipyard's gate, Yuval could smell the grain dust in the air; hear the locomotives all along the port, thrusting and screeching; hear the hydraulic whine of grain elevators and bucket loaders, loading barges heavy and low; and see the blinding electrical arcs of welders mending the hulls of ships and barges.

He laid down his sea bag, took a gulp of water, felt the early morning sun on his forehead, and waited for his boat to get to port. No less than an hour later, he saw the M/V Liza Ann, with two grain barges in tow, billowing gray smoke over the riverbank's Cyprus trees. Her flag hung limply in the stiff, still air.

The job was one Yuval had done many times before, running line-haul between New Orleans, Baton Rouge, and the Houston Shipping Channel, with six heavy barges in tow. A month being the very earliest they would return, Yuval knew he would get no Sunday off on the M/V Liza Ann—an ancient, rusted tub of Missouri steel—under the command of Captain Larry Guidry—an old, remorseless, Louisiana steel worker. Trying to find anything to look forward to, he thought to himself, he may see some porpoises in the brackish water of the Galveston Bay.

By noon, she had tied off, refueled, loaded her crew's meager provisions, and set off once more with her westbound tow. Motoring down a primitive, cypress-lined canal, the M/V Liza Ann slowed before a withering, termite-ridden lock. The sun began to fall. The captain eased her through. Yuval, through the mosquitos, payed and heaved slack in time. The lock horns blew, the gates parted, and a pristine, still, river-like waterway opened before him.

Yuval coiled his lock-lines on the hooks hanging from the M/V Liza Ann's push knees, quietly catching his breath; took one great, round look over the wide, green, intracoastal waterway; smelled its warm, earthy mist, nearly thick enough to bank their tow; and saw the gulf-bound pelicans swoop behind the tree line.

The M/V Liza Ann's gently undulating wake reflected the horizon's smoldering, orange glow. The sun melted into the western tree line; shimmered, dimmed, and burned red like blood; and fell beneath the delta, overcome by the weight of the starlit sky. Yuval stood fast on the bow of the M/V Liza Ann, feeling the night's gentle wind thicken his hair; gazed into the Milky Way, its million colors glittering above; and felt, almost inexplicably, tears of sadness filling his eyes.

The days crept by. One day, while painting the hull, Yuval sang a melody which satisfied him. The next day, though, he could not remember it. He felt tired all day, every day; at night, he could not get one moment of rest. He wondered if wisdom could come from it. He feared nothing would come from it.

The last day came as every last day ever did. He packed what clothes of his had not been torn, laid on his bunk, and closed his eyes. He reflected on his past month—what had he accomplished? He ate beans, cornbread, and beef; raised wires and rigging into the sun; and tore, stained, and soaked his clothing in sweat.

But what did he want? His mind shook and stirred as he put into words everything that he had, for so long, understood in his soul; he wanted to find a place with people who loved him, with people he loved, where he did not need to sweat, where canned beans did not exist, and where there was no captain but God. He accepted with grief that that boat—that the intracoastal waterway, the Gulf of Mexico, and even the wide Bering Sea—may be some people's homes. It was not, and never would be, his own. He realized he was wasting his time.

Back at the shipyard, he cashed in his last boot voucher, threw away his seabag, and jump-started his truck. He made a promise to whoever may have been listening; he would never step foot on a rusted workboat again.

But as to what he would do instead, he had not put in nearly as much thought. He quickly spent three quarters of his remaining money, passing three months with four separate girls, in two separate states; spent two nights at his mother's apartment in Portchester, to his mother's immense delight, and to his mental grief; rented a room in a three-story apartment, two streets away from the interstate in Yonkers; failed to find the courage to visit, or even call, anyone else in his family; and in his darkest moment, as his space heater cut through the cold winter air, wanted only to fade away.

7

The Box

DIASPORA

One morning, Yuval kept his covers pulled tightly around him. Staring into the blanket above him, he warming his body with his breath. A pair of old earplugs silenced the clatter of his old, uninsulated windows, shaking within their worn channels with each gust of wind.

He checked the time on his phone—1:30 a.m.—and tried to remember when he fell asleep. He only remembered that, when he laid his head on his pillow, the sky seemed to be getting dark. Knowing he must have somewhat slept, he could lie awake for the rest of the night—staring at his breath in the light of his Nokia phone, reading through old messages—with some degree less of guilt.

He looked through his contacts, pausing at every name and number, forcing himself to put into words why he could not call one or the other. Every time, he found an excuse. This happened frequently, similar to when he would open his shared refrigerator, forcing himself to explain why he was not hungry for this or that, or when he would gaze out his window, looking for new reasons why he could not join the passersby.

He rubbed his eyes, turned off his phone, rolled over in his bed, and took a painkiller from a bottle on his windowsill. The pill allowed him to fall asleep.

Late in the morning, he nearly finished a pleasant dream. His phone interrupted him, vibrating next to his pillow. Yuval opened one eye to see the caller ID—his mother. He sighed. He normally let her calls go to voicemail. But as it continued to ring, he looked at the time again—nearly noon—felt a multifaceted guilt, thought about what he was accomplishing by ignoring her, and answered it.

"Hi Mom," he said dryly, rubbing his eyes.

"Yuval! It's so good to hear from you! How are you doing?"

"Fine."

"Oh, good! So, I had Deborah over today," she began, already making Yuval regret picking up the phone.

"You remember Deborah, right? We went to an Israeli dancing class before *Pesach*, and her son Gideon—you two used to have playdates—"

"—Mom," Yuval interrupted, thinly veiling his frustration, massaging his temple, rising from his bed to find his pants. "I'm busy. What—ugh, is there anything else?"

"Well, yes, okay. So I was at her house," she began, as Yuval let the phone fall from his ear, "and when we moved, she took some of my things to keep in her attic. There's this one shoebox—

"Is that all, mom? You have some stuff for me?" he asked, exasperated at her inability to summarize her own points succinctly. He expected most of her calls to devolve into her trying to give him random keepsakes and junk.

"Well, I also know the best tabbouleh place, and it's not too far from…" she continued.

Yuval, at that moment scanning through the Rice-A-Roni and chicken bones in his fridge, suddenly perked up.

"—Oh! Uh, I am actually free for lunch… where is it?"

A few minutes later, he opened his door, smelled the cool air, and squinted his eyes. He realized he had not been outside in days.

His Geo Tracker sat neglected a few streets down. Throwing away the parking ticket on his windshield, weathered by the rain, he fueled his truck with the ten dollar bill he kept in his glove box.

Pulling up to the restaurant, he saw the white-clothed tables through the window and glanced down over his sweatshirt and paint-covered jeans. At least, he said to himself, his underwear was new.

Stepping through the door, Yuval felt the Jordanian restaurant's warm, heavy, welcoming air. He sighed, the smells of roasting meat, saffron rice, and various teas surrounding him. To his surprise, however, scarcely more than a few old, well-dressed couples sat in the restaurant's far corners. Despite the life and motion he sensed coming from behind the kitchen's doors, the restaurant was ethereally quiet for lunch time.

His mother was late, too, as he had expected. After being seated alone, he availed himself of the restaurant's spiced tea, advertised proudly on the front of their menu. Twenty minutes later, his mother arrived.

He watched her as she came through the door—a little smaller and a little older—and smiled politely when she pulled out her chair.

Yuval hardly said a word, letting his mother ramble about Deborah, Gideon, and similar nonsense. But by the time the waiter had brought him his food, he had satiated his hunger, and the last sip of his tea had turned cold. He decided he had enough.

"Alright mom, this was nice, but I gotta get going—"

"Oh! Okay, but don't you want your box?"

Noticing the shoebox sitting by her feet, he remembered that was, ostensibly, the reason why he came.

"Yeah, sure, I'll take it," he said. Lifting it up, he was surprised by its heaviness. "What's in here?" he asked.

"Oh, just some old things. Take a look."

Yuval opened its cover, printed with drawings of colorful flowers and green vines. He gave it a cursory thumb through and saw the usual school papers, childhood toys, and class photos he knew she hoarded in her cupboards and on the top shelves of her closets. To his surprise, however, he picked out a drawing he remembered fondly from grade school—one he had not seen in nearly twenty years. His mother, more receptive than Yuval would believe, paid close attention to the sudden shift in his eyes.

In pink, red, green, and blue, at the age of nine, he put into watercolors the magnolia tree that once shrouded the whole of their old house's backyard. He saw the sun, hanging low behind the hill above their house, casting streaks of watery purple and red through the clouds; saw the magnolia's pink and white flowers in their rare, full bloom, just moments before the first of its petals would fall; and saw the weedy, wild grass rising against its trunk, jutting through the filigree of their dark, wrought iron bench.

He remembered the exact evening he painted it, feeling the March breeze blowing through their breakfast nook window. The fresh scent of brownies his sister and mother had baked together, resting next to their kitchen sink, filled the room. The feeling of his father's cold, suede jacket, moments after he came to hug him, tickled his face.

"You were quite the artist," his mother said.

Yuval looked at her, suddenly noticed how much of his emotion his face betrayed, and collected himself.

"Th—thanks, mom," he said, looking away, though allowing her to see the tip of his smile. "Let's do this again, sometime."

"Yeah, I'd love that Yuvi!" she gushed. "You know, the secret to this tabbouleh is the extra lemon they put in—you know how I know that? I asked the chef, and—"

As she enthusiastically went on, Uri smiled and nodded, happy to let her tire herself out.

Back in Yonkers, two hours later, he locked his door, closed his curtains, and like a child on the last morning of Hanukkah opening his first present, poured into his box. His heart fluttered as he sorted through his treasures. In his hands, he held an entire childhood's worth of birthday and Valentine's Day cards; years of family photos, with younger likenesses of him, his family, and his friends; and vibrant watercolor impressions of landscapes, portraits, and everything else that had held meaning to him at one point in time.

But beneath it all, he found more than his own memories. He saw Polaroid pictures of his sister and brother, stacking Jenga blocks with himself as a toddler; found ancient photos of his college-aged mother and father, in dark sepia, smiling hand-in-hand during a hike to the peak of Mount Meron; and digging further, found newspaper clippings, college applications, and even that obscure family name *Vostęvskie,* on his father's old ID cards.

Yuval saw one last family photo on the very bottom, picked it up, and felt a lump come to his throat. He saw his young, smiling mother, whom he had treated with cold indifference for nearly twenty years of his life; saw his college-age sister, long gone from the state; saw his school-age older brother, living in that very city, presently unaware Yuval had even moved back; and saw his father who, with seven years having passed since Yuval had seen him, surely had lost the dark color of his beard.

He closed the box, pushed it under his bed, and laid on his mattress. Staring at the ceiling, hours passed by as his memories floated by his eyes, mercilessly accosting him. When the sun set, he shut off his light, closed his eyes, and hid under his covers. Another day had passed. Now, he would have to endure another night.

One may have wondered who, or what, spoke to Yuval at that moment. Some unaccountable being saw Yuval in his cloud of sadness, curled up on his bed; wrapped his arm around him, pitying him; and just when Yuval could no longer breathe, and He had forced the first of his tears to leak from his eyes, breathed into Yuval's soul:

"Yuval! All that you need is in front of you. And yet, you refuse to loosen your eyelids' grip, fearing you may cry! Do not be so foolish. Why do you fear to cry? Open your eyes. Cry..."

Yuval heard this voice. He shook his head as if to insist he cannot, but felt the lump in his throat rise. His face grimaced and flushed with warmth. He took in an uneven, truncated breath, and for the first time in twenty years, felt warm tears flow down his face. The arm holding him did not let go, gently petting his hair. Yuval buried his face into His shoulder.

The voice did not tell a lie. After God had opened the floodgates of his heart, two decades of his soul's calcification gently peeled away. Laying on his bed, staring silently at his ceiling through glassy eyes, he gasped in sudden realization.

The truth showed itself before him like a distant light on a dark, snowy night. He threw his blankets off, sat up, and jumped to grab his box. Digging through the papers once more, passing the drawings and photos he remembered so well, he took a hold of the documents on the bottom that he brushed right over without a second thought.

"Vostęvskie..." he read, finding his father's Argentinian identity card once more. He had heard this name in passing moments throughout his life and knew his father had changed it at some point in the past.

Yuval found his phone, its battery dead, and hastily plugged it in. As he steadied his breath, clarity settled on his mind like a blanket of clean, white snow. He was not old—only twenty-eight; his life had not been long, but had only just begun; and he realized, to his profound relief, no matter what he may have once said or done, his fate had not been set in stone.

His phone powered on. He dialed his father's number, no longer in his contacts but still clear in his memory. The phone rang for no longer than a moment.

"Yuval?" his father answered.

"Dad," he said, suddenly worried whether calling him was the right thing to do. He choked up.

"Yuval? Is everything okay?"

"Yeah, dad…" Yuval managed to say. "Look, so—mom gave me this box of old stuff, and I found some of your old ID cards. I thought about asking you—"

"—Ah, you're getting worried you'll never look as good as me, I see."

They both chuckled. A moment passed in silence.

"Well, whatever it is you need to ask, I'm sure I can answer you better over a glass of wine. I don't have any grape juice… but if you don't tell mom, you can have a sip of mine."

"I've missed you, dad."

"I've missed you, too."

"Text me your address," Yuval said, already leaving out his front door.

"Of course, son."

Yuval got in his car. Driving towards his father's apartment in New Jersey, a smile began to rise from his lips. Watching this all, a nameless being, having extended his arm through distant space and endless time, gently lifted it off of Yuval's shoulder. With precious little strength left to give, He resumed His divine and eternal contemplation.

8

In Diaspora

DIASPORA

Whatever catharsis Yuval felt that night, visiting his father's apartment in the south-side of Hackensack, he gave back to Uri twofold. He came through his creaking door, glancing around the shabby, but not overtly unkempt, single room apartment. His father had been living there since his divorce. An open bottle of wine stood in the corner of his all-purpose kitchen table, but Yuval smelled no alcohol on his father's breath. His hair had grown gray and silvery, but maintained its characteristic ear-length waves. All things considered, his father seemed well.

Uri poured them both hot coffee he had just brewed; cleared away from the table some books, letters, and term papers he had been grading for his adjunct professorship; and they sat down together. Each smiled at the other, beginning their reconciliation with banal and kind conversation. Yuval looked healthy, Uri was looking well, the building seemed nice, and so forth. Nor did either exactly remember anymore, or even understand, what had precipitated their years-long disconnection—at least, not enough to feel any need to mention it. Though Uri did not ask, or even very much care, what Yuval's specific purpose for visiting was, he could tell Yuval had been holding something on his tongue. When they had both been silent for just a moment too long, Uri took another sip of his coffee, and Yuval asked him his question.

"Dad—why did you change your name from Vostęvskie?"

Uri looked him in the eyes. He set his coffee back on the table. Seeing his son's face glowing with deliberate energy, he understood his thought process; at his very same age, he realized, he had been very little different from his son. It appeared to him that Yuval had made his same, first mistake—believing that one's happiness could be discovered elsewhere in the world, hiding in every place except where one has already been. What he did not expect, however, was for Yuval to see the foolishness of that path so early and with so much strength. He had seen his error, and in order to rectify it, he needed to know, in the simplest of terms, where he, his father, and the rest of the Wests, were *from*.

As far as his exact question, Uri realized that it was rhetorical; for Yuval to be asking it, he must have already understood the answer. But after a moment of thought, he took a breath and told him, "You're asking me about the *Vostęvskies*? I'll tell you about the Vostęvskies, if that's what you want."

Yuval nodded.

"You know, Bubbeleh, my throat is a little too dry to tell a story," Uri said, winking at his son, shaking his empty glass from side to side. Yuval laughed, getting up to pour his father another glass.

And so Uri told him the story, as best as he knew it, from the bits and pieces he had heard from his father, Meir, who had once heard bits and pieces of it from Aaron. Having once been a Vostęvskie, he could not overlook the parts of that story that involved himself. But starting from his retelling of his short time at war in Lebanon and his remarkable accolades that he had withheld, the stories that he related to Yuval only increased in surreality and wonder. Leaning closer to his son, he related the few visages he had of his father, fleeing from the Nazi's as a stowaway; of the village he had been born in, called Tolevoste, where he may have once been a fiddle instructor; of how they weathered winters of nine months per year; and of how their family had lived in that village, he believed, since no less than time immemorial. Finally, leaning even closer, and whispering as if there was someone else there who could hear, he divulged the Vostęvskies' most enigmatic tale of all; that they had once been makers of fine kosher wine, transforming one hundred acres of buckwheat into grapevines.

In fleeting vignettes, Yuval looked at himself, his siblings, his grandmother whom he had seldom seen, and the grandfather who he had never known—and saw their lives for what they truly were—dried leaves tumbling in the ever-blowing wind. But Yuval remembered the realization he had come to just hours earlier—he was still alive. If what his father spoke of was true, what stopped him from following that story to its conclusion? He decided he would go to Poland, track down this *Tolevoste*, and see for himself what was still there to be found.

He told his father his new plan. Uri hesitated to respond. He had once considered tracing his ancestry in a similar way. He remembered vividly the day he asked his own father, Meir, if he had ever considered visiting Tolevoste again. His father responded curtly, marking one of the few occasions he would ever mention Tolevoste to him in his life.

"If you go back to Tolevoste, you will be wading through a river of Jewish blood," he had said, quelching the thought.

Nearly forty years had passed since that day. Uri knew that all the blood his father had once spoken of had long been washed away. He did not fear visiting for what he might find. His only fear was for what may *no longer* be there to find. He did not let his son know of this fear, however.

"That's an excellent idea," Uri said, getting up to pour himself another cup of coffee. He found the spare sheets to make Yuval a bed on the couch, kissed his son on the forehead, and the two went off to bed.

Though more time elapsed than he had planned, the following year, Yuval did make the trip. At the start of his spring break from SUNY Maritime—which he applied to with his father's help the very next day—he landed in Warsaw Chopin airport, early in the morning. He caught a bus directly from the passenger terminal, showing Tolevoste's name alongside nine others on its display sign. He traveled the thirty-five kilometers west, and got off at Tolevoste's bus stop alone. On its main road, with wild flowers along its adjacent river bicycle path, few cars passed by.

He heard the village's chirping insects, smelled the grass, and felt the sun. He noticed a few people nearby, mostly walking further east, seemingly enjoying the pleasant weather as well. He walked down the road and soon discovered the town square. As far as first impressions went, he liked what he saw.

The road—wide enough for comfort, but tight enough for one to recognize the face of another from across the street—had a clean and bright orange tint. Small, clean homes behind tall, wild bushes sat perfectly welcoming to, and perfectly withdrawn from, the wide, bright sidewalk. Even the cars rolled by slowly and peacefully, as if implicitly maintaining Tolevoste's temperate pace.

He had made no specific plan for that trip—he did not need to. Knowing well enough that at least one inn would have a vacancy, he decided he would stay or leave according to what he saw fit. His only goal had been to make it to the town square—the only image he could find of Tolevoste, prior to his visit, from the internet.

With no stoplights, the few cars not parked yielded to children and mothers on bicycles crossing the square, riding around the modestly-decorated garden at its center, showcasing the same flowers he had seen on the roadside. An old lady in a light pink sweatshirt sat on an iron bench, her grocery cart by her side, eating a carrot; a faint smell of boiled vegetables came from several directions.

He noticed, in particular, one brick property across the square. He could not read the sign, but gathered that it may have had an administrative function in Tolevoste. He had an idea and made his way there. Through the wooden door, a young receptionist, with papers neatly stacked around her, greeted him with a smile.

"Do you speak English?" he asked her. She did.

Yuval briefly explained his entire purpose—he was a tourist, had a familial relationship to the town, was Jewish, and sought to trace his family line. The woman looked confused, but Yuval could not be sure if it was his English that confused her.

"Let me try to explain again—"

The woman politely lifted a finger and asked him to wait for one moment. Going through a back door, she came through to the lobby not one minute later with someone who purported to be an assistant to the mayor. Gently placing his hand on Yuval's back, he introduced himself, asked Yuval where he had come from, and gestured for him to come to his office to explain his intentions further.

Yuval thought nothing particularly strange of it. He followed him through the single-story government building, passed an events board with posters and children's drawings, and sat opposite the assistant's desk.

"So, please explain to me how we can help you?" the man asked in his strained English.

Yuval spoke more slowly this time, but expressed his purpose no differently. The assistant listened attentively and somewhat somberly, allowing Yuval to go into greater detail—about his grandfather, Meir, about the Nazi invasion, about Tolevoste's nine-month winters, and about the vineyard of one hundred acres which his family of Vostęvskies had once laid claim to.

The man scratched his stubble as Yuval politely waited for a reply. He took a breath, looked down, and sighed.

"My son," he began, with no less warmth than before. "It looks like you are somehow mistaken. I do not know the name of *Vostęvskie*, but I can say something without a doubt. Not only is this not wine country, and there has never been a winery here before, but no Jews—not by the name *Vostęvskie*, or any other—have ever called Tolevoste their home before."

Yuval tilted his head.

"I'm sure my grandfather was born here. This is the only Tolevoste in Poland, right?"

"During and after the war," the man began, somewhat interrupting him, "people assumed new names, created fake identities, laid claims to all sorts of land for all different reasons... I am saying nothing about your grandfather—it was a hard time for us *all*. The best I can say is reality is different from what you have heard. I mean," he continued, chuckling, "I am sorry to laugh, but the idea of a winery in Tolevoste—that is quite the story! No, there has never been such a thing here. In fact, even your description of Tolevoste does not match the truth—while we have winters, they are mild. In fact, never in our history has a winter lasted anywhere near nine months per year!"

Yuval sat in silence, unsure of what to say. The man's confidence caused him to vacillate, but surely, he thought, the existence of such a winery could not be erased from the Earth. Why would his father lie? Something *must* have remained of one hundred acres of grape vines. As he sat in thought, an idea alighted him.

"A cemetery! There must be a cemetery here. I'm sure there is a Jewish grave somewhere in town?" Yuval interjected.

If he could poke just one hole in the assistant's story, he might be able to discover more. But the man pursed his lips, shaking his head with feigned compassion.

"I'm sorry, young man. There is not one Jewish name in our cemetery," he insisted. "You can see for yourself if you like."

He did nothing overtly to ask Yuval to leave, but something in his response gently intimated the meeting had ended. Yuval nodded, realizing he had used up the extent of his amicable welcome. He shook the man's hand, pushed in his chair, thanked him once more, and briskly left the building.

"The library. I know there is a library here," Yuval said, feeling his heart beginning to pound.

The library stood no more than one block away on the same road. Sweating, he walked through the doors, and as politely as he could, asked the librarian at the desk if they had a record department. Once more, this woman gave him a confused look.

"Do you speak English?" Yuval said, now failing to hide his growing exasperation.

"Yes," the middle aged woman said curtly.

"Okay. Where are the records of the Jewish families who used to live here?" he said. "Has there ever been a winery here?"

With the same reserved expression, she recited the same line he had heard just before—*Jews had never lived there before.* If he wanted to read about wineries, she explained, she could find him a book, but he would surely see Tolevoste is not the place for one.

Yuval felt physically ill. The color in his face drained away.

"There is not a single record?" he asked again, unable to believe it was true.

The woman stared at him with an apologetic expression, raising her hands into the air before her. But just as she did, she remembered one curiosity that she had seen some years before. Yuval saw her eye's shift away in thought.

"Want to follow me?" she asked him, walking around the desk.

In the very back of the library, past a few men on computers and children playing quietly on the floor, she took him to a back room. There, one small bookcase, kept cloistered away, held the extent of Tolevoste's rare archives. She wiped away cobwebs covering most of it, fingered through a top shelf, and spoke to him.

"This is something we have—in *Hebrew*. It is the only such thing like it."

Yuval took the book from her hand, bewildered; somewhat correctly sounded out the Hebrew author's name—*Yitzhak Leybush Peretz*—and opened the cover. He did a double take; looked back at the librarian, smiling with a shrug; and tried to make sense of what he saw. The only evidence of any Jews ever living in Tolevoste was one book, with a square cut into almost every page, taking the form of a clandestine place to hide some small trinkets or coins. What Yuval did not see, however, were the small initials scrawled in the top corner on the very last page—*M.V.*

"Do you want it?" the woman asked sympathetically. "We do not have much of a use for it."

"No," Yuval said with a scowl. "Neither do I." He gave the bizarre book back to her, smiled dryly, thanked her, and walked away.

He did not want to go anywhere else in Tolevoste—there was nothing more he needed to see. He walked back down the road to the bus stop with his head down, contemplating the reality as he now saw it. It seemed to him, more likely than not, that *something* of the story of the Vostęvskies was not as it seemed. But with an aching heart, he understood it did not matter anyway. It made no difference if Jews once lived there, if his family ever had a winery anywhere, or if the whole story was an allegory invented over time—for any West, Vostęvskie, or any Jewish family who may have lived in Tolevoste, there was no longer anything there.

With thoughts like these weighing on his mind, he lifted his head. A pleasant, warm smell from down the road filled the air. He felt his stomach rumble; looked ahead of him, searching for the source of the scent; saw what he figured to be a small, unnamed restaurant, partially hidden by the vines draping down its façade; and decided he should get something to eat before leaving.

Yuval opened the restaurant's light, creaking door; let his eyes adjust to the soft, evening light coming in through its windows; went up to the counter, behind which stood a portly old woman, with a soft and patient smile; ordered the first thing he saw on the menu—*wieprzowina* soup; and sat down alone to wait for his meal. Within minutes, an old man with a frayed apron—her husband, Yuval sensed—came through the kitchen door with a large, wooden bowl. Yuval looked down at what he ordered, set perfectly in front of him beside a heavy, steel spoon. He saw hearty chunks of pork, braised in a red wine sauce, topped with cream and fresh garden herbs. Taking in the scent, he was pleasantly surprised that he had ordered precisely what he had smelled from outside.

He did not ordinarily eat pork, but more so out of habit than intention—he did not keep *kosher*, after all. He picked up his spoon, touched the soup to his lips, smiled, and decided it was good. God, seeing what He always knew would come to pass, watched without judgment as Yuval began enjoying his bowl.

Yuval suddenly felt a tap on his foot—startled, he peered under the table. There, he saw a small, black cat pawing at his shoe. He chuckled. She rubbed against his leg, looked up into his eyes, and quietly mewed. For a moment, Yuval felt an uncanny, ineffable connection. The old woman, watching from behind the counter, called out to him.

"Don't worry! She is well fed," the old lady said to Yuval in heavily accented English. "Always begging, that one."

Yuval smiled, put his fingers by her face, and felt her rub against his hand. He liked cats. Grabbing a small chunk of pork, he offered it to her; she pulled it from his hands, dropped it on the ground, and hastily cleaned it off the floor.

"Okay, now. Go on," Yuval said softly. But the cat only stared back. "Well, you're not getting any more."

Yuval finished his meal, paid his bill, thanked the old woman, and left. Following his feet, the cat only separated from Yuval the moment he walked out the door. On his way to the bus stop, in a better mood, Yuval decided he should visit Polish restaurants more often back in New York. After all, he had a dish he knew to look for.

However, as far as the source of that particular recipe, Yuval would know just as much about it as the old man who had served it to him, and one Chana Vostęvskie from unknown generations ago—that is to say, he would know nothing of it at all.

God, in deep meditation, peering through just one eye, saw Yuval leaving on the Warsaw bound bus. For just one moment longer, he watched as the descendant of the extolled winemaker, Chaim Vostęvskie—and the seven-times great grandson of Yitzhak Vostęvskie, who had long ago wrathfully thrashed a cat against a stone well—was cast into immutable doubt over whether any of his history had ever even happened at all.

He sighed, shed one celestial tear, closed His eyes, and turned His face away.

DIASPORA